THE YOUTH OF GOD

The Youth of God

A Novel

Hassan Ghedi Santur

MAWEN ZI
HOUSE

We acknowledge the support of the Canada Council for the Arts for our publishing program. We also acknowledge support from the Government of Ontario through the Ontario Arts Council.

Cover design by JD&J Design LLC

Author photo: Emmanuel Jambo

Library and Archives Canada Cataloguing in Publication

Title: The youth of God : a novel / Hassan Ghedi Santur.

Names: Santur, Hassan Ghedi, author.

Identifiers: Canadiana (print) 20190087471 | Canadiana (ebook) 20190087617 | ISBN 9781988449739
 (softcover) | ISBN 9781988449746 (HTML) | ISBN 9781988449838 (PDF)

Classification: LCC PS8637.A67 Y68 2019 | DDC C813/.6—dc23

Printed and bound in Canada by Coach House Printing

Mawenzi House Publishers Ltd.
39 Woburn Avenue (B)
Toronto, Ontario M5M 1K5
Canada

www.mawenzihouse.com

For my father

Stories of your kindness and generosity inspire me to be a better man

For reason, ruling alone, is a force confining;
and passion, unattended, is a flame that burns
to its own destruction.

Therefore let your soul exalt your reason to the
height of passion, that it may sing;

And let it direct your passion with reason, that your
passion may live through its own daily resurrection,
and like the phoenix rise above its own ashes.

—KAHLIL GIBRAN, *The Prophet*

1

M R ILMI LOVED THE VIEW from the window of his classroom.
Every season had its charm, but this was his favourite time
of the year when the leaves on the giant maple tree outside were at
their greenest. He watched the branches sway in the wind. A storm
was gathering, he could tell—the sky looked dark and foreboding. A
breeze brought in a scent of freshly mowed grass. The soft sound of
the rustling leaves beckoned memories of the big tree that grew in his
childhood home, memories that were quickly interrupted by the shuffling of pages, the creaks of chairs, and the occasional cough.

Mr Ilmi turned around from the window, leaned against the pane
and watched his students writing their final exam. It was mid June and
in a few days the school year would end. So much had happened that
year, yet so much remained the same.

Since the events that occurred in late winter, he had in varying
degrees felt rage, powerlessness, and sorrow. But above all else, regret:
he should have done more to prevent them, he should have foreseen
them.

Mr Ilmi's eyes scanned the classroom and for a moment they rested
on Nuur, sitting at his desk at the centre of the first row. He saw Nuur
hunched over his exam papers, his eyes fixed on the questions before
him. He seemed at ease. He was born to learn. But when Mr Ilmi
blinked, it wasn't Nuur sitting there at all but Tisha, her fingers twirl-
ing one of her long braids.

Lately, Mr Ilmi had been experiencing these moments of magi-
cal thinking with alarming regularity. He saw Nuur when he least
expected to. In these illusory sightings, Mr Ilmi saw Nuur not as he
was but as he remembered him. What Mr Ilmi remembered most

about Nuur were his large, dark eyes that seemed to conceal so much. It was rare to encounter such a strong presence of inner life among the parade of teenage boys who passed through his classroom every year. But it seemed to Mr Ilmi that there was more than just the presence of an inner life in Nuur. His entire being seemed to have been comprised of certain ineffable qualities that had made him an enigma.

"Bismilahi rahmani rahiim." Nuur mouthed these words as he washed his right foot in the sink of the boys' washroom. He had fifteen minutes to perform his ablution, pray, and get to Mr Ilmi's biology class.

As he washed his foot, he caught a glimpse of himself in the smudgy mirror above the sink. The lanky frame, the dark complexion and narrow, pointy nose separating his high cheekbones—his features, he thought, lacked the grace and charm that drew everyone, especially girls, to his older brother Ayuub. But Nuur had made peace with his appearance, for he recognized that there was more to him than what appeared to the naked eye. He carried a secret world inside him that no mirror in the world could ever reflect.

He heard voices outside. Quickly he finished washing, and just as he was jamming a bare foot into his black sneakers, the door swung open.

James Calhoun entered, followed by his entourage of two, both overweight and overdressed for early October, in baggy jeans and hoodies. They had a habit of walking several feet behind James, who liked to stroll the hallways of the school with the swagger of a tin-pot dictator.

James had a big, bald head like that of a cross between a baby's and a pit bull's. "You better not be doing what I think you're doing," he said, as he made towards Nuur with his usual stylized and menacing limp.

"I'm not doing anything," Nuur said in a quivering voice.

"Don't lie to me, bitch," James snarled, his breath smelling of nachos and cigarettes.

"I'm not lying."

James turned to his sidekicks, both grinning with anticipation, ready to do whatever was required.

"You were washing your stinking feet in the sink, the same sink we use to wash our hands and faces. That's fucking disgusting," James said, his voice louder with each word. "What do you think we should do about this, boys?" he asked, without turning to look at his posse.

"I was just making wadu, to get ready for prayer," Nuur whispered, hoping to elicit from them some respect for God, or failing that, compassion for his devotion to God.

"Making what?" James seethed.

"A wadu."

"The fuck is that?"

His two friends sniggered.

Nuur felt a panic rise up from deep within his guts, telling him to fight or flee. Fighting was out of the question. That would be like slapping a pit bull in the face. As soon as he tried to move, he felt his slender bones, for he had no muscles to speak of, crash into the large, surprisingly soft body of James. Nuur struggled to maneuver his way between James and the other two boys.

"Where the fuck you think you're going, bitch?" James said. With his warm sweaty hands, he grabbed Nuur by the back of his neck and shoved him towards the middle of the three stalls of the washroom. Nuur stumbled onto the linoleum floor, his head an inch away from the hard marble of the white toilet bowl. His kufi, the small white cap he always wore, fell into the toilet with its several large, brown residues left by the last flush.

"He looks thirsty, boys. You think we should offer him a cold, refreshing drink of water?" The two sidekicks outside the stall chuckled approvingly.

Nuur felt James grab a fistful of the collar of his qamiis, the long brown robe under which he wore a white t-shirt and pair of khakis. It was an ensemble that made him look like a darker, smaller version of Osama bin Laden and the butt of jokes in the school's hallways. He was used to kids calling him Osama or Bin Laden or Al-Qaeda Boy in class and in the hallways and most especially on the rare occasions when he was brave enough to venture into the wild, wild West that was the school cafeteria. He had resigned himself to the endless taunting and name-calling that came his way for wearing a qamiis to school; for growing a big, bushy beard at seventeen; and for wearing a little white head cap that gave him an air of piety and screamed weakness when all the other boys at the school looked like extras on the set of a Kanye West music video.

Nuur knew that no amount of begging or appeal to the better selves of the three bullies would save him from getting his head dunked in the filthy water. He also knew that a speck of toilet water would be enough to nullify the absolute state of cleanliness that his prayer required.

It was a swift, unpremeditated move. As soon as he caught a glimpse of the space between the floor and the metal divider between the stalls, Nuur shrugged off James's clasp, dived onto the cold, dusty floor, slid into the adjoining stall and locked the door. James and his minions pushed and pounded with ferocious anger. Nuur stood up on the rim of the toilet bowl, lest they grab his legs and drag him out.

Any one of them could have mustered enough force to break the door down and retrieve Nuur from his hiding place, but apparently it seemed to require too much effort for the meagre entertainment value of roughing him up. Nuur thanked Allah for their lack of resolve.

"I'll get you, bitch," James muttered.

"Yeah, bitch," another boy echoed.

"Better fucking believe it," boy two chimed in.

Nuur heard them shuffle off one by one. He waited a few moments until he was sure they had left, then stepped down from the toilet bowl and lingered in the stall for a moment to recite the Fatiha in his head and offer his gratitude to God. He made sure not to let any of the Quran escape his lips, the boy's washroom on the second floor of Thistletown Collegiate Institute was too profane a place for the holy words to be spoken out loud.

He came out of the stall and looked around. All was quiet. Confident that the three bullies were gone, he opened the door of the adjacent stall and stared at his lovely, white kufi sitting in the smudgy bottom of the toilet. There was no hope of rescuing it. But come payday next week, he would go to the Somali flea market on Rexdale and Martingrove and buy himself a nice new kufi.

Suddenly he felt better. The prospect of buying another, better kufi gave him just enough strength to go to his afternoon biology class even if it meant being in the same room as those thugs. Biology was his favourite subject. He wasn't going to surrender it to those boys the way he did his head cap. The possibility of learning something new fortified Nuur and lifted his otherwise dim spirits.

3

M R ILMI SKETCHED A CRUDE diagram of the human brain on the blackboard and drew a thick line in the middle that separated the two hemispheres. He created several smaller regions of the brain with a few wiggly diagonal lines.

While Mr Ilmi was busy drawing the diagram, the twenty or so students in his class took advantage to flirt, insult, and make plans with one another, their voices becoming progressively louder. Finally, Mr Ilmi turned around. The room grew quieter but not enough to conduct a lesson. He walked to his desk, sat on the edge and faced his students. He made a mental note of who had bothered to show up for his one o'clock, twelfth grade biology class. The usual suspects, Derek, Mustafa, and Liban were absent again.

"So, who can tell me what that is?" Mr Ilmi asked in a dignified but gentle tone. The room went silent. It never ceased to amaze him, how these kids, mostly Somalis, with a few Jamaicans, a couple of East Asians, and a smattering of Whites, listened to him when he spoke, even though all he ever heard from his colleagues was how they spent the first twenty minutes of every class trying to get them to shut up.

Mr Ilmi took some pleasure in thinking that it was something about him, his character, that they responded to, respected, and even feared. But he knew it probably had more to do with the colour of his skin. As the only Somali teacher and as one of only four black teachers in the entire school, he had somehow gained the students' trust. He was one of them. As one of them as a teacher could be.

"So? Who can tell me what that is?"

"A map of Africa," Duran said, always the wisecrack, always yearning to get laughter but just as happy to settle for being laughed at. It was his lucky day. He got a few genuine chuckles.

"Ha-ha, very funny," Mr Ilmi said.

"The human brain," Nuur said in his usual shy voice, from his seat in the centre of the first row. His quiet intelligence and dignified manner had made him a favourite with Mr Ilmi.

"Can you name any part of the brain for me, Nuur?" Mr Ilmi asked, staring into Nuur's large, dark eyes that seemed to conceal so much. He often wished he could be this kid's shrink, talk to him in private, have him confide whatever troubles made him look so solemn, so beyond his age.

Nuur stared at the diagram on the board for a moment, tilting his head ever so slightly. "There is the cerebral cortex on the upper right corner."

"Excellent," Mr Ilmi said as he made a little dot on the area in question. "Go on."

"And there, at the bottom is the hippocampus and—"

Before he could continue, a voice yelled, "Sit on my hippocampus, Osama!"

The class broke into riotous laughter, and Nuur turned his head down to his notebook.

"That's enough!" Mr Ilmi said, raising his voice in class for the first time in days. All became quiet. "One more comment like that, James, and you'll be in detention for the rest of the day. Now, please apologize to Nuur."

"For what?" James asked, his famous temper already showing.

"You know what for, James. Apologize, so that the rest of us can learn about the human brain."

Silence. The whole class stared at James, waiting to see if he would stand his ground, as he had done many times before, and risk another detention.

"I'm waiting, James."

"Okay. Fine. Sorry," James blurted.

"Sorry for what?" Mr Ilmi asked.

"I said sorry already. Fuck, what do you want from me, man?"

"An apology without acknowledgement of what you're apologizing for is meaningless."

Another long pause, testing Mr Ilmi's patience. "Please leave the class."

"Okay. I'm sorry for calling you Osama. There. Happy?"

"Very," Mr Ilmi said with a smile. "Thank you, James. Go on, Nuur," he said to the poor boy, who looked mortified by all the fuss made on his behalf. Mr Ilmi's heart ached for the boy. There was a pitiable vulnerability in Nuur's eyes, a combination of innocence and wisdom that he wished he could shield from the constant ridicule that could easily turn it into something hard and ugly.

Mr Ilmi looked at the clock on the wall. In ten minutes the entire class would head for the door as if breaking from prison. "Okay. Listen up, folks. Here is your homework for the weekend. You will each choose a part of the brain, you will research every bit of information you can get on it and present your findings to the class. I want to know the role of your chosen part of the brain, how it has evolved in the human animal, and what happens to it if it gets damaged or diseased. In short, I want to know everything. Diagrams, pictures, and any other visual aid you can think of is encouraged. Oh, and remember, I have been Googling longer than you have been alive. So cut and paste from Wikipedia at your peril."

"How are we supposed to do research if we can't even Google?" Lola whined. A pretty, overweight girl, Lola often wore pink sweatpants that proclaimed JUICY in large letters on her ass. A big hit with the boys.

"There are things called books. Scientific journals. Magazines. They're housed in a little place we like to call the public library. The city is littered with them. Use them. That's why your parents pay taxes."

The entire class sighed audibly as though going to the library and taking out a book was akin to forced labour. "Have a good weekend," Mr Ilmi said as the boys and girls began their frenzied escape. "Hey

James, hold-up," he said to James, who was almost out the door. Mr Ilmi waited until the last of the students had left.

"Man, I already apologized to Al-Qaeda Boy."

"You couldn't really have meant it if you're still calling him that, could you?"

"I'm just playin' with him. It don't mean nothing."

"It doesn't mean anything."

"It doesn't mean anything," James repeated, mimicking his teacher in that irascible way of his.

"That's better. But that's not why I called you."

"Then what, my girl is waiting for me at the bus stop. You know how chicks get when you keep 'em waiting."

"Yes, God forbid I should keep you love birds apart longer than necessary. But I need to ask you about Faysal. I know you two are friends."

"Yeah, we tight."

"Have you heard from him? He hasn't been in class for three days."

James chuckled. "Guess you didn't hear, eh?"

"Hear what?"

"Ain't you got no TV, man?"

"Heard what, James? What happened to Faysal?" Mr Ilmi demanded, surprised at himself, for Faysal had given him nothing but headaches since he walked into his class at the start of the semester.

"He got shot in the ass," James said with a laugh.

"What!"

"Chill, Mr Ilmi. He's cool. Just embarrassed is all. Has to sleep with his ass up in the air. That's harsh, yo."

"Yes. That is harsh," Mr Ilmi said, relieved that Faysal's injuries were of the embarrassing variety rather than the tragic. "Do you know which hospital?"

"Humber. Me and the crew saw him yesterday. For real, though, my girl is waiting. I gotta go."

"Okay. Thanks, James."

The boy made a beeline for the door, his jeans almost halfway to his thighs. "James," Mr Ilmi called out to him.

"Yeah," James answered, one hand on the door frame.

Mr Ilmi took a moment to speak. "Take care of yourself, will you?"

James nodded with a smile and disappeared into the weekend. Finally, alone in the classroom, Mr Ilmi went to the blackboard, stood there looking at the diagram of the brain he had drawn for his students. He had been a teacher for fourteen years and it never ceased to amaze him how fond he became of his students each year, even the ones he disliked, and there were a few. There was always a part of him, however small and well concealed, that cared about them, about their evolution as people, and feared for their safety.

A few years before, when he returned to school in September after a vacation in Kenya, he found out that Nalah, one of his favourite students had been killed in a car accident. During the summer break, she had gone back to Lebanon, and while she was on a weekend trip to Baalbek with her family to see the temple ruins of the Roman era, their chartered van had driven off the road. Nalah, her cousin, and her half-brother were killed instantly. Mr Ilmi had felt a deep sorrow and anger at the unfairness of the world. He held it together in Principal Terry's office as he listened to the details of Nalah's death, but as he walked back alone in the deserted hallway, he broke down and wept.

Mr Ilmi wiped the board, put his notebooks in his brown leather satchel, and left the classroom feeling happy about the week's work. As he strolled through the now almost empty hallways towards the parking lot, it pained him that he hadn't learned to take more joy out of his job. Sure, he liked the actual task of teaching biology, telling these kids about the wonder that was the human body and the innumerable chemical and molecular interactions that made it work so beautifully. Every once in a while, he even fantasized about the possibility that something he said about liver enzymes or cortical remapping might stick with a student and cultivate a love of science and possibly lead to their one day becoming a doctor. But Mr Ilmi didn't dwell on this particular fantasy, for it invariably led to regrets.

Why had he abandoned his own dreams of medical school? When he came upon that proverbial fork in the road and had the option of applying either to medical school or teacher's college, why didn't he take the harder road, the one less traveled? And it seemed no matter how many times he asked himself that question, the answer was always the same useless, nondefinitive muddle of excuses and half-assed assessments of his character, his grit, his ambition, but never of his intellect, for he had always known that he had in him to be a good, possibly even a great surgeon. *Too late now*, he thought as he got into his dusty black Toyota and turned on the ignition. Futile pondering now.

———

Later that night Mr Ilmi did what he almost always did after work. He had dinner with his wife Khadija. He hated her cooking. She had been in Canada for two years and she still cooked like an old Somali woman. The vegetables were so overcooked they might as well have been puréed. The rice was so oily it tasted like it was fried. Plus, there was the issue of spices. She used so much cumin and garlic and hot pepper that the natural taste of what he was eating was often impossible to tell. But he could never bring himself to complain. It was bad enough she was making him dinner well into her first trimester. He had tried on many occasions to tell her that she didn't have to cook for him, he had spent most of his life taking care of himself. He wanted her to relax, sleep, read the countless beginners' English books he had purchased for her. He wanted her to learn English fast, so that she could go to university and be anything she wanted. But she had brought with her some antediluvian notions of what a good wife should be, and she would not waver.

As he sat across from her at their large dinner table in their small apartment on Dixon Road and Kipling Avenue, chewing on a piece of lamb, he wondered once more what had happened to his life. How did he, at the not-so-young age of forty-three, find himself in an apartment he hated, in a neighbourhood he despised, with every intension of leaving it when he got a full-time teaching job and could make enough money to move to a more interesting neighbourhood of the city? But the most vexing of the endless questions that rattled around in his head as he watched his wife eat her dinner contentedly was how he had traveled halfway around the world to Nairobi to marry a woman with whom he had spoken on the phone no more than a handful of times and whose picture was sent to him by his uncle as an email attachment like a business document.

If someone had told him, back in his days at Queen's University, that his future wife would come into his life practically a stranger, he would have laughed at them. He had carried a fantasy, a vision of the day he would meet his future wife. It would be at a party and they would lock eyes across the room and walk towards one another, unable to resist the visceral, gravitational pull of their attraction. Or he would be moving into his new building somewhere far away from here, his suitcases by his side, and a beautiful woman would walk into his elevator and they would make the kind of eye contact one never forgot and over the next couple of weeks they would continue to bump into each other until one day one of them would invite the other over for dinner on a Friday night. And that would be the beginning of a great romance. They would go to the cinema to see the latest Almodóvar film. They would kiss in the rain. He always wanted to kiss a woman in the rain. He had been certain that that was in his future.

Never did his vision of romance include several long-distance phone calls from his uncle Ahmed in Nairobi, his dead mother's only brother and the only true father figure he had ever had. Never did Mr Ilmi imagine that his loneliness and desire to have his "adult" life commence as soon as possible would make him fall victim to his uncle's powers of persuasion.

"My cousin Mubarak called me today," Khadija said in her Southern Somali dialect, breaking Mr Ilmi's mental inventory of what might've been. He was glad for the interruption to his litany of regrets.

"Oh yeah," he said in his most benevolent, husbandly voice. He nodded and asked a few follow-up questions as she told him about Mubarak, who had recently opened a small shop in a bazaar in the suburbs of Johannesburg. She had a cousin in South Africa, an aunt in Amsterdam, and two other relatives in Nairobi. Her extended family alone illustrated the migration narrative of their people. Since the outbreak of the civil war in Somalia in 1991, every family he knew, including his own, had been scattered across the globe. He even had a close cousin in Auckland, New Zealand. Since the death of his mother, who had kept her family together in Toronto, his three living brothers had fled to such far-flung places as San Diego, Copenhagen, and Istanbul.

After dinner, Mr Ilmi and his wife retired to the large sectional brown leather sofa that overwhelmed their small living room. Within days of her arrival in Toronto, Mr Ilmi took his new bride to Leon's and asked her to choose the furniture she liked. He now wished he had contributed a bit more to the selection process. He shifted in his seat a couple of times as he tried to interest himself in the Bollywood movie he had rented for her. No matter how hard he tried, he could never understand the appeal these films held for her.

He massaged her feet and gazed at her face as she watched the movie, her eyes watering at the romance and melodrama unfolding on the screen—a story about two lovers kept apart by class. He desperately wanted to know what she was thinking at such times. He longed to know the contents of her mind. One of the things that fascinated him and, truth be told, troubled him about her was how devoid of opinions she was. She didn't seem to possess any deeply held convictions about the world around her or even about her own life.

This was most painfully manifested in her attitude towards sex. She neither enjoyed nor hated it. She preferred neither one way nor another. She neither instigated it nor stopped its occurrence. She seemed to have made peace with the whole business of sex as a messy and unfathomable but all the same necessary function of life, and she was not about to look into it any further. It felt to Mr Ilmi that there was in his wife's past a fateful day when she had come to realize the futility of struggling against fate, and she had made a pact with Allah that she would not resist His plans for her if He spared her the fates that befell many of the girls she had grown up with in the impoverished coastal town of Kismayo in South Somalia. Allah seemed to have kept His end of the bargain. Khadija was lucky enough to be married to a kind, good-looking man. She got to escape her meagre existence in Kismayo, sharing a small room with her three younger sisters. And now she was expecting a baby. God had been good to her and it seemed to Mr Ilmi that his wife's way of showing her gratitude was to not ask for anything more. If this was as good as it was ever going to get in their marriage, Khadija seemed to have accepted it. And that night, as Mr Ilmi watched his wife enjoying her Bollywood film, looking so content, he vowed to try to be content as well.

4

WHEN THE WEATHER WAS GOOD, Nuur liked to walk home from school. The thirty minutes between his school and his apartment building at Kipling and Dixon were his most precious of the day. Sandwiched between two places he hated—home and school—those meagre thirty minutes gave him some time to be alone, to think and make plans, and on rare occasions to entertain visions of the life he might one day lead.

Twice a week, however, he had to head straight from school to his part-time job at Hamar Cade, the Somali restaurant on Rexdale Avenue where he worked as a waiter, busboy, and dishwasher. As he served or wiped the tables, he often wondered what it would be like to go to a restaurant, share a good meal and jokes with friends, and when it was all over, get up and leave the remains for someone else to clear. Nuur's family was not the kind that went out to restaurants together. He had no memory of eating out with his mother, father, and brother, to celebrate a special occasion like a birthday. Even at home, they never ate together. His mother ate in the kitchen, usually over the sink, and his father was always away, driving his taxi from early in the morning until night. And so on most days, it was just Nuur and his brother at the dinner table.

Nuur's brisk walk from school to home would end abruptly, as he inserted the key into the lobby door, cutting off the sweetly meandering and stimulating interior monologue that had played in his head. His consciousness—a word he had come to learn recently in Mr Ilmi's class and become quite fond of—gave him the feeling that there was more to his life, some delicious, almost secret quality about his existence that he couldn't account for but which he possessed nonetheless.

His consciousness felt to Nuur like a palace in whose vast rooms he could roam freely, each wondrous chamber naturally opening into another without end. His consciousness was as vivid as a dream and as welcoming as home.

As Nuur slid the key into the lock to open the door to his apartment, he took a deep breath to prepare himself for an encounter with his mother. He hated this about himself. His need to fortify himself in order to face his mother rather than looking forward to seeing her made him feel like a bad son. For this act, he knew Allah's wrath would someday fall upon him. Didn't Allah say in his holy book that the key to paradise lay at the feet of your mother? If he wanted to be among the chosen, those who would gain access to eternal paradise in the hereafter and drink from its rivers of honey and sit under the giant tree with Mohamed, Isa, Moses, Ibrahim and all the other prophets, then he had to banish these ill thoughts about his mother. Surely, God could see the feelings he harboured in his heart. And he was certain that God would not be pleased with them.

The apartment was dark and he turned the kitchen light on. There was no boiling pot on the stove. No smell of food. It wasn't a good sign when his mother failed to make dinner. The evening wouldn't be pleasant. He looked into the living room and didn't see her in her usual spot on the sofa, yelling on the phone, demanding divorce from his father, who had recently moved to Rochester, Minnesota, and taken a second wife.

Nuur dropped his backpack on the dining table. He heard what sounded like whispers followed by several quick moans. He dreaded days like this when he came home from school and found his mother in bed, still wearing the baati she wore to bed the night before, crying and cursing the day she met his father. Nuur walked into the narrow hallway leading to his mother's room and realized that the moans were actually coming from his room, which he shared with his older brother Ayuub. He opened the door.

"Subhanallah!" he cried out, startled by what he saw, and stepped back in horror. His brother Ayuub was splayed out on the bed, his hands cupped behind his raised head, watching a girl on her knees, her head bobbing up and down upon him. The pretty Somali girl, who was about Nuur's age, with long curly hair, jumped up, shocked and embarrassed. Ayuub turned away and struggled to shove his erect cock into his sweatpants.

Nuur stepped out and shut the door behind him. He grabbed his knapsack from the dining table and rushed out of the apartment, invoking Subhanallah repeatedly under his breath, all the way down the dim, urine-scented, green-carpeted corridor to the elevator and down to the lobby. Outside, he felt the cool autumn breeze on his face. He stood at the building entrance, wondering where to go. He had to get as far away from that abomination as he could, and so he marched and ran to the one place he knew he would never feel like an intruder.

For the entire twenty-minute duration of his walk to the mosque, Nuur tried to banish from his mind the filth he had just witnessed in his bedroom, in the very room where he offered his morning prayer, where he memorized the Holy Quran for his weekly lessons at the mosque. He cursed Ayuub for defiling the one place in the world that was his and exposing to his eyes what no decent Muslim should ever witness. He cursed his brother. He also prayed for him. He prayed to Allah to forgive Ayuub, who didn't know what punishment awaited him. He also begged God to show Ayuub mercy on the Day of Judgment. The thought of his brother burning in hellfire brought tears to Nuur's eyes. He prayed to Allah to spare his brother's soul. He prayed for his mother to be happy. He prayed for his dad to come back. Praying, he reached the threshold of the mosque.

As he walked into the two-storey, red-brick building, Nuur felt a deep and comforting sense of having come home. This was where he spent every Friday afternoon praying and listening to long lectures on the Quran and the Hadith, the sayings of the Prophet. He felt an urgent need to pray, to cleanse his mind from the lewdness he had seen.

He sprinted up the stairs to the ablution room, where he rinsed himself, making sure to thoroughly wash away his perspiration after his long walk. Having made his ablution, he came down to the prayer hall and tossed his school bag to a far corner. He had a math test to study for, but he could not bring himself to worry about such worldly things.

Nuur stood facing Mecca in the east and began to pray, reciting the Fatiha under his breath. But thoughts of his brother kept creeping into his mind. He wanted to pray for him. As he lowered himself to the ground to prostrate to the Almighty, the all-knowing, the creator of the seven heavens, he thought about Surah An-Nisa which warned of God's wrath against those who surrender to lewdness and lust.

He stayed in prostration much longer than required and asked Allah to guide his brother and deliver him from himself. Warm tears ran down his cheeks and he wiped them away with the sleeve of his qamiis. As he finished praying, he turned his neck to his right, then left, and whispered, "asalamu alaykum." Peace upon you. Nuur noticed the imam of the mosque watching him. For almost a year now, he had seen Imam Yusuf giving sermons, leading Friday prayers, and quietly reciting the Quran to himself in a corner. Never before had he caught that solemn, learned, awe-inspiring figure looking directly at him. Imam Yusuf was a short, thin man whose meagre features belied the booming, melodious voice that poured effortlessly out of him. On Fridays, during his sermons, there inevitably came a moment when his voice rose up with righteous fury and indignation, resonating around the prayer room, as though it carried waves of molecular disturbances from the great beyond.

The imam had a habit of looking down from his pulpit at the worshippers who sat before him on the carpeted floor. He would look into their eyes as he read verses from the Quran, translating them simultaneously from ancient Arabic into his stiff, formal English. But for some inexplicable reason, whenever his gaze panned across the prayer hall, it skipped Nuur and landed instead on the man sitting next to him.

This had happened so often that Nuur took it for granted that there was something about him, some flaw visible only to Imam Yusuf that made him unworthy of his direct gaze. Seeing the imam looking directly at him now, Nuur couldn't help but think that he had made some error in his prayer. Nuur got up quickly, grabbed a copy of the Quran from a nearby shelf, walked across the prayer hall, as far away as he could get from the imam's gaze and sat with his back against the far wall.

Just as Nuur began to recite a verse of the Quran under his breath, he looked up and he noticed Imam Yusuf sitting opposite him. It was eerie, almost miraculous, that one second the imam was at the other end of the hall, and the next, here he was, sitting cross-legged before him like the Buddha.

"Asalamu alaykum," Imam Yusuf said in a voice so gentle, it could lull a baby to sleep. Without the amplifying speakers it had a sweet and beguiling, almost seductive tone.

"Walaykum salam," Nuur said, trying his best to simultaneously steady and soften his voice.

"You speak Somali," the imam said.

"Uh, not well."

"In that case, I will practice my English with you," the imam said with a smile. Nuur couldn't help staring at his hennaed full beard and the bare skin over the upper lip—in strict accordance with the pre-scribed style for a devout Muslim man: full beard, no mustache.

"I take it you were born here?"

"Yes."

"Mashallah," the imam said. He had a habit of constantly uttering this phrase whose meaning in English Nuur had never understood. Was the imam implying that it was a good thing Nuur was born here, or that it was a sad thing deserving of pity?

"I won't bother you too long—" the imam said.

"Oh, you're no bother at all—"

"I just wanted to introduce myself. My name is Imam Yusuf Abdi. I have seen you in the mosque often, but I never introduced myself.

Forgive me," he said as he extended his hand to Nuur.

"I should be asking for forgiveness," Nuur replied and shook the imam's hand. It was warm and soft. It reminded him of his father's hands, which were always warm, even in the dead of winter. He noticed that the imam sounded happier, almost cheerful, than he did up on the pulpit giving his fiery sermons. Now as he sat across from Nuur, there was no evidence of that fervor. Instead, there was a surprising gentleness in tone and demeanor. Nuur wondered if his senses had been deceiving him all this time, making him fear the good and kind soul sitting before him.

"What is your name?"

"Nuur."

"Mashallah," the imam repeated. "Do you know what your name means?"

"Light. That's what my mother told me."

"She's right. May Allah bless her . . . Is everything all right?"

Nuur hesitated. "Yes . . . why?"

"I noticed that when you were praying, you looked . . . emotional. Am I wrong?"

"No."

"Is anything troubling you?"

"No."

The imam began to rise up, as though to walk away.

Nuur felt a pang of guilt. "Well," he said clearing his throat a little.

The imam sat back down, crossed his legs again.

"What do you do when someone . . . " Nuur's words trailed off.

"Go on, son."

A warm feeling washed over Nuur, when he heard this most revered imam call him *son*, even though he knew that it was what the imam called all the boys who came to the mosque. Nonetheless, something about this man calling him *son* made sense to him like the revelation of a destiny. "What do you do when someone you love is on the wrong path?" Nuur said.

Imam Yusuf folded his arms across his chest and stared down at his lap in a gesture of reflection. "The wrong path," the imam repeated, taking it for granted that there were only two paths in life.

"Yes, the wrong path," Nuur said. "The path to hellfire."

"Subhanallah," Imam Yusuf said softly with a dramatic shake of the head. "Why do you think this . . . this someone is—"

"He dropped out of high school," Nuur said.

"Going to school is not a religious obligation, son."

"He talks back to his parents."

"I see . . . go on."

"He smokes too."

"Cigarettes?"

"Yes. And . . . hashish."

"Subhanallah," Imam Yusuf whispered.

"And . . . " Nuur stopped himself, feeling as though he had arrived at an invisible boundary.

"And what? It's okay, son. No one has to know. Whatever you tell me stays with me."

"He commits zinna."

"Subhanallah," the imam said again, sounding genuinely scandalized. "How do you know this, son?"

"I have seen it with my own eyes."

"You have?"

"I walked in on him. They were in the room that we share. I saw them committing . . . " Nuur stopped, unable to say what he saw. "I feel like he's walking straight into hellfire and there is nothing I can do to stop him. So when you saw me crying, I was praying for him. I was asking Allah for his, his . . . salvation." That word, *salvation* didn't feel right to Nuur for some reason, as though it didn't belong in the Islamic lexicon, but he didn't know what else to call what he had been praying for.

"Who is this person?"

Nuur remained silent.

"It's alright, son. You can tell me."

"My older brother. His name is Ayuub."

"I see."

"I don't know what to do, Imam Yusuf," Nuur said, with a quiver in his voice.

"There's nothing to be done."

Nuur looked at the imam, a feeling of betrayal creeping into him. "Why are you saying that?" he asked, his voice rising a little. This was his older brother he was talking about, his only brother, the one he had spent much of his childhood looking up to, imitating, idolizing, the one whose approval, with the exception of his father, he sought the most. The brother who had jumped into the deep end of the swimming pool to rescue him when Nuur made the mistake of getting into their neighbourhood pool while the lifeguard was on his lunch break. Nuur was twelve then, and Ayuub fourteen. And this imam was telling him there was nothing he could do to rescue his brother from a fate worse than death?

Imam Yusuf remained silent for some time, as though waiting for a revelation telling him how to handle this moment, calling upon all his religious training, the years of studying at madrasas in Somalia, then in Riyadh, Saudi Arabia, and finally in Cairo at the famed Al-Azhar University.

"Do you know the story of Abu Talib?" Imam Yusuf asked at last.

Nuur shook his head. Suddenly the sound of the call to prayer pierced through Nuur like a blade. He looked at his watch. It was Maqrib. Sunset prayer had already come.

"Tell me the story of Abu Talib," Nuur said.

"Another time," the imam replied, his voice almost drowned out by the prayer call.

"No, tell me now," Nuur said, a note of desperation in his voice. He was convinced that hearing the story of Abu Talib would help him rescue his brother from the eternal punishment that surely awaited him.

"Patience, son. Patience," Imam Yusuf said and got up in one swift movement that belied his age. He gave Nuur a quick fatherly pat on the shoulder and walked away.

Later, after the prayer, Nuur went up the stairs to the second floor of the mosque. It was a drab hallway, with blue paint chipping off the walls and dim florescent lights overhead. A few old bookshelves were lined against one wall. He searched for the imam's office, passing several closed rooms that he imagined were storage closets. A strip of light leaked out from under the door of the last room, which had to be the imam's office. He knocked lightly on the door.

"Come in," Imam Yusuf called out and Nuur opened the door.

"Nuur, come in, son."

"I'm sorry to bother you."

"Come in and close the door."

Nuur closed the door behind him and stood there. The office was messy, stacks of religious books everywhere. Imam Yusuf was putting away what looked like a bundle of money into a pale green plastic bag.

"I can come back another time, if you're busy."

"Nonsense. Sit down."

Nuur looked around to find a seat. The two chairs in front of the imam's desk had banker boxes on them.

"Move one of the boxes and sit."

Nuur did that.

"I was hoping to hear the story."

"The story?"

"The story of Abu Talib."

"Oh yes. Indeed. The story of Abu Talib." Imam Yusuf paused for a moment as if to recall the story. "Do you know who Abu Talib was?"

Nuur shook his head.

"Abu Talib ibn al-Muttalib was the leader of the Quraysh clan. Do you know of the Quraysh?"

Nuur nodded. Quraysh was the clan the Prophet belonged to.

"Very well. Abu Talib was the uncle of our Prophet Mohamed."

Nuur and the imam said the customary "Peace be upon him" in unison. "Abu Talib was an important man, very influential in his day. And when the Prophet's father died, Abu Talib took on the task of raising Mohamed, since our beloved Prophet was an orphan. He raised and loved him like his own son. And when the Prophet received the revelation—do you know the story of the revelation?"

Nuur nodded again.

"Excellent. You are well read. It pleases me to see a young man your age take his faith seriously. As you know, not many boys your age do. They are too busy with mindless entertainment. Sad. Very sad!"

"You were saying after the Prophet—"

"You are eager to hear the story. Very well then. After the message from Allah came to the Prophet, he had no choice but to spread His word. But the Quraysh clan, they did not take this new religion too well. It was a perilous time for the Prophet. He was shunned by his community. He made many enemies. But his uncle protected him. Loved him. He never wavered in his support."

Nuur began to wonder what this story had to do with his brother Ayuub's misdemeanours.

"You see, the Prophet with his new message was disrupting the wicked ways of the Quraysh tribe. He was becoming a revolutionary figure. His life was in grave danger, but his uncle was always there for him, protecting him. But the curious thing was, all around him people who heard of the Prophet's message of truth were converting to the new faith. But Abu Talib never did. When Abu Talib was on his deathbed, the Prophet rushed to his bedside and stayed with him, pleading with him to recite the Shahada, 'There is no God but Allah,' to save his soul."

Nuur heard the imam's voice crack a little as he said those words, as if it were he at that bedside fourteen hundred years ago, trying to save his uncle's soul.

"And so the Prophet's beloved uncle died a pagan. And we all know what happens to the unbelievers."

Nuur nodded. "So you're saying . . . "

"I'm saying, Allah guides only those whom he wishes, my son. You can try. I can try. But only Allah can save your brother."

Nuur couldn't believe what the imam was telling him. How could he see his brother's soul in peril and not do anything to help him? Feeling dejected and oversold on a story whose meaning remained a mystery to him, Nuur stood up, thanked the imam and headed for the door.

"Remember, Nuur. Allah guides whom he wishes."

As he left the mosque, Nuur vowed that if he couldn't save his brother's soul from hellfire, he would do the next best thing. He would love him and be by his side just as the Prophet stayed by his uncle's side.

5

M R ILMI STOOD AT THE BACK of the hospital elevator, which was almost as big as his bedroom. He imagined what it would be like riding these things up and down every day in full doctor's regalia: those lovely baby-blue scrubs, a stethoscope dangling from his neck, a neat little cap on his head. Just then, two young doctors waltzed in and pressed the tenth-floor button. They seemed completely oblivious to his presence. Their indifference seemed to shout: We are doctors! We save lives! You're a mere civilian! They carried on their conversation about a patient they had just operated on. Mr Ilmi moved a little closer to hear them better. He didn't catch everything but he caught enough to know that it had something to do with endometriosis and the removal of ovaries. He wanted to know more about the procedure but the elevator came to his floor and he had to get off.

He looked for room 732, taking his time to glimpse into the various rooms and the patients they held. Some had visitors. Others were completely alone. A peculiar desire to keep the lonely ones company came over him.

Finally, he came to room 732. The first bed was occupied by a very old white man who could have been a hundred. Mr Ilmi walked up to the second bed, which was next to the window. There he was, Faysal, lying face down, his ass raised, though not quite up in the air as James had described it. But it was nevertheless an embarrassing position for anyone, especially a teenage boy for whom looking cool was of the utmost importance.

As if he sensed the presence of someone behind him in his vulnerable state, Faysal twisted his neck to see who it was.

"Hey, Mr Ilmi. What's up?" he said, sounding a little intoxicated.

"Hello Faysal, how're you feeling?"

Faysal tried to change his position and winced with pain.

"No, lie back down," Mr Ilmi said in a tender voice as though he were talking to his own child. Faysal obeyed and relaxed, pressing his head sideways against the flat hospital pillow. Mr Ilmi then produced a small box of donuts he had bought downstairs in the lobby and put them down on the bedside table, within easy reach of the boy.

"Thanks, man. You didn't have to. But thanks," Faysal said. He reached for the box and took out a donut. Mr Ilmi watched him take a couple of bites and smiled.

"James told me you got shot."

"Yeah, in the fucking ass, can you believe that?"

Mr Ilmi tried not to stare at the boy's raised backside but it was hard to ignore.

"So, what happened? Were you in a fight?"

"Would you believe me if I told you it wasn't my fault?"

Mr Ilmi shook his head. He would've liked to nod, but he knew Faysal's proclivity for trouble all too well.

"I'm serious. Me and my boys went out to a club down on Richmond—"

"You're underage, how do you even get into a club?"

Faysal gave him a knowing look. "So I dance a couple times with this chick. And I kiss her, nothing wrong with that, right?"

Mr Ilmi nodded.

"How the hell was I supposed to know she had a maniac boyfriend? Hours later me and my boys, we're walking to the subway, this black car with tinted windows pulls up to the curb, we stop to look and the window rolls down slowly and I see the silver tip of a semi. We turn and run . . . " Faysal stopped as if trying to recall an important detail.

"And?" Mr Ilmi asked.

"And that is it. That's all I remember. A couple of inches to the right and my pelvic bone would've been fucked for good. My wallet saved my ass. Can you believe that shit? Took some speed off the bullet."

"Wow." Mr Ilmi said. He didn't know if he believed Faysal's account of what happened or at least his innocence in the ass-shooting incident. He had heard about Faysal's gang activities, which included selling drugs and explained the many pairs of $150 trainers he owned. But Mr Ilmi sat there and nodded as if he really did believe Faysal's version of events. He was relieved that the incident hadn't ended in tragedy. He bent down and grabbed his leather satchel from the floor, fished out some papers and gave them to Faysal.

"What's this?"

"Your homework."

"What? I got shot and you want me to do homework?"

"You weren't shot in the head."

"They got me on Vicodin and Demerol and shit. I've been hallucinating about little furry bunnies with evil red eyes."

"I expect you to have all these chapters read and the review questions completed when I visit you next week."

Faysal put the papers down on his bedside table and sighed at the injustice he had to endure. The best part of getting shot in the ass was not having to go to school, and now Mr Ilmi was taking away that consolation. He buried his face in his pillow in a dramatic gesture. Just then, Faysal's father walked in.

Mr Ilmi got up from his seat and extended his hand to the short, balding man whose eyes showed a kind of existential weariness. "Asalamu alaykum," he said to the man, who shook his hand indifferently.

"Hi dad, this is my biology teacher, Mr Ilmi."

"Good to meet you, Mr Ilmi," the father said in Somali.

"I just came by to visit Faysal and bring him some homework."

"It's no use," the man said. "His mother and I tried everything, he's gonna end up in jail or killed."

"Dad, why you gotta be like that?"

"Be quiet! See what I have to deal with, Mr Ilmi."

"Listen to your father," Mr Ilmi said, trying not show his irritation at the certainty with which the man predicted his son's demise. *No father should say such things to a son,* he thought. "I must get going," he said. "Take care of yourself, Faysal. And it was nice meeting you," he said to the father.

"Thanks for the donuts," Faysal said, as he reached for another one and stuffed it into his mouth.

"No problem. Take it easy," Mr Ilmi said and headed for the door.

———

Later that night, as was their tradition, Mr Ilmi watched another interminable Bollywood film with Khadija after dinner. When the film ended, Mr Ilmi wanted to go to bed with his copy of Antonio Damasio's *Descartes' Error: Emotion, Reason, and the Human Brain,* which he'd started the previous week. It had captivated him. Khadija, however, needed him to get more medication for the severe heartburn she had been suffering due to her pregnancy.

Mr Ilmi shuffled off to the bedroom and put on a pair of his faded jeans and his jacket. As he was leaving the front door, his wife was putting on the second of the three Bollywood movies he had rented for her. It was going to be a long night. She waved to him as he closed the door. As he walked the long, badly lit hallway to the tiny elevators, he felt the stirrings of what he could only identify as the gratification of a desire to be alone, to contemplate his life and its current trajectory.

Mr Ilmi had been anxious all week about the coming birth of their child, and he wanted to talk to Khadija about his concerns and fears, imagined and real. She, on the other hand, was content to wait and accept whatever Allah had in store for them. Mr Ilmi had concluded that as far as she was concerned, having a baby is what happens when two people got married. End of story. As he got into the elevator and pushed the button for the parking basement, he was overcome with envy of his wife and her ability to accept life as it presented itself. But underneath his envy stirred a dim current of resentment. She possessed something he yearned for, yet she was unable or unwilling to share it with him.

It was ten in the evening and the aisles of Shoppers Drug Mart were practically deserted. He took his time, meandering about with his metal basket in his hand, in no particular hurry. After picking up three bottles of Khadija's heartburn medication, he strolled along the men's aisle and picked up a shaving cream and a deodorant; he stopped by the magazine stands and flipped through a newsmagazine, before moving on to the men's glossies showing successful-looking, well-groomed men. He tried his best to curb his envy. He picked up a copy of *Esquire*, whose cover showed a beaming Leonardo DiCaprio swinging a golf club. In the background were beautiful green hills and a distant blue ocean. He had never been on a golf course and now longed to be on one. He had never even considered golf to be a legitimate sport, yet all the same now he wanted to play golf. He desired a life that included trips to golf courses. Deep into these thoughts of the impossible, suddenly he heard the voice of a woman beside him.

"Arsenio! Oh my God! Is that you?"

His heart sank. Without looking, he knew who she was. No one else ever called him Arsenio. More than ten years had passed since he last saw her, and he was shocked to see her still looking so young, so unravaged by time. Her hair was shorter now, a bellowing mass of wavy curls that lent a kind of easy glamour to her face. She was wearing a black business suit with a knee-length skirt and red high heels, the kind of well-coordinated sexy professional outfit whose intent seemed to be to intimidate and arouse in the boardroom. She moved in for a tight embrace.

"Oh my God!" Mikeila wailed. "I can't believe this. How are you?"

Mr Ilmi's mouth had gone dry. His tongue was stuck to the roof of his mouth. After an eternity, he finally managed to produce a barely audible human voice. "I know. Yeah, I am . . . " He trailed off. He wanted to drop his shopping basket and run. It was painful to look at her, full of smiles, so genuinely happy to see him.

"How are you doing?" he said at last.

"Fuck, it feels like a lifetime ago, eh," she said.

He had always admired her openness, how easily she talked, without inhibitions. He remembered the first time she said "fuck" in his presence. They were at a bar in downtown Kingston, both seniors at Queen's. They were on the dance floor, some tuneless techno track was on that they found impossible to dance to and so they wrapped their arms around each other and swayed back and forth to their own rhythm. "I think we should go back to your place and fuck," she said without so much as a smile. No woman had ever uttered those words to him and he nearly came in his pants.

"What are you doing here?" he asked and instantly regretted it. It came out more hostile than he intended, as if he were saying, You have no business being in my neighbourhood, back in my life.

"I was just driving through and remembered some stuff I needed. I have an early flight to catch and I—" She stopped midway and asked: "What about you? You still live around here?"

"Yeah, a couple of blocks from here . . . at Dixon and Kipling. Do you work around here?"

"No, downtown."

"A bit out of your way, no?"

"I was visiting a business that I'm rating."

"Rating?"

"I work for a financial rating agency."

"Nice. So I guess you did end up getting that MBA after all."

Mikeila nodded. "And you, what do you do?"

"I . . . I teach now . . . high school," he said. He was about to say, "I am a teacher," but he always had a hard time saying those words. He felt like a fraud saying that. He considered himself as someone who taught rather than a teacher. To him being a teacher was not just a job. It was a calling—like being a nun or priest.

"You're a teacher. That's amazing," she said. Her glance fell on his shopping basket.

"Heartburn, eh?"

"Oh that. For my wife."

He wished he could take those last words back.

"You're married! That's fantastic, Arsenio."

He had a bodily, almost painful reaction to her calling him Arsenio. It was a nickname she gave him one night during their first week as a couple. He was lying in his bed in a little room on the third floor of a giant Victorian house near the campus that he had rented with five other guys. They were sweaty and spent from sex, and she bounced up and turned to him. "We need a name for you."

"What?"

"A name. For you."

"I have a name. Bashiir, remember?"

"No, I need to give you a name only I know."

She took his face in her hands and looked at him for a moment. She had a way of looking at him that made him feel seen, as if for the first time in his life. "Arsenio," she said, like a mother looking at her child and finding the perfect name for it.

"Arsenio?"

"Yes! Arsenio. As in Arsenio Hall."

"Why Arsenio?"

"Because you're funny like Arsenio."

It was true. He used to be funny in his former life, but he had lost that along with the many other traits he had surrendered to time.

"Because you're goofy like Arsenio," she continued.

He gave a boyish, hissing laugh the way Arsenio Hall did on his nightly show.

"And because you fuck like Arsenio," she said and kissed him on the mouth.

"Oh, I do, do I?"

She nodded.

"And you know how Arsenio fucks?"

"I have a terribly overactive imagination."

"And is he good in your imagination?"

"The best," she said. They laughed together. They kissed. And then kissed for the rest of the night and that's how it was between them. That is how it was for a long time.

That was the one time in his life when he was properly in love. *How it was then is how it should always be*, he thought to himself as he stared at Mikeila. He tried to remember why they broke up. Who said what cruel thing to whom? Who broke whose heart? Who uttered the final words? He couldn't remember any of it now. Over the years, he often wondered if he would ever see her again. And if he did, what would that moment feel like. And now that he was in the middle of that moment, he didn't know how to inhabit it. She felt foreign to him.

As though Mikeila knew what he was feeling just then, she put a hand on his arm. He caught a fleeting glimpse of an elegant diamond ring on her ring finger. "It was nice seeing you," she said with a smile.

Was. The word echoed in his head. This chance meeting that he had played in his head for so many years had already leapt into their shared past.

"It was nice seeing you too," he replied. They smiled at each other for a long time until it felt awkward. She moved closer and laid a soft kiss on his cheek, so soft he barely felt her lips. "Take good care of yourself," she said, finally taking her hand back from his arm. She turned and walked away towards the cashier. As she retreated he waited to see if she would turn around for one last look at him. She didn't.

It was then that it hit him—the magnitude of his naïveté—of his mistake. He genuinely believed all those years ago that what he felt for Mikeila was the first of many to come. It was inconceivable to him that it might never happen again. He remembered that warm overcast day in early May when she told him she was going back to Trinidad to visit her parents, after which she would start her graduate studies at Cornell. They had been fighting the entire month leading up to that day and it seemed like a good idea to spend the summer apart.

He stood behind a shelf and watched her pay at the cashier. He looked on as she smiled one of her benevolent smiles at the cashier and headed for the door. *Mistakes were made,* he said to himself as he gazed at her walking through the sliding glass door of the store and disappear into the night.

———

Mr Ilmi stood at his usual spot in the classroom, leaning back against his desk to face his students. He was pleasantly surprised that he had a full house this afternoon. Even the three amigos, Derek, Mustafa, and Liban, who hadn't bothered to show up for the last three classes, were present.

"Okay. Who is up first?" Mr Ilmi asked. Silence. Not a single shuffle or cough. "All right, you leave me with no choice but to pick one of you myself."

They squirmed in their seats, they looked away so as not to meet his eyes.

"Okay, Duran, you're up first," Mr Ilmi said.

"I'm always the first to go," Duran protested, looking aggrieved. "Why it always gotta be me?"

"I know, I know," Mr Ilmi said in his best mock sympathetic voice. "The tragedy of your life." There was a smattering of laughter from the others. "Just think of it this way, Duran. You will be the first to finish your presentation and get back to your seat."

The idea of getting the ordeal out of the way and returning to his daydreaming won Duran over and he hoisted himself up and staggered to the front. He stood hunched over, opened the folded papers in his hand, and began to read. "The temporal lobe is a part of the brain . . . "

"Hold on, Duran," Mr Ilmi said. "Aren't you forgetting something?"

Duran looked dumbfounded. "I don't think so."

"Think again."

Duran looked around for a hint. It was no use. The rest of the class looked just as lost. "The cap, Duran. What did I tell you about wearing a baseball cap in my class?"

"Oh that."

"Yes, that."

"My bad."

"Continue."

Duran took off his cap and adjusted his shirt, which looked about four sizes too large for his thin frame. He held up the paper a few inches away from his face and started reading again. "The temporal lobe is a part of the brain that is home to the primary auditory cortex and . . . "

"Duran."

"Yes, Mr Ilmi."

"Where is the auditory cortex?"

Duran, looking bewildered, stared at his teacher.

"If I produced a diagram of the brain, would you be able to show us where the auditory cortex is?"

A long pause. "Yes."

"Yes?"

"Maybe."

"Which is it? Yes or maybe?"

"Both."

"So it's a definite yes and a maybe, simultaneously?"

"Yes. I think so."

Mr Ilmi looked defeated. He stayed silent for a few moments, then he looked at Duran and said, "I tell you what Duran, why don't you redo the presentation tomorrow. I will ask you the same question, and when I do, I want you to be able to show me on the diagram every part of the brain that you mention. Does that sound fair to you?"

Duran nodded his head like a toddler and walked back to his seat.

"All right. Who's next?"

They all looked at each other.

"Janet, why don't you show these boys how it's really done."

Janet got up with her usual smile. She proceeded to distribute around what looked like a professionally produced brochure. She handed one to Mr Ilmi as she took to the podium next to his desk.

Mr Ilmi gave the brochure a quick glance and was impressed by the multicoloured labeled diagram with little thought bubbles that succinctly explained the functions of the hippocampus.

"For my presentation, I chose the hippocampus," Janet proclaimed. "So what is the hippocampus?" She paused dramatically, giving ample time for her rhetorical question to land. "It is one of the most important parts of the human brain. Without it, we would never be able to find our way around this school or walk back home after school."

Some of the students chuckled. Maybe it was her voice. Janet had a way of talking like an over grown baby with the IQ of an astronaut. Mr Ilmi watched as she pontificated on the role that the hippocampus played in spatial navigation, expertly referring to her diagram. She showed the class the location of the hippocampus in each side of the brain, in the medial temporal lobe, just under the cortical surface. She explained how the hippocampus helped us develop spatial memory and navigation, and she drove home the point that without this small feature in our brain, we would all be truly lost. Just when Mr Ilmi thought he could not be more impressed with Janet's thorough knowledge of the hippocampus, she moved onto what happens when this part of the brain gets damaged by an accident or a disease like Alzheimer's. In short, Janet's presentation was everything Mr Ilmi could ask for. Janet was just another confirmation of his suspicion that the girls in his class and everywhere else, were outperforming the boys in every subject. He secretly hoped that when his wife finally gave birth, it would be a little girl they put in his arms.

"Thank you, Janet," Mr Ilmi said when she concluded. "Nicely done!"

Janet gave another one of her shy smiles and walked back to her seat.

"All right. Who wants to follow that?" Mr Ilmi asked facetiously. There were no takers. "James, your turn."

James, who usually never turned down an opportunity to get

attention, hesitated for a moment, no doubt nervous about following the great Janet. "Cool," he finally said and strutted up to the front of the class, bringing with him his black and red Toronto Raptors jacket. Facing his classmates, giving a dramatic shiver he put on the jacket. Mr Ilmi thought he wouldn't be surprised if some day he saw James in a gangster film, playing the part of a crazed, violent drug dealer or a ruthless pimp.

"So you know why I shivered and put on my jacket?" James asked and waited for a response. "Because my brain told me to," he answered himself, in a deadpan tone.

The class broke out into laughter.

"Actually, it was my hypothalamus . . . It's true. My body felt cold and to feel warm, I put on my jacket so I can function better. Oh, and check this out," he said. Taking his jacket off, he made a ta-da gesture. "I got warm, so I took it off. The hypothalamus is so freaking cool. It regulates our body temperature. It tells us to eat when we're hungry so we don't starve to death. And when we get thirsty, it sends a signal to our body saying yo, give me some H2O."

More laughter. Even Nuur let out a chuckle. And so James proceeded to entertain the class with his antics concerning the hypothalamus. Evidently he had done his reading, and Mr Ilmi was surprised. When he had finished, he grabbed his jacket and headed back to his seat. The class gave him a roaring applause.

Mr Ilmi said, "We have time for one more, the rest we'll continue tomorrow." He scanned the room. "Nuur, your turn."

Nuur gathered his notes, went and stood before the class, and cleared his throat a little too loudly. His qamiis, his kufi, his beard, everything about him looked out of place.

"I want to tell you about the amygdalae today," he said, his voice deep but cracking ever so slightly, his nerves about to give way. "We have two of them. The plural is amygdalae and the singular, amygdala."

He walked up to the blackboard and drew a large diagram of the brain, and deep in the centre he drew two small shapes, each the size of an almond. "We've all had this experience. It's late at night, you're walking home and you hear the sound of footsteps behind you. You sense danger. You quicken your pace. Your heart starts to beat faster and faster . . . Or you're watching a movie. A cute baby is wailing. He's in distress. No one comes to help him. You feel sad. You wish you could help the baby, comfort him . . . Or you're walking from school, and on your way you pass a food stand and buy a cinnamon roll, you bite into it and bam, for an instant, you're five years old, in your pajamas, your dad just walked in with a box of warm cinnamon rolls for you and your brother, and suddenly your heart breaks because you remember your dad. You miss him so much and become sad. All these complex impulses and sensations and thoughts, good and bad, are processed by the amygdalae. These two tiny nuclei control and trigger our responses to, and our engagement with, the world around us. They receive input from sound, touch, taste, and so on. The amygdalae help us form long-term memory. They inform what we fear, hate, love. They help us experience emotions in other people. When someone cries, we don't laugh. When we see someone laugh, we often laugh with them. The amygdalae are kind of like a diary of our body. They record and remember trauma. They remember fear and anger and happiness. In short, the amygdalae make us who we are. There are even recent studies that suggest a strong link between the amygdalae and sexual orientation."

"So Ryan likes to blow guys because his amygdalae make him do it," Andy, one of James' sidekicks, blurted. A smattering of nervous half-laughter. Unlike James, Andy always struggled with the timing of his bad jokes.

"One more comment like that and you will find yourself in the principal's office," Mr Ilmi barked, his temper getting the better of him. "Continue, Nuur."

Mr Ilmi looked on as Nuur went through his presentation, occasionally consulting his notes. But it was clear that Nuur didn't need notes. It was as if he knew things by instinct. Nuur had an uncanny ability to digest complex material, run it through his own unique mental processor, and give it back fully and genuinely comprehended. Nuur was the reason Mr Ilmi loved teaching. Every once in a while, a student walked into his biology class endowed with the kind of nimble mind that made teaching a pleasure.

It was clear to him that standing before him was a natural talent, a unique mind that given the right opportunity and guidance could blossom into a first-rate intellect. Janet was prepared and competent. In fact, the girl was so competent she could run a small country. James showed a knack for communication and he had a wonderful sense of the theatrics about him. But Nuur showed the potential of a serious scholar, someone who possessed what it took to go very far in life.

Mr Ilmi was lost in his thoughts when he realized that Nuur had finished his presentation and was staring at him, waiting to be dismissed.

"Thank you, Nuur. That was wonderful," he said as he looked at his watch. It was two minutes before the end of class. "Eli, Hussein, Tanisha, Lola, Abukar, and Rodriguez, your turn tomorrow. Make me proud," Mr Ilmi called out as the students started gathering their belongings.

Mr Ilmi watched them file out of the room. "Nuur, may I have a word with you?"

Nuur sat back down.

Mr Ilmi sat on the edge of his desk and gave a long look at Nuur, who had a worried look on his face. "Why the amygdalae?" he asked.

Nuur looked puzzled. He glanced down at his notes, as though the answer were written somewhere in them.

"It's okay, Nuur. It's not a quiz. I'm just curious, that's all," Mr Ilmi said with a gentle smile.

Nuur remained quiet for a moment. Then he spoke. "I don't know. It seemed more . . . I don't know, it felt important, like if I understood the amygdalae then maybe I could understand myself." He paused and made a face. "That sounds dumb. I can't really explain it."

"No, it's not dumb at all. Far from it." Mr Ilmi said. "And what did you think of your presentation?"

"I wish I had more time to work on it. I could've done it better."

"Yes. You could've. But as it was, you did a fine job."

"Thank you, Mr Ilmi."

"Don't ever lose that, though."

Nuur gave his teacher an intent look, trying to make sense of what he had just said.

"That feeling, that you could've done better. Don't ever lose it," Mr Ilmi explained. "It's what separates the good from the great." He said this with the conviction of a man who wished he had someone tell him the same thing when he was Nuur's age, someone to tell him he had it in him to do better, be better.

"I'm gonna be late for calculus, Mr Ilmi."

"All right, off you go."

6

EVER SINCE HIS FATHER LEFT and took a second wife, Nuur had come home from school to find his mother Haawo usually still in her baati, the long, formless cotton dress that she loved to wear to bed. She would be sprawled on the overstuffed olive-green living room couch, talking on the phone with one or more of her three sisters who were scattered around the world. Her calling card gave her five hundred talking minutes for just ten dollars, and she went through several cards a week. These two- or three-way calls spanned the globe, with his Aunt Jamila in Stockholm, Aunt Zaynab in Dar es Salaam, and Aunt Luul (his favourite) in Dubai. They consoled her and also admonished her for still crying over the man who had discarded her. The one who could be relied upon for admonishment was Aunt Luul. She was the strongest and feistiest of them, a no nonsense feminist who would be horrified, however, to be described as one. For her, a feminist was synonymous with a lesbian.

Most afternoons, when Nuur came home, his mother hadn't made dinner. He would drop his knapsack and go straight to the kitchen and prepare the only dish he knew how: pasta and sauce, with ground meat from their neighbourhood halal market. But today, when Nuur opened the door, he was met by the intoxicating scent of his mother's cooking. There, in their small kitchen with its oppressively dark brown cabinets and beige linoleum tiles was his mother, standing by the sink, peeling potatoes. On the stove were three pots. Nuur smelt a heady mixture of basmati rice, broiled goat meat, and sautéed vegetables.

"Hooyo, seetahay?" Nuur asked. This was his standard Somali greeting for his mom. She turned around and greeted him with a radiant smile he hadn't seen in months. Haawo came towards him and hugged him, keeping her arms stretched wide so as not to smear him. Nuur felt the warm perspiration on her cheek when she pressed it against his. "What's all this?" he asked.

"Dinner," Haawo replied.

"You're cooking again," Nuur said in a tone that represented at once a statement of fact and a question.

"I'm making your favourite, rice with goat meat," his mother said.

"That was dad's favourite, actually."

"You love it too," Haawo insisted.

Nuur hated to contradict her so he let it go. He heard the sound of the shower running. "Ayuub is back?"

"Your father is home," she said nonchalantly, as though he'd just walked in from a long day of work. She turned her back to Nuur and resumed chopping vegetables on the cutting board.

"When?"

"He came to his senses and has returned to his family. Praise be to Allah."

"Yes, praise be to Allah. But when did he come back?"

"This morning, after you went to school."

"Mom, you're divorced. You asked for a divorce and he granted it, remember?"

"Your father talked to an imam in Minnesota. The imam told him the divorce wasn't valid. It was done out of anger."

"Of course it was out of anger. Happy people don't divorce."

"He only granted me the divorce because I demanded it, out of anger."

"That's ludicrous. What kind of imam has he been talking to?"

"Nuur, don't be like that. You've always been a baari boy."

To hell with being baari, he wanted to say, but kept quiet. He had so fully accepted himself as baari, the obedient son, that he found it impossible to be anything else. He had to be baari. Even though he felt like walking to the washroom and dragging his father by what little hair he still had and throwing him out of the apartment.

As he stood in the little hallway outside the kitchen, he felt consumed by a kind of rage that at once scared and thrilled him. He heard a sound and turned his head to see his father, Ismail Adan Farray, standing outside the washroom. Everyone who knew him called him Farray on account of his index finger, half of which had been cut off in a work accident in the early eighties in Casablanca, where he had been studying during the day and working as a carpenter at night. He had a towel wrapped around his waist, and his thinning hair was brushed back to reveal the sculpted features of his face and his big, bushy eyebrows that Nuur and Ayuub would brush with a tiny comb when they were little.

For months after his father left, all Nuur had heard from his mother was a torrent of curses, calling on Allah and all the prophets to make Ismail Adan Farray's new wife barren. That frantic cursing gave way to bitter resignation to the fact that no amount of praying for his testicles to fall off would bring him back. Now, just when Nuur had gotten used to that, his father had returned.

"I don't get a hug?" his father said, approaching him. He came and stood before Nuur, who was now inches taller than him. They stood in silence as though sizing each other up for a fight. Then all of a sudden Nuur felt his father's arms, still warm from the shower, engulf him. After a moment's hesitation, Nuur lifted his arms and embraced his father and for a brief moment he felt like a little boy who knew nothing of life but the simple and joyous sensation of being hugged by his dad.

Nuur couldn't believe how light his father's body felt pressed against his own strengthening chest. Gone was the stout belly of previous years. Significantly diminished were the broad, muscular shoulders that he used to ride on as child, his little legs dangling on either side of his father's chest. In the midst of the embrace, Nuur couldn't help the thought that his father had returned to fatten and restore himself before returning to his new life in Minnesota.

"How are you, my boy?" his father asked. "It's good to see you again."

"Good to see you too," Nuur said, hoping that if he forced himself to utter the words, Allah would make them true. Ismail touched his son's beard as though they were the feathers of an exotic bird.

"What's happening here?"

"It's the Sunnah of the Prophet Mohamed. Peace be upon him," Nuur said firmly.

His father gave a sarcastic chuckle, with that touch of venom he reserved for the sanctimonious imams who loitered about the courtyard of their apartment complex asking him why they hadn't seen him at Friday prayers. He turned to his wife and said, "You forgot to tell me our son has joined the Mujahedeen."

Nuur was relieved to see his that father had not changed, that he still possessed a fear of religion, which manifested itself in his contempt for anyone who displayed overt piety. Nuur believed that his father also envied the certainty with which the pious moved about in the world, a certainty he must've secretly yearned for.

Nuur sat down with his parents at the dinner table. With little appetite for food and even lesser desire to be sitting facing his father, he moved his food around on the plate, trying to eat out of politeness. His eyes finally met his father's and they held each other's gazes.

"Is this a temporary fashion thing or do you plan to keep it for the rest of your life?" his father asked, putting down his fork with deliberation.

"Keep what?"

"The beard. Your beard."

"Forever, Inshallah," Nuur said rather proudly.

"You think you're going to find a professional job with a beard that big?"

"Why not?"

"Why not?" Ismail turned to his wife. "Talk some sense into your son."

"Maybe I will be so good at my job that they won't care how big my beard is."

"Don't be naïve," his father said. "Cadaan people will always care about how big your beard is." He used the generic word *Cadaan* for all white people the way some white people said *blacks*—not as mere description of skin colour but as a category of people who shared a particular character defect.

"Cadaan people will always want you to look like them, talk like them, think like them. They like to surround themselves with people who are just a little different, to make life a bit more exotic, add a bit of colour to their bland lives, but not so different that it challenges their sense of the world. Cadaan people don't like to be challenged with the presence of too much difference. It scares them."

Ismail spoke with the confidence of a man who had known these Cadaan people intimately all his life. "Their tolerance has a limit," he continued, emphasizing *tolerance* sarcastically.

"Really?" was all Nuur could come up with, in the face of his father's confident assertions.

"Yes, really," his father said, pushing away his plate.

"When was the last time you were around these Cadaan people?" Nuur asked.

"Meaning what?"

"Meaning, you don't know any, Dad. In all the years we lived here, I've never seen you so much as shake the hand of a Cadaan person. You don't work with them. You don't socialize with them. You live in a self-imposed ghetto—"

"What's your point?" His father snapped. There was a limit to how much challenge, rhetorical or otherwise, Ismail Farray was willing to allow from his son.

"My point is, you say their tolerance is limited when in fact your tolerance is even more limited."

"Come on, you guys," Haawo interjected. "Let's just eat and enjoy each other's company?"

Nuur sat back. "So how long are you staying, dad?"

"What's that supposed to mean?"

"It's just a question."

"Why don't you say what's really on your mind, son?"

"It's a simple question really. How long do you plan to stay? Three days, a week, a month, forever?"

"Watch it, boy!"

"You guys, come on!" Haawo said impatiently, glancing back and forth between her son and her husband.

"You must've been spending too much time with your brother. You're becoming just like him."

"And what's that, exactly?"

"Too clever for your own good."

"Have you heard from your brother lately?" his mother asked Nuur, desperate to change the direction the evening was headed.

"No, mother. I haven't seen Ayuub in four days."

"Does he do that often, disappear like that?" Ismail asked.

There was a long pause.

"Well?" Ismail asked.

"Sometimes," Haawo said meekly. Nuur noticed his mother reverting back to her old self around his father. Meek. Hesitant. Deferential. Sometimes Nuur wished Auntie Luul was his mother. She would've known how to put his father in his place.

"And you just let him . . . " Nuur's father paused, as if searching for the right word, " . . . roam free. Let him come in and out like it's a hotel?"

"What's she supposed to do, tie him to his bed?"

"I'm talking to your mother!"

"Sometimes he stays at his girlfriend's house," Haawo said at last.

"So this is what Somali parents have come to now, allowing their daughters to have boys sleeping over?"

"She's not Somali," Haawo said with a sigh.

"What?"

"Her name's Lisa," Haawo said in a soft voice, as though not to let the neighbours find out that her beloved son had gone off and shacked up with the dreaded Cadaan girl. This had been, in fact, Haawo's worst nightmare, that one of her sons would end up bringing home a white girl. Nuur knew that his mother wasn't too worried about him bringing a white girl home. Or any girl for that matter. She believed he was too awkward around girls and the task of choosing a wife for him would eventually fall on her. And like any good Somali mother, it was a task she more than looked forward to. She longed for the day when her son would sit across from her and utter the words, "I'm ready, mother. I want a wife." She would clasp his face in her soft, hennaed hands, kiss him on both cheeks and say, "Mashallah! I know just the perfect one for you," and she would start making frantic calls to relatives all over the world to spread the news. The news of a young Somali man looking for a young Somali wife traveled faster than CNN's breaking news.

Nuur watched as his father fumed in his seat, but he tried not to show his delight. "Look what happened," Nuur wanted to say to his father. "You go off for one year and your beloved Ayuub has shacked up with a Cadaan girl, probably giving you a little mixed grandchild even as we speak, and your other son, the one you barely speak to, has joined the enemy—those pious, holier-than-thou, mosque-going, qamiis-wearing simpletons you've spent your entire life mocking." He wanted to say all those things that would hurt his father the most and demonstrate to him his inability to make his two sons in his own image. Whatever respect and affection he had once felt for him had vanished. As a boy, Nuur had gone to pathetic lengths to make his father notice him. He had struggled to be allowed into the warmth of the exclusive club of his father, mother, and older brother. It came like a revelation now that there was no club anymore. All that was left of it was a mother who had surrendered her pride and dignity, a father who had abandoned his family for the tits of a girl young enough to be his daughter, and an older brother who changed girlfriends like socks.

Nuur was overcome with a longing to get up, put on his shoes, and walk to the mosque. He could still make it to evening prayer if he walked fast enough. He yearned for a feeling of . . . he didn't know what exactly, except that he wouldn't find it sitting at this table with his mother and father.

———

Hours later, returning from the mosque, Nuur walked home with a mixture of emotions roiling inside him. What he could register clearly were shame and regret. He had prayed, read a few Surahs from the Quran, and done his calculus homework until he saw the lights turning off, telling him it was time to go home. Spending a few hours at the mosque had always had the effect of cleansing him of whatever anger or anxiety had pestered him during the day. He regretted the rage he harboured for his parents. As he entered the apartment building and took the elevator, Nuur vowed to be kinder to them, for Allah promised paradise for those who were good to their parents. He walked in the long, dimly lit corridor to his apartment feeling drained. He longed for sleep, the kind of deep, restorative sleep from which one might wake up changed.

It was late and Nuur didn't want to wake them up so he opened the door as quietly as he could. Just as he was taking his shoes off, he heard muffled voices. He wondered if his parents had started to argue already. *That didn't take long*, he thought to himself. But it became clear to him that what he was hearing was the sound of his father in a sexual climax. It hit him like a punch in the gut. He turned around, opened the door, and ran for the elevator. He tried hard to banish the images forming in his head: his mother naked, splayed out, debasing herself for the pleasure of the man who broke her heart; his entitled father greedily taking what he wanted, whenever he desired. In that instant, he hated his mother even more than he hated his father.

It wasn't until he staggered out into the cool, damp air of the night and took a deep breath that he felt calm enough to walk. He didn't know where to go, so he went towards the little courtyard in the centre of the complex of apartment buildings. In this parkette, with its small sandbox, a monkey bar, and three swings, he had spent many summer afternoons as a child, playing while his mother sat on a bench with other Somali mothers watching over their children and sharing the latest news from the war back home.

Nuur walked across the sandbox to the swings. He dropped his school bag on the ground and sat on one. The cold metal chains holding the seat sent a slight shiver through him. He began a slow, rhythmic swing, back and forth, back and forth, gazing at the amber lights of the apartments around him, until they blended into a luminous mass.

He braked with his foot on the ground and came to an abrupt stop. He let go of the chains and sat motionless on the rubber seat for a long time, peering at the little boxes of light in the buildings. In each of those boxes were crammed entire families, five or six or seven souls. Each of those boxes was a life, glimmering, however faintly, with the hope and tenacity that had carried them across continents.

Staring hard enough at the boxes, he discerned vague forms of their occupants. Many of them were Somalis who had come to Canada in the early nineties, fleeing the civil war or the refugee camps in Kenya or Ethiopia, ending up here and calling it home. Among Somalis the world over, this neighbourhood in Toronto had become famous as simply "Dixon," named after the main street that ran next to it. Nuur had borrowed from the local library a book called *From Mogadishu to Dixon: The Somali Diaspora in the Global Context*. He found it interesting but dry and academic, full of statistics and lacking life.

Six buildings, some twenty floors each, the white brick had faded to grey, the windows were dull, and the balconies filled with tattered suitcases and the debris of uprooted lives. As the nineties gave way to the new millennium, many Somalis left for other parts of Canada, especially Alberta, to chase their dreams.

Nuur heard laughter coming from the entrance of one of the buildings. He made out four guys. He wondered if one of them was Ayuub. He imagined Ayuub in his girlfriend Lisa's bedroom, or hanging out with his friends Ahmeday and Fathudin, passing a joint, talking about girls, while Tupac or Jay-Z blared out of a CD player. There was a time when Nuur and Ayuub would lie in their beds, listening to *Me Against the World* or *Life After Death*, while Ayuub pontificated on the brilliance of Tupac's lyrics or Biggie's genius with rhyme. But when Nuur gave up hip-hop for taped Quran recitations, their long, rambling chats that had lasted deep into the night slowly ceased and became a memory of an era whose faint melodies Nuur could still hear if he sat quietly, like, say, in a park late at night.

As though his mind had willed his brother into being, Nuur saw the unmistakable figure of Ayuub crossing the parking lot, heading for their building. Nuur felt a pang of joy and called out twice. Ayuub stopped and stared in his direction, then started walking across the parkette towards him.

Nuur made out a smile on Ayuub's face as he passed under a lamp. "I thought it was you," he said when he got closer and raised an arm for a quick fist bump. He went and took the adjacent swing.

"What's up, little bro?"

"Nothing. Just chilling."

"Just chilling?"

"Yeah."

"Cool."

Ayuub took out a cigarette and lit it. The brothers glanced at each other for a moment then broke out into inexplicable chuckles, the kind they had shared in the past for so many unsaid or unsayable things. Without warning, Ayuub reached for Nuur's kufi, put it on his head and moved it from side to side as if modeling for a prospective buyer. "What do you think?"

"Nice. It suits you," Nuur said.

Ayuub laughed. He put the kufi back on his brother's head and said, "Suits you better." They smiled at each other in agreement. "So, what'ya doing bro, sitting here all by yourself this hour of the night?"

"Just had to get out of the house."

"Old lady driving you crazy?"

"Don't call her that."

"What? She *is* old." Ayuub took another drag of his cigarette, then said, "I'm just kidding around."

"I know."

Nuur remained quiet, trying to figure out how best to break the news to Ayuub that their father was back. He had a good reason to worry about how Ayuub might react. The previous year, when Ayuub decided to drop out of high school, just before their father left for Minnesota, the two had gotten into one of their biggest fights. Unlike their previous fights, which had ended with Ayuub leaving the apartment for a few hours, his father had grabbed Nuur's library copy of *Catcher in the Rye* that was lying on the dining table, rolled it tight, and started hitting Ayuub with it.

Ayuub took each of those ferocious blows with heroic stoicism that surprised Nuur. Their mother had screamed at their father to stop, but the blows kept landing. All Ayuub could do was cover his face with both hands, leaving his head exposed. Perhaps the spine of the book landed on a vein. Suddenly a thick stream of blood started running down Ayuub's face, and his father's hand froze midair.

"Look what you did! Look what you did!" his mother said, sobbing and cursing her husband. "May Allah punish you for this, Ismail Farray. May Allah punish you!" Two days later, his father left for Minnesota to visit his brother and for a brief change of scenery that became a year and yielded a new wife.

"Dad is back," Nuur said at last and waited for his brother's reaction. But Ayuub said nothing, as he made the tiniest back and forth motion on the swing and looked straight up at the lighted windows of the apartments. Nuur felt certain that he was thinking about that incident, when their mother had finally called an ambulance. The head wound turned out to be nothing more than a cut on the scalp but it marked them all in some unique way. They never spoke of it.

Nuur watched his brother take the last drag of his cigarette. "I can't believe she took him back," Nuur said at last. "After all that drama and the screaming on the phone, she still took him back."

Was it love, Nuur had wondered? Or loyalty to the life they had shared for almost twenty-five years, before fleeing their home in Mogadishu for short stays in Kenya, Italy, and the United States, finally settling in Dixon in Toronto into an apartment whose living room was no bigger than the veranda of their home back in Mogadishu? A villa with two maids, a gardener, and a driver. Such was the life Ismail Farray had provided for his young family thanks to an illustrious career as the architect of some of the most popular hotels in Mogadishu, including Hotel Juba and Hotel Al-Uruba. His work had included many international trips aboard Somali Airlines. On one of those flights Ismail Farray met a beautiful flight attendant called Haawo. In four months, they were married, went to Rome for their honeymoon, and soon thereafter Haawo became pregnant with Ayuub. Her sky-blue flight attendant's uniform with the little white stars was never worn again. Nuur wasn't even conceived when that life came to an abrupt end one bright morning in January 1991.

"So is he back for good?" Ayuub asked.

"Not sure how long he's staying," Nuur said. "What I don't get is, why make all that fuss and all that drama if she was just gonna take him back?"

Ayuub cleared his throat and spat on the ground. "She's fifty years old, bro."

"So?"

"So give her a break. A Somali woman after a certain age has a better chance of being killed by a terrorist than finding another husband."

"That's ridiculous!"

"Is it? How many Somali men do you know who wanna marry a fifty-year-old woman with two grown-ass boys?"

"A fifty-year-old man," Nuur said, rather proud of his answer.

Ayuub gave one of his throaty laughs. "Fifty-year-old Somali men wanna marry twenty-year-olds, preferably twenty-year-old virgins."

"So be alone then," Nuur said, speaking not only about his mother but about all the middle-aged Somali mothers whose husbands had taken second wives.

"Easy for you to say, bro. To you being alone is a phase. To her it's a life-sentence. You have your whole life ahead of you. What does she have to look forward to? An empty apartment and a stack of long-distance calling cards, that's what. So don't judge, bro. You have this whole black-and-white thing about life. You gotta allow some room for messy shit. We all make choices. Some good ones and some really shitty ones. That's life. So don't fucking judge."

Nuur glanced at his brother's profile and tried to remember the last time they talked like this. Like men. Like friends. Ayuub turned to Nuur and reached for his beard and gave it a light tug. "When you gonna get rid of this, man?"

"It's the Sunnah of the Prophet, peace be upon him," Nuur said.

"Well, the Prophet, peace be upon him," Ayuub said imitating his brother's pious tone, "lived fourteen hundred years ago. You live in the twenty-first century."

"So?"

"So, cut it off."

"But I like it."

"Seriously dude, how the hell do you expect to get laid looking like that?"

Nuur turned away. Sex was the one thing they never discussed. On this subject, there was a chasm between them as wide as the ocean. For one thing, Nuur never had any and Ayuub had too much, but there was also a difference of philosophy. Nuur looked forward to his wedding night when he would experience for the first time whatever pleasure and beauty came from sex and be happy knowing that he came to it the right way, the way Allah prescribed it in his holy book. Ayuub, on the other hand, seemed, at least to his brother, as though sex was what he did while waiting for something else to happen.

"Were you headed home when I called you?" Nuur asked.

"Yeah. Needed to get some clothes."

"So what, you're living with Lisa now?"

"Yeah, pretty much."

"Is it serious?"

Ayuub became quiet, as though searching for the right words. "She's pregnant. So yeah. I guess it is."

Nuur felt a sharp pang of something that was at once shock and thrill. He was horrified that his brother was bringing a new life into the world without the sanctity of marriage. He was committing an innocent child to a life of being called illegitimate in the living room of every Somali family they knew. But there was also a part of Nuur that knew that there was no such thing as an illegitimate child, there were only illegitimate parents. And that part of him won out and he was happy, happier than he had felt in a long time, knowing that in less than a year, he would become an uncle. Nuur placed his palm on the back of Ayuub's neck and gave it a gentle nudge. "I'm happy for you and Lisa."

"Thanks, bro," Ayuub said. He paused a moment, then added, "I'm going to Fort McMurray."

Nuur felt a sudden shiver. Fort McMurray was a world away. He had heard awful stories about Alberta. Not a month passed these days without news of another young Somali man's body being found in some snow bank or muddy ditch somewhere. Drug war, was all the police would say. Some fifty murders unsolved. Unsolvable? Not worth solving? Nuur tried his best to put all that aside and be happy for his brother's newly found sense of direction, even if that pointed far into the west, farther than anyone in his family had ever ventured.

"Fathudin is coming with me," Ayuub said, as though to allay Nuur's obvious fears. "Fathudin's older brother lives there with three other guys. They each pay like three hundred a month for rent. Can you believe that? Think of all the money I could save. He says the place is crawling with recruiters looking for guys to work in rigs up north. Twenty-three dollars an hour. Can't beat that."

"Sounds amazing," Nuur said. "Sounds like you have it all planned out."

Ayuub nodded. "There is no future for me here, bro. Don't wanna end up like dad."

Nuur nodded.

"Man, this place, you don't get out while you can, it'll swallow you whole," Ayuub said. "Get out while you can, bro. Get out before it's too late." A long pause. "Everyone is getting out."

"Everyone" was an exaggeration, still the Somali population in these apartments was nowhere near what it used to be in the late nineties, when the vast majority here was Somali. But the gang wars of Somali teens, reenacting the clan battles back home, and crackdowns by police and security guards with their German Shepherds had chased many Somali parents away, as they found themselves, once again, fleeing violence.

"Look at my friends," Ayuub continued. "Yasiin and Omar went back to Mogadishu. Suleyman and Jabriil went to Alberta, and Mohamed . . . " Ayuub's voice trailed off, but Nuur knew what his brother wasn't saying. Mohamed, one of Ayuub's best friends, the boy who had lived three floors below them and with whom he had walked to school everyday and played basketball, was shot dead last June. His shirtless body was found lying at the base of a tree with three bullet holes in his chest.

"It's like we needed twenty years to get it through our thick heads that this ain't our home," Ayuub said, his voice cracking a little. "This here," he said, looking around, shaking his head, "is no place for us."

Nuur nodded but he didn't know why he was nodding. This was his home, the only place he had ever known. But he didn't know how to put that feeling into words, so he stood up, stretched and reached for his schoolbag on the floor. He lugged it onto his shoulders like a little boy.

"You think he's asleep by now?" Ayuub asked.

"Not sure. Probably not," Nuur replied.

"Then sit down and keep me company."

"Don't you wanna see him?"

"Not tonight. Soon, but not tonight."

Nuur sat back down on the swing, his knapsack still on his back. His brother took out another cigarette, lit it, and took a long drag. He sighed with what seemed to Nuur was happiness bordering on bliss. Ayuub offered the cigarette to his little brother who shook his head.

"Oh, don't be such a pussy. Just one drag."

Nuur hesitated a moment, then took the cigarette from his brother. He inhaled it deeply, creating a small, transient light in the darkness between him and Ayuub. He let out a deep, violent cough, eliciting a peel of laughter from Ayuub. When Nuur recovered from his coughing fit and his brother from his laughter, they sat silently on their respective swings and stared ahead at their building.

7

"A s my African Express flight from Nairobi made its slow descent into Mogadishu, I looked out the window of the plane and saw the shore of the Indian Ocean. The blue water and white sand dunes looked exactly as I had left them. A warm and welcoming feeling of home enveloped me."

In a shaky voice, Mr Ilmi read those words from several pages he had printed out the night before. He took a sip of water from a bottle on the side of the podium. He tried his best to shield his eyes from the expectant gazes of the audience in front of him. He felt their hunger for the profound lessons he had learned from his return to Somalia after twenty-five years. Or, failing that, an exciting adventure story from him.

A month ago, this had seemed like a good idea. Mr Ilmi received an email from his former classmate and good friend from Queen's, Kayin Akinsanya, a boisterous Nigerian. They had met in an undergrad course on The African Novel and their heated debates about the legacy of colonialism on their beloved continent became famous among their circle of friends. Kayin was now the chair of the African Studies Department at the University of Toronto. He invited Mr Ilmi to speak at the awkwardly titled symposium, "Unraveling Somalia: Interrogating the Politics of Diasporic Identity." A month before, Mr Ilmi had relished the thought of standing in front of an audience, telling it about what he had witnessed recently in Mogadishu. When he returned from Somalia, Kayin was one of the first people he had called. A few minutes into their telephone conversation, Kayin, in his still pronounced Nigerian accent said, "Eh, you must come to our symposium then. You must tell us the things you saw."

Over the phone, the idea of taking part in a symposium had sounded exciting, but Mr Ilmi wished he had turned down his good friend's invitation. For all his other ambitions, Mr Ilmi had never fancied himself a writer. He knew he didn't possess the gift of synthesizing his complex emotional and sensory experience at seeing his hometown after over two decades into a thirty-minute, provocative, and inspirational speech. Pride had caught up with him, but he soldiered on with his prepared remarks. Mr Ilmi felt a single bead of sweat trickle down the small of his back. He remembered the words of one of his professors in teacher's college; his advice for dealing with first-day teaching jitters was to find one student, lock eyes with him or her and talk to that one student. Mr Ilmi's eyes desperately scanned the length of the William Doo Auditorium. His eyes finally fell on Nuur, whom he had invited to the symposium. He had wanted to take Nuur out of the humdrum of his life in a suburban high-rise and introduce him to a part of the city he wished someone had taken him to when he was Nuur's age. Now as he stared at Nuur's face, he felt grateful for the manageable, trusting audience of one.

"I closed my eyes and saw myself as a boy, swimming at Liido, Mogadishu's most famous beach. It was a Friday afternoon and I was spending the day at the beach with my family. As a giant wave hit me, I felt the sting of the salty water in my eyes. I smelled that peculiar earthy, salty scent of the ocean, an aroma I had not experienced anywhere else in the world. From the air, the water looked as cool and inviting as it had done when I was a boy. A part of me thought: maybe things aren't so bad after all. But it didn't take long for the Mogadishu of my memory to clash with its reality now. On our way to the hotel where I was to stay for the next five days, we drove along Maka al-Mukarama, the most prominent boulevard in Mogadishu. And there it hit me just how bad things really were in this city of my childhood. Two decades of bombardment had turned it into an unfamiliar city. Buildings with gaping holes where doors and windows should've been, garbage-strewn sidewalks, hills of sandbags—these were all that remained of that once beautiful street. Mogadishu, this city of over two million people, still teeming with so much life, was a war zone.

"The SUV we drove in, courtesy of a well-connected cousin in government who had promised to make my stay in Mogadishu safe, zigzagged the road to avoid craters left by mortars. It was driven by an armed driver with a bodyguard sporting an intimidating Kalashnikov. The bodyguard, a short, sweaty, hairy mass of compact human flesh told the driver to slow down. Before us was a fast-moving convoy of grey armored vehicles with AU—for African Union—written on the back. Afraid we might be mistaken for a suicide bomber, the bodyguard advised the driver to put some distance between us and the convoy. Large parts of the city, however, were still controlled by Al-Shabaab, the terrorist group."

Mr Ilmi thought he was sounding too much like a novice reporter from some Western country, on his first foreign assignment, stringing together seemingly important facts for the edification of an ignorant reader. He ploughed ahead.

"From the window of the car, I watched a one-legged man with a crutch, trying his best to navigate the uneven, unpaved sidewalk. One of the many walking wounded I would encounter during my stay. I wondered what had happened to his leg. Did he lose it in one of the countless battles that had taken place here? How did he get around a city so unfit for the handicapped?"

That's better, Mr Ilmi thought. Less affected. More observational.

"At last, we got to the hotel. A heavily fortified oasis of white walls and well-kept gardens. The green courtyard, the lawn chairs, the tea trays and the animated conversations of the well-heeled guests were almost enough to make me forget that I was in one of the most dangerous capitals in the world. The aroma of Somali tea, a concoction of loose leaf tea, ginger, and cinnamon steeped in boiling water and served with milk and sugar, was a delicious, Proustian experience transporting me back to a lost time. A time that will never be regained."

A Proustian experience? What the hell was I thinking? Mr Ilmi thought. He hadn't even gotten past *Swann's Way.* Mr Ilmi was suddenly overcome with an all-consuming dread about the futility of his enterprise.

"Since security concerns made going out after sunset unwise, I entertained myself by exploring the old hotel. One evening, I stumbled upon one of its many patios, the wrought-iron railings remarkably in good shape. I spent a good chunk of time alone on that patio on the top floor overlooking old Mogadishu. Laid out before me was an impressive tableau of wreckage lit by the setting sun. Every direction I looked there was something that was once a prominent landmark in my childhood. To my left was what remained of Hotel Al-Uruba, its lovely arabesque windows still recognizable. To my right were the remains of the red-brick façade of the old parliament building, and straight ahead stood the Italian cathedral or, more accurately, one wall of it."

Mr Ilmi took another swig of water. "The next day, I left the hotel early to visit my childhood home near the famous Bakaare Market. On our way, we drove by the now dilapidated National Theatre. I asked the driver to stop so I could take a few pictures. It felt wrong to just drive by the place where I saw my first play. I was thirteen then."

As he read this sentence, Mr Ilmi's mind recalled scenes from that play—a Somali version of Romeo and Juliet—a melodrama about two young lovers from two warring clans. His father, Yasiin Ilmi, who loved the theatre, had taken him to see it. He was an Arabic literature professor, an authority on *The Arabian Nights,* and a lover of all things to do with storytelling. But much to his father's disappointment, Mr Ilmi never took to storytelling. He loved facts—observable, quantifiable, scientific facts.

"I tried to focus my camera on the fading block letters on the façade of the building that read, The National Theatre," Mr Ilmi continued. "Suddenly, I heard the angry screams of a thin, young man, front teeth stained from too much khat, a Kalashnikov dangling from his shoulder, and two, long bullet belts wrapped around his bony torso like a shawl. He had taken offense to my photo-taking. Livid, he demanded that I stop. The driver and the guard, who were equally armed, exchanged angry words with him. He looked as though he hadn't had a decent meal in weeks. I tried to explain to him that I was taking a picture of the theatre, not of him. I tried to placate him by deleting a few of the offending photographs. Miraculously, this worked. The boy disappeared as quickly as he had materialized. Still a bit shaken by the altercation, we moved on to the one place in Mogadishu I wanted to see more than anything else: my childhood home. Unfortunately, that part of Mogadishu was contested ground between the forces of Al-Shabaab and the government, who often exchanged fire between them. Our driver instructed me that we could stay here only for a few minutes."

Mr Ilmi took a deep breath and wished he had written this section of his speech with more sensory details. He wanted to linger here and tell the people what it felt like to witness his childhood home in ruins. "On our way to my home, I had played all sorts of scenarios in my head about how I would feel when I finally saw the house I grew up in. It was a white, five-bedroom villa with a beautiful garden behind a blue metal gate."

Mr Ilmi occasionally looked away from the paper in front of him to find a few older men and women nodding, as though they too could remember the homes they had lost to wars. As he continued to read, his mind drifted back to that hot, windy day. He could hear his voice telling the audience the story but his mind was back in Mogadishu.

———

Mr Ilmi sat forward, practically thrusting himself into the small space between the front seats of the car to give the driver directions. They went downhill from Maka al-Mukarama along the nameless street that ran past his house. Gone were the stores, trees, and cafes that once lined the street. Nothing was familiar. There was no sign of the photography shop where they had their family portrait taken; or the two-storey orange villa with a dog tied to the gate; or the dusty playground where he and his friends had played football—it was overgrown with cactuses. There was an eerie silence all around. It felt as though at any moment a forgotten landmine could explode under their car, or a teenager with an Uzi might emerge from behind one of the cactuses and spray them with bullets. Anything looked possible, and this knowledge sent a wave of fear and thrill through him.

The driver finally managed to plough through a sand hill where Mr Ilmi thought had stood his childhood home. All that was left of the house were the foundations, showing the divisions of the various rooms. It looked as if a hurricane had come and left behind a mere blueprint on the ground.

He stepped over a few large rocks whose origins he couldn't tell and stood in the middle of what would have been his mother's bedroom where, in 1998, his half brother Isaaq, who had never fled the war, was killed with his new wife. Isaaq and his wife of three weeks were in bed when a mortar came through the ceiling, instantly killing them. Mr Ilmi kicked the sand with the front of his shoe and felt the slippery texture of a tile under the dirt. It was a blue ceramic tile. He squatted down and with his hand brushed away the sand and dust until the tile was fully visible. There was a thick crack across it. Mr Ilmi burrowed his fingers under each side of the tile and tried to lift it. It wouldn't budge. He used all the strength he could muster to dislodge the tile, until it finally gave way, breaking into two, and Mr Ilmi fell back on his bottom.

He got up and dusted his khaki pants with his hands. The thought occurred to him that this small tile the colour of the ocean was the only remnant of his home that he could take with him back to Canada. So he put one piece of the tile in his pocket, threw the other away, and walked back towards the SUV. Entering, he closed the door quietly as though afraid to disturb the ghosts of Isaaq and his wife and all the squatters who had sought shelter in his home and met their untimely end there. He closed his eyes and gave himself up to the comforting sway of the car as it navigated the sand hills, rocks, mud holes, and everything else that twenty years of war had wrought.

———

Mr Ilmi continued his speech, moving on to recount his trip to a feeding centre run by a distant relative, who wanted to show him the good work her NGO had been doing, and to tell him—he thought—While you cowards fled to the West, we have been here saving lives.

"It should have been only a twenty-minute drive to the district of Wadajir and the nutrition centre, but due to the condition of the roads, it took us almost an hour. I was shown around the compound and introduced to a few of the thousands of women who regularly came to the centre for their daily rations of food. In the past year, a severe draught had made life in the countryside impossible. Crops had failed. Livestock had all but disappeared, and thousands of mothers carrying children with bloated bellies had been streaming into Mogadishu from all directions. I saw mothers sitting cross-legged on the ground, nestling on their laps their severely malnourished children; some babies were so emaciated and weak they could barely keep their eyes open. I was puzzled by the complete absence of the fathers of the children. Somalia had always been a country held together by women. My eyes fixed on a little boy whose name I was told was Raage. His lifeless body seemed to hang from his mother's arm like a rag doll. The mother told me in a dialect I found hard to understand that she had walked nine days from Baydhabo Region, one of the worst afflicted areas. But what's stayed with me to this day is the almost inaudible wail of a toddler who was being placed in and out of a weighing scale. He looked as though he wanted to let out a deafening cry but his body was too weak to produce any sound.

"With the horrific cries of malnourished babies still in my head, my guide took me inside a walled compound where close to a thousand mothers and their children were lined up, waiting for their turn to fill their buckets, plastic bags, and pots with porridge, a spoonful of vegetable, and a single banana. Their only meal for the day. It was the ultimate portrait of indignity. And I was reminded of the words of our nation's most famous novelist Nuruddin Farah, whom I once heard on a radio program saying about Somalis: 'It's hard to be dignified when you're being rationed.'"

Mr Ilmi paused for a moment to give the audience time to digest those words, for he felt them to be such an eloquent summation of what had become of his people. He continued, "Later that day, I was invited to an early dinner by a good friend of my mother who had never left the country. We ate at a new private club where Mogadishu's business elites and returned diaspora congregated. As we feasted on mango salad and succulent goat meat, the absurdity of my day nagged at me."

Mr Ilmi turned to the next page, to be confronted by two pages of a rant, a diatribe against the evils of clan-based society, the brutality and carnage that the warlords had visited upon his country, and the ineffectual efforts of the United Nations and Western NGOs. But Mr Ilmi saved his most venomous attack for Al-Shabaab, a group whose perversion of his faith allowed them to justify unspeakable acts of violence against their own people. But here in front of the seventy or so people who had gathered to hear a piece of travelogue, an adventure story, a political rant seemed wrong, self-indulgent. Mr Ilmi quickly scanned the length of the page to see if any of it could be salvaged. He made a quick editorial decision to chuck the entire two pages and moved on to his final paragraph.

"In my last night in Mogadishu, I tried to write down some of my thoughts and feelings about the absurdities of life in the capital. I was a jumble of contradictions. I felt grateful for having left Somalia before the outbreak of the war and to have made a life for myself in Canada. But I was also filled with shame for leaving the city of my childhood after only five days. It felt as though, once again, I was abandoning it."

He heard his voice crack, cleared his throat, and took a gulp of water from the bottle. He glanced up at his audience as though to seek an answer for the tears that suddenly filled his eyes. "Sorry," he said and looked back down at the page. "But I forgave myself for these contradictions." Mr Ilmi continued, his voice gathering strength and conviction. "Somalis are, after all, a people of profound contradictions. We are fiercely loyal and proud. But we can also be cutthroat. We can be nauseatingly patriotic but also sell our nation out for personal profit. We are a country famous for astonishing folklore and poetry. But we're also a place where hands are chopped off for petty theft, adulterers get stoned to death, and girls are raped with impunity. The following morning, as my plane taxied for take-off, I was unwilling to say goodbye to my hometown. I did my best to banish the catalogue of horrific images from my head, and instead I thought of the famous resilience of my people."

———

Mr Ilmi answered questions, shook the many hands that greeted him, and thanked Kayin for the invitation. Then he signaled to Nuur that it was time to go. As he buttoned up his coat in the cold November night, Mr Ilmi looked up at the clear sky and noticed the tiny stars that dotted it. A sharp pang of gratitude hit him. "So?" Mr Ilmi said to his student in a tone of muted excitement. "What did you think?"

Nuur paused for a moment as though he were running the entirety of Mr Ilmi's speech in his head, selecting the parts that warranted comment.

"Well?" Mr Ilmi said, a slight impatience creeping into his voice.

"How old were you when you left Mogadishu?" Nuur asked as if no other part of the speech had left an impression on him.

"Thirteen, just about to turn fourteen," Mr Ilmi said. "Why do you ask?"

"It sounded like . . . you sounded like, I don't know, like you left a part of you there."

Mr Ilmi drew in a sharp cold breath. He took pride in his ability to adapt and move on. But his lecture had betrayed him. Nuur was right. They walked quietly for several minutes on a small, tree-lined path beside the music building. To their right, the office towers of down-town Toronto glimmered in the distance. To their left, the windows of the old, ivy-covered music building showed a small group of students rehearsing a chamber string piece. The deep sound of a cello cut through Mr Ilmi's heart. He slowed down to take in the melancholic piece, which he recognized as Bach's Cello Suite No 1 in G Major, and his heart was filled at once with the loss of things he couldn't name.

For two years while attending teachers' college, this campus had been Mr Ilmi's home. Late at night, after his last class of the day, he would walk for what felt like hours, a heavy backpack slung over his shoulders, a sandwich in one hand and a carton of chocolate milk in the other. This was his favourite part of the city, with the old ivy-covered buildings and the shuffling sounds of student's feet as they crushed the autumn leaves under their feet, young men playing catch football on King's College Circle, the chatter of young women. He had loved it all. He wished he could go back and make different choices. Live a different life. As Nuur and Mr Ilmi continued their silent walk towards Bloor Street, Mr Ilmi felt at home. And it hit him: the reason he had invited his favourite student tonight was to show him a way of life, a mode of existence he felt certain this youth had no ways of imagining. It was his duty not only to teach the boy biology, which was what he was paid to do, but to take him out of his world of degradation. Nuur had it in him to infiltrate and make his own this rarefied world of ivy-covered buildings and shimmering glass towers that the invisible visible minorities of this city thirsted for but few of them ever got to enter, much less make their own.

Mr Ilmi stole a few quick glances at Nuur to look for signs of discomfort in the pricey eatery they sat in. All around them were men and women in fancy designer clothes, basking in the glory of their entitled accomplishments. But Mr Ilmi saw no outward signs of discomfort on the boy's face. He looked at Nuur's outfit for the evening— a crisp white qamiis and an equally pristine white skullcap that gave him an aura of purity. He couldn't help but admire the boy for his confidence, his unwillingness to accommodate the tastes and expectations of the people he shared the city with. He remembered the countless ways he had diluted his identity when he was Nuur's age, desperate to fit in. When torn blue jeans were in, he bought them; when baggy pants that tripped him when he walked were all the rage, he had to have them. He had longed to be thought of as one of "us," until he became old enough to realize that there was no "us," and being "in" was relative.

"So have you thought of universities, or a major?" Mr Ilmi asked, munching on a piece of bread. In his mind, it was a foregone conclusion that Nuur would go to university.

Nuur nodded at his teacher's question.

"And?"

"I'm leaning towards premed," Nuur said in a tone that signified to Mr Ilmi that the boy was trying out these words, seeing if they came out strong and plausible or mangled and possibly deranged.

Before Mr Ilmi could seize the moment and encourage his student, their waiter arrived with their food, a steak and steamed vegetables for him and a grilled salmon fillet and rice on the side for Nuur. For some reason, it hadn't occurred to Mr Ilmi that Nuur wouldn't eat the meat or the chicken in a non-Muslim restaurant since they would not be halal. "If you could go into any area of medicine, what would it be?" Mr Ilmi asked. He watched as Nuur thought about the question, pausing to take a sip of water.

"Oncology," Nuur said at last with a little ambitious twinkle in his eyes, the way the other boys in class said "basketball player" or "hip-hop star" when he asked them about their ambitions.

"Oncology? Okay. Why oncology?"

"It's the last frontier of medicine."

"The last frontier?" Mr Ilmi asked, puzzled but also genuinely interested in what this boy in white qamiis and skullcap was thinking. He could feel Nuur loosening up, his real self, whatever that might be, beginning to emerge.

"Think about it, thousands of researchers around the world have spent billions of dollars for decades trying to find a cure for cancer. And sure, they've developed some amazing treatments but never a cure. We haven't fully grasped the complexity of cancer cells, their ability to perpetuate in the most hostile environments. I bet you money they'll find a cure for AIDS before they cure cancer." Nuur smiled.

Mr Ilmi watched Nuur as he dug his fork into the fish and took a big bite of it. There was a kind of hunger in the way he ate, not mere hunger for food, but the kind of hunger that betrayed deeper deprivations.

"How is it?"

"Not bad."

"Not bad?" Mr Ilmi said with a chuckle. "*Toronto Life* gave this place four stars out of five."

"The restaurant that I work at makes the same fish and rice for a fraction of the price."

"I didn't know you worked at a restaurant."

"At Hamar Cade, on Islington and Rexdale. Ever been there?"

"No. Not yet. Is the food as good there?"

Nuur nodded. "And cheap too. Two people can eat there for fifteen bucks."

"You know, it's not all about the food. Presentation, atmosphere, music, service. It's all part of the experience of eating out, having a good time."

Nuur nodded but looked unconvinced.

"Can I ask you something?" Mr Ilmi said, unsure of how to phrase his question.

Nuur gave another one of his nods.

"Why do you dress like that? I mean, why don't you wear regular clothes?"

"I'm a Muslim," Nuur said as if to imply, "duh."

"I know. But I guess what I mean is, we're Somalis. It's not exactly our custom to wear qamiis, is it? It feels like some kind of Saudi colonization through fashion or something."

Nuur took in Mr Ilmi's wardrobe for a moment as if evaluating it, making a mental commentary on it. Mr Ilmi wore navy pants, a blue shirt, and, over it, a brown sports jacket. An outfit that made him look like a dark-complexioned mannequin in the windows of The Bay. "That's not exactly our traditional attire, is it?" Nuur asked casually pointing with his fork to his teacher's ensemble.

"Well, no. But we wore this back in Somalia. It's nothing new for us."

"Some would say you've been colonized. Fashionwise."

"By whom?" Mr Ilmi asked.

"The Italians. The Brits. Take your pick," Nuur said.

Mr Ilmi couldn't help but chuckle, acknowledging the rhetorical touchdown his student had just scored against him.

In all the years he had been teaching, rarely had Mr Ilmi witnessed a student like Nuur. He was a mass of contradictions. He was painfully shy, but give him an argument to defend or a presentation to deliver and he shone like one of those actors who claim to be shy but display their innermost selves on stage every night in front of hundreds of people. He was well-mannered and polite, but every once in a while, there were flares of rage, as if he might just strangle you with his bare hands, if pushed. A prodigious intellect lurked behind those dark, almond-shaped eyes, but there was also a considerable tilt towards dogma and rigidity of thought. Mr Ilmi wondered what would become of him.

———

For the past few weeks Mr Ilmi had been reading in bed a chapter a night from his book on Descartes, while his wife slept soundly next to him, her back turned to him, her soft, gentle snore providing a soundtrack. She had recently started her second trimester and was now sleeping upwards of thirteen hours a day. He watched her, lying on her side facing away from him, peaceful and vulnerable as a child, as though worry had not been invented yet. He envied and also resented her anxiety-free existence.

He wondered what she dreamt about in her sleep. Not once had she shared with him her dreams or thoughts. It felt to him that there was a whole world in her mind that he knew nothing about and the thought filled him with sorrow. He longed for access into that black box. Perhaps, in her sleep, she dreamed about the boy she had wanted to marry. He had heard bits and pieces about Nuruddin, a young man who came to Khadija's father and asked him for her hand in marriage, only to be turned away because he was without a job and incapable of taking care of himself let alone a wife. Nuruddin had stood outside her house for two whole days in the rain, pleading with her father to let him see her one last time. *Maybe in her dreams, she is rejoined with her beloved,* Mr Ilmi thought. He turned his gaze back to his book. Every night, he got into bed, kissed his wife good night and opened the book with the hope that he would, at last, discover what Descartes's error was.

"I think, therefore I am," perhaps the most famous statement in all of Western philosophy. Descartes had coined it in 1637, and centuries later it moved Mr Ilmi almost to tears, as though the five, simple words were the answers to the questions that plagued him. Who was he? For almost all his adult life, Mr Ilmi's idea of himself as a being was founded on the notion that he *was* because he had the ability to think. It was never, I feel, therefore I am. Or: I believe, therefore I am. Being constitutionally averse to belief, he was distrustful of people who ran around telling people about their beliefs. It was his thoughts that he valued above all else. He knew them as intimately as he knew his private parts. He never doubted that he had a soul, that there was more to him than the sum of the perishable biological material that made up his physical presence. But the relationship of his body to his soul and his thoughts, and the consciousness they produced and the conscience that arose from that consciousness, still remained a delicious mystery to him. He knew with every fiber of his being that his conscience was uniquely his own. Even as a child in Mogadishu, sitting cross-legged in the Quranic school next to his house, he knew that the sense of conscience, of right and wrong, that the Quranic teacher tried to inculcate into him was not his own, and therefore always remained to him suspect.

And so to be confronted with the notion that he, like Descartes, had been in error all along troubled Mr Ilmi deeply. According to Damasio, the author of the book he held in his hand, this was Descartes's error: "The abysmal separation between body and mind . . . the separation of the most refined operation of the mind from the structure and operation of a biological organism."

This was a revelation. It felt as if Gabriel had flown into his bedroom and commanded him to recite: "You are NOT your thoughts!" Mr Ilmi berated himself like a schoolboy. How could he have believed all this time that his thoughts, that fleeting jumbled mass produced by his brain, was somehow separate or separable from his body? It turned out that his most refined thoughts, his conception of God, of art, of love and joy and despair had always been one and the same with his most basic biological functions.

Mr Ilmi reread the last page of the book. He closed it, turned off the light on his nightstand and shut his eyes. But his mind was still alive with thoughts—or was it his body? He longed to wake up his wife and talk to her about his discovery. He desperately needed someone with whom he could kick around these ideas. He placed a gentle hand on his wife's back, between her shoulder blades. He felt the dampness of perspiration through his wife's baati, the matronly cotton dress she wore to bed every night. She stirred under his palm. He thought about all the changes taking place in her body and wondered what it must feel like to be the site of so many biochemical interactions and changes that made it possible for her to sustain the life of their unborn child? He marveled that a life lived within her. He moved closer and placed a soft hand on Khadija's shoulder and for the first time in two years of marriage, he felt the love for her that he had hoped one day he would feel.

Mr Ilmi had been hopeful when he married Khadija and brought her to Canada that one day he would wake up to find himself in love with her, the way he had observed his mother and father in love, who were also practically strangers when they got married. The easy way they laughed at the same things, their subtle, desirous glances when they thought no one was watching, the way she cared for him when he fell sick and the deep grief she fell into when he passed away—these moments he witnessed as a young man were for him the confirmation that his mother and father did find in each other not only love but shelter.

Would he and Khadija find the love his mother and father did? Mr Ilmi had often fretted about this. Now finally he was filled with a sense of its possibility, and for now that was enough to sustain him.

And just as worries about his future with his wife subsided, a whole new set of worries invaded his mind. In the dark, he tossed and turned and thought about the baby she was carrying. A pang of fear tore through him. What kind of a father would he be? He wanted to be a different kind of dad than his own father had been. For all his wonderful qualities, his father was, for all intents and purposes, absent, spending most of the year away teaching at universities in Lagos, Tunis, Alexandria, and once even as far away as Malaysia. And the three months he was at home, he spent either in his library or out with friends at his favourite Italian cafe in downtown Mogadishu, gossiping about the latest shenanigans of the dictator Siad Barre's regime.

Mr Ilmi did not resent his father's absences, for in Somalia, child-rearing was by tradition the domain of mothers. But as sleep descended on him and the slow fall into unconsciousness began, he resolved that it was time this particular Somali tradition be changed in his family.

———

Mr Ilmi left the teachers' office where he had his lunch on most days, and as he maneuvered his way around the busy hallway on his way to his afternoon biology class, he heard a loud crash that sounded like somebody being slammed against the lockers that lined the walls. As he turned around he felt certain that the boy who was being ruthlessly banged against the locker was Nuur. His heart quickened as he rushed towards the commotion.

When he reached the scene, Mr Ilmi found that the boy getting roughed up was not Nuur but Christopher, a small and skinny boy from Ukraine. Mr Ilmi felt a twinge of shame at the relief he felt to discover that it wasn't Nuur who was getting beaten up. But he also knew that all teachers had one kid who occupied a special place in their hearts. He couldn't help it, it was human nature, he told himself.

Mr Ilmi was not surprised to find that James was the perpetrator of the slamming "Hey! Enough of that!" he yelled.

"Enough of what, Mr Ilmi?" James said, letting go of Christopher with his usual grin of pure delight.

"Are you all right, Christopher?" Mr Ilmi asked.

"Of course, he is. Aren't you, Chris?" James said.

Christopher, too petrified to contradict James, nodded.

"See, Mr Ilmi? Little Chris here is just fine."

Mr Ilmi wanted to send James to Principal Terry's office, but that would probably get Christopher into bigger trouble with James. He couldn't stomach the possibility of Christopher being pummeled by James and his posse in some deserted part of the school with no one to rescue him. Mr Ilmi often found himself mired in these moral quandaries as a teacher. It seemed to him that much of his day was spent weighing one bad option against another.

"You have five minutes before your next period. I suggest you head towards your classes immediately," he said and continued down the hallway, which was still crowded with students getting back from lunch and heading for their afternoon classes. He caught a glimpse of Nuur entering a room that was often used for student meetings and other special purposes. Mr Ilmi closed the door behind him. Curious to see what the boy was up to, Mr Ilmi went over and knocked on the door couple of times. There was no answer. He slowly turned the door handle and took a step inside.

At the back of the classroom, behind a few desks stacked with chairs, Mr Ilmi found Nuur prostrated over a small olive-green prayer mat on the floor. He watched Nuur get up and recite the Fatiha, the first verse of the Quran, under his breath. He had a look of such solemn concentration that it was as if nothing else mattered in the world. He looked at peace in a way Mr Ilmi had never felt. He watched with envy as his student prostrated again.

Mr Ilmi had seen devout boys come and go during his fourteen-year teaching career. What set Nuur apart from the others was the intensity of his spiritual devotion, and while Mr Ilmi admired it, it also scared him. Although Mr Ilmi was not raised in a particularly observant home, he had imbibed a cultural reverence for Islam. Over the decades, that reverence had been tempered by a growing wariness of religion and in particular of Islam, or more accurately the kind of Islam he had been encountering in his neighbourhood lately. He had observed in his Somali neighbours a conformity in appearance and opinion that was exasperating. What had happened to the diversity in thought and dress that he had known back in Somalia? The Somali Muslims he met nowadays seemed to be stripped of any individualism, any semblance of uniqueness.

Nuur had finished his prayer. "Asalamu alaykum, Mr Ilmi," Nuur said in a voice that seemed to have been rendered even softer by the prayer he had just finished.

"Walaykum salam," Mr Ilmi replied, doing his best to soften his voice as well. "I didn't mean to bother you—"

"It's no bother," Nuur said and got off the floor. He began to roll his prayer mat, but stopped midway to ask, "Would you like to pray?"

"Oh no, I'm good," Mr Ilmi said, unable to think of a better way to decline an invitation to pray. "I mean, I have a class in ten minutes," he said, well aware of the fact that ten minutes was more than enough time for Thuhur, the afternoon prayer.

Mr Ilmi watched Nuur's face for the look of judgment he often saw in religious people for those who were not observant. But he saw only a neutral look. He watched Nuur roll up his prayer rug, cram it into his knapsack, and put on his sneakers. "I wanted to give you something before class," Mr Ilmi said.

"Really?"

"It's just a book." Mr Ilmi opened his leather satchel and took out the book that had occupied his nights for the past few weeks. He handed it over. "I finished it last night and I thought you might like it."

"Thank you," Nuur said and read the title, mouthing the words slowly as if considering their meaning. "I didn't realize Descartes made an error," he said with a smile.

"Then you're in for a surprise . . . hold on to your hat."

Nuur let out a soft laugh. Mr Ilmi couldn't tell if he found the joke funny or was just being kind to his teacher's attempt at humour.

"What's it about?" Nuur asked.

"Have you ever heard of the statement, 'I think, therefore I am?'"

"Of course," Nuur said.

"What do you think it means?"

Nuur sat on the edge of a desk and became quiet.

"There is no right or wrong answer."

"I think," Nuur said then paused. "What I feel he's saying is . . . " He paused again. He let out a soft chuckle that seemed to Mr Ilmi half nervous and half excited. Mr Ilmi chuckled too, in accompaniment. "I think what Descartes is saying is . . . when we think, that is when we are ourselves the most."

"Hmm. Interesting," Mr Ilmi said

"Yeah, I think that's what he's saying." Nuur paused again to reconsider, then said, "No. That's dumb."

Mr Ilmi enjoyed watching Nuur take delight in the act of thinking. "Now remember, Nuur, there's never a dumb answer, just a lazy one."

"So what does it mean then? 'I think, therefore I am'?" Nuur asked.

"Well, that is for you to find out. Read the book. Think about it. Think about what it means to think. Think about what it means to be. What does it mean to say: I am."

8

"AND THE CALIPHATES, Subhanallah, spread our diin, as far west as Spain and as far east as China. And while the Europeans, the so-called civilized race, stumbled around in the dark ages, killing each other, pillaging villages, raping women, Muslims were building a civilization, perfecting physics, mathematics, architecture, medicine. And do you know why?" Imam Yusuf asked the seven bearded youths seated in a circle around him. Nuur wanted to answer the imam's question but he didn't know if it was a genuine question or another one of the imam's sentences that ended with a question.

"Because the Muslim ummah of that day had faith," the imam said, his voice rising to a crescendo. "Because they had faith in the Almighty and they obeyed his commandments. They did not pick and choose those they wanted to obey and disregard those they felt to be too cumbersome or uncool. Having faith is not strawberry picking season. You do not get the privilege of choice. Now that is something the caliphate understood because they had the fear of Allah in their hearts."

Nuur adjusted his posture as he listened. So rapt was his attention that he didn't realize that his left leg had gone numb from the cross-legged position he'd sat in for too long. He discretely uncrossed and extended his left leg. Numerous questions had been rattling around his head these last few days and finally someone, a learned man who had studied at the most prestigious Islamic university in the world, was sitting before him and giving him the answers he yearned for. Nuur nodded at the words that poured out of Imam Yusuf's mouth as if at a sonnet written just for him. He had heard similar arguments from other Muslims before, but they always lacked the essential element of conviction. Now, sitting in this circle, listening to Imam

Yusuf, he experienced a revelation, a clear and convincing epiphany about the centrality of faith in the life of a Muslim man. Nuur felt a swell of gratitude in his heart. He was grateful to Allah for bringing Imam Yusuf into his life.

Why was the Muslim ummah in the sorry state it was in?—that was the primary question that plagued Nuur these days. It seemed to him that not a day passed when the news media didn't bring another evidence of the Muslim ummah's degenerate condition. From Iraq to Palestine and from Chechnya to Somalia his brothers and sisters were constantly being tortured and humiliated: they were bombed in their homes, blindfolded and dragged in their own streets, their lands were confiscated, their beloved Prophet was caricatured, their holy book was tarnished. Now someone was giving him an answer. Nuur watched as Imam Yusuf took a long, dramatic pause and glanced down at the red carpet, his finger tracing its intricate patterns. Every gesture of the imam had a way of adding to the dramatic tension that made Nuur and his fellow students sit still, holding their breaths, lest they miss something of the life-altering wisdom spilling forth.

"My sons, we are a people enslaved," Imam Yusuf finally resumed, his voice barely above a whisper, as if he were about to break into tears. "Our people are indeed enslaved but we can't blame the kafir." The imam had a way of spitting out the word *kafir,* infidels, as though a tiny insect had flown into his mouth. "We can't blame the kafir because it's we who have abandoned our faith and our duty to Allah, and for that we will taste the bitter fruits of hellfire. Oh my beloved sons, how can we expect to ascend to the heights of this world and the hereafter when we neglect the teachings of the Holy Quran and the Sunnah of our Prophet (peace be upon him) and instead chase the teachings of the kafir. Subhanallah. We enslave ourselves for years to obtain the Masters' and PhDs of the infidels, but those pieces of paper will not save your souls on that most grave Day of Judgment. We strive for the honorifics of the kafir while we abandon the teachings of our faith," the imam continued. "Have no doubt, that's what we are seeing in the world today. Look at every Muslim country, not a single one of them practices true Islam and the Sharia. It's too hard, you say. I can't get up at five in the morning to pray. I can't fast for a month. I can't give away a part of my wealth in the name of Allah. You love this dunya, this world, more than you love aqira, the hereafter."

Nuur began to feel as though Imam Yusuf was talking to him directly, accusing him of loving this world far too much. The imam was right.

"This dunya is an illusion, my sons. A mirage. Do not be fooled by it!" Imam Yusuf's voice rose once again in that melodic and righteous way that reminded Nuur of Martin Luther King's famous speech, which he had watched last semester while preparing a history presentation on the American Civil Rights Movement. The contents of their speeches might have been different but the cadence was the same.

"This dunya is but a mere second compared to aqira, which is everlasting. You must banish the temptation of shaytan, which comes to you every night, whispering into your ears, filling your hearts with desire for this world. A true Muslim does not live for this world but for the hereafter. A true Muslim renounces this dunya and prepares for the one to come. A true Muslim loves death, for it ushers paradise. Do you understand me, my sons?"

Nuur was confused. He wanted to say yes! but he wasn't sure if the imam was actually expecting an answer. He heard the seven other young men in the circle say yes in unison, but by the time Nuur joined them in their affirmation, the moment had passed. He said yes by himself, in a shaky, uncertain voice.

"Make no mistake, my sons, shaytan wants nothing more than your company in the hellfire. He wants as many of you as possible in the pits of hell, where you will spend eternity. You must not allow shaytan that victory. You must remain steadfast in your faith. You must resist his charms every time he comes to you with his deceitful overtures." Imam Yusuf took another pause and lightly padded down his huge, hennaed beard as though it needed to be contained. "Every time shaytan whispers in your ears and says: Look there, and you turn your gaze to find a pretty thing strutting her stuff on the street, you must say: istaqfurallah."

A couple of boys sniggered at the expression on Imam Yusuf's face as he articulated the words *pretty young thing*. An expression of disgust mixed with ... . what? . . . Nuur couldn't tell. It was the same expression that he saw on the imam's face whenever he talked of "Women in the West." Listening to him, Nuur often got the sense that these women conspired together with shaytan to lead young men like himself to the gates of hell.

"Shaytan would like nothing more than to see you engage in zinna. He wants to see you surrender to the pleasures of the flesh. Be aware of the flesh, my sons, for it's the flesh that will lead you to hellfire. I was like you once, young and eager. I know of what I speak. I know what it's like to be a young man. But you must be strong in your faith. You must be vigilant! This is your jihad, my sons . . . Ever walked down Yonge Street?"

A few of the boys chuckled. Nuur couldn't tell why. What was he missing?

"You know what I'm talking about. All that filth. All that human flesh for sale on every billboard, on every street poster, making a mockery of God's beautiful gift to man."

What's Imam Yusuf on about? Nuur wondered. What flesh for sale? What gift to man?

"I've spoken too much," Imam Yusuf said, looking around the circle, making eye contact with each of the young men, sporting a consoling smile. "Any questions?" He said to no one in particular. He looked around and prepared to get up. But Dahir, a short, chubby boy whom the other boys had nicknamed "Cade" on account of his extremely light complexion raised his hand.

"Yes, Dahir?" Imam Yusuf asked with an exaggerated show of eagerness to be of assistance. Everyone who came to these Sunday lectures at the mosque knew that if you had an embarrassing question you wanted answered by the imam, Dahir was your boy. He was fearless.

"These *temptations* you talk about," Dahir said. "I can't watch a basketball game on TV without a million ads with half-naked women."

That elicited a few chuckles.

"What's your question, son?" the imam asked, losing his patience.

"How do I deal with all those temptations? I wanna stay pure. Honestly, I do!"

"Don't watch the games."

"But I love watching NBA. It's my only source of entertainment."

"Then don't watch the commercials. Look away."

"The thing is," Dahir started, taking delight in his captive audience. "The thing is, as young men, we have these feelings, these urges that Allah has given us, right?"

"Go on," said the imam.

"And since I'm not married and I don't wanna commit zinna, what are my halal options?"

"What are you asking me, exactly?"

"I guess what I'm asking is . . . is it a sin, taking matters into my own hands, so to speak."

The circle broke into open laughter, prompting the imam to give a "simmer down" gesture with his hand.

"Dahir is asking a serious question. This is a serious issue for Muslim brothers. Less so for our beloved sisters, for Allah has not burdened them with that particular affliction to the same level." Imam Yusuf took another dramatic pause. "The Quran says nothing of this matter, directly. But we as Muslims have another great source of wisdom at our disposal and that's the Hadiths, the sayings of our Prophet, may peace be upon him. One of those Hadiths narrates that the Prophet had said: 'Oh group of youth! Whoever from among you can marry, should do so because it keeps the gaze low and it protects the private parts. And those who cannot marry, should fast because fasting breaks the lust.'"

"Hmm. That's it. That's your answer. Just fast?" Dahir said.

"Yes."

"For how long?"

"However long these temptations last."

"I'm seventeen. They last forever."

Even Nuur couldn't help laughing.

"No one said faith is easy, son. If it were easy, we would all go to Jannah. But not all of us will go to paradise. In fact, the vast majority of humanity will reside, for eternity, in the pits of hellfire." Suddenly, the group got serious. Talk of hellfire had a way of scaring these rowdy boys into silent submission.

"You all have a choice, my sons. You can either follow the righteous path of the Prophet and be among the believers, or you can join the ungrateful infidels who remain oblivious to Allah's warnings. Choose wisely!"

With that warning, Imam Yusuf stood up in one swift movement as though he had been practicing how to get out of a cross-legged position all his life just for occasions like this, when he needed to make a memorable exit.

9

Mʀ Iʟᴍɪ ᴡᴀs ɪɴ ᴛʜᴇ ᴋɪᴛᴄʜᴇɴ helping his wife with dinner, chopping lettuce, when he heard a soft, hesitant knock on the door. He washed his hands and went to get the door. Looking through the peephole, he couldn't see anyone. He opened the door and still couldn't see anyone. He looked down the hallway and saw the figure of what looked like Nuur heading for the elevator.

"Nuur, is that you?"

Nuur turned around. "Yes. I'm sorry, Mr Ilmi. I didn't mean to disturb you on the weekend but . . . "

"Is anything the matter?"

Nuur walked back to Mr Ilmi's door. "No. Everything is fine."

"You sure? You look—"

"No, I'm fine. I'm great actually." He took out Mr Ilmi's book from his backpack. "I finished it this morning, and I wanted to speak to you. But it's the weekend, and you wanna spend time with your family, so I'm just gonna . . . "

He turned to go.

"Wait. Wait a minute, Nuur," Mr Ilmi said. If this had been any other student who had come to his apartment to discuss a book with him, he would've thought they were high on something. But this was Nuur, and Mr Ilmi was certain he had never so much as touched a cigarette let alone drugs. "Why don't you come in," Mr Ilmi said.

"It's all right, we can talk about it at school next week."

"Nuur, don't be silly. You're here now. Come in," Mr Ilmi said in his stern, teacher's voice.

Nuur stepped into the apartment and took off his coat and scarf. "I think I figured out the error. It took me a while to get it, but I think I understand now," he announced as he struggled to take his shoes off.

"Okay, slow down. First things first. Let me introduce you to my wife."

Mr Ilmi noticed that Khadija, having heard the voice of a young man had already gone into their bedroom and covered her hair and shoulders with a garbosaar. She knew her husband didn't care whether or not she covered herself, but it seemed that she could never let go of what had been drilled into her since childhood.

"This is my wife Khadija," Mr Ilmi said to Nuur. And to her he said, "This is Nuur, one of my students."

"Barasho wanaagsan," Khadija said in the demure voice she reserved for male guests.

"Nice to meet you too," Nuur replied reflexively then remembered that he was talking to another Somali. "Barasho wanaagsan," he said.

"We're just about have dinner, you must stay," Mr Ilmi said, ushering Nuur into the living room. He caught Nuur glancing at his watch quizzically. "We have dinner early around here," Mr Ilmi explained.

"I can come another time—"

"Nonsense. You'll have dinner with us."

After a few forkfuls of pasta, Nuur put down his fork and took a sip of his water. "I'm a person. I'm a human being," Nuur said quickly, as if trying to get that off his chest. "I know that because I think. I have thoughts."

"Okay."

"So that makes me different from animals." He took another sip of his water, this time a bigger sip, more like a gulp, as if to lubricate not merely his throat but his mind. "But maybe animals have thoughts too. We just can't know what they think."

"You're right. We can't know that," Mr Ilmi conceded.

"What makes me who I am is not just my ability to think but what I think when I actually think . . . " Nuur paused for a moment as if to make sense of what he was saying.

"Go on."

"I guess what I mean is, the ability to actually know my own thoughts, to make sense of them is what really makes me, me. You know what I mean?"

Mr Ilmi nodded a bit timidly, not quite sure what Nuur meant. Khadija had been silently staring at the two men absorbed in abstruse talk, and she quietly got up and went away. Soon they heard the sound of an Indian movie.

"We're all different, right?"

Mr Ilmi nodded, his head turned towards the sound of the television. It was a quiet Sunday night and there was no other sound, it seemed, in the entire universe.

"We're the people that we are because we have different thoughts," Nuur went on, "But then, what happens when a lot of people have the same thought? Like collective consciousness. Like those people who get brainwashed."

"Brainwashed?" Mr Ilmi said.

"Yeah, like those people in that compound in Guyana who got brainwashed by their leader, whatshisname? And they all killed themselves. Does that mean they weren't individuals with distinct consciousness?"

Mr Ilmi nodded again to encourage his pupil, but Nuur didn't seem like he needed any encouragement. Once he got going, it was hard to stop him.

"Okay. So I'm who I am or what I am because my thoughts are what makes me who I am . . . No. That can't be right. My thoughts are my own creation, so obviously they can't determine who I am. If anything, it's the other way around, right? So I am who I am because I'm the generator of my thoughts. So the person that generates the thoughts or ideas or perceptions, that is the I that exists. But then that doesn't really answer the question of who this *I* is. I mean this person, this entity running around doing all this thinking and having all these ideas, who is that? . . . " He paused, but Mr Ilmi knew that the boy was not finished. "Our brain is just an organ. Like a spleen or a kidney. I mean, if you really think about it, the human brain for all its awesome complexity is essentially a computer that helps us process the world around us. So, therefore, to say who we are comes from the computational activity of our brains makes no sense—it's like saying a Mac is a person because it can compute things. For a Mac to be a person, to be an I, it needs a body, and that needs to be connected to a computational centre, the equivalent of our brain for it to even come anything close to an I. Right? Say something. What do you think?"

"Right. Of course. Right." Mr Ilmi said with a bewildered smile.

"Wait a minute. Hold up," Nuur started again. "If the brain needs the rest of my body to do its job, how can anyone claim I'm who I am because my brain has the capacity to generate thought. You can't base who you are on your ability to think. There has to be more. Right?"

"Is that a question?" Mr Ilmi asked. "What is that 'more'"?

"I mean, you need more than to merely think to be able to say, 'therefore I am.' You need an essence, a soul, or something that does not depend on a body or a mind. Something that transcends the body and the mind, something like a soul. And you need a body to sustain that thing, that soul, because you can't have all these body-less souls floating around. I mean, what is that? That's just creepy, right? What you need is a place for the soul to do its job."

"The soul has a job?" Mr Ilmi asked, barely following.

"Sure it does. The job or function of the soul is to make each of us . . . irreplaceable. I think that is why the Quran tells us, if you destroy one human life, it's as if you destroyed all of humanity. Because there's nothing else like an individual human soul, it's unique. It's irreplaceable."

"Interesting." Mr Ilmi said, taking a sip of his water.

At this point Khadija appeared with two cups of tea and some buskut, large, flaky Somali biscuits. Nuur blushed and said, "Sorry. I've taken up too much of your time . . . I've spoiled your Sunday evening."

"Not at all," Mr Ilmi lied. He knew that the young man needed someone he could talk to, someone to counter whatever deleterious notions he was picking up at the mosque. "Have your tea, then I'll show you something."

Nuur finished his tea and said, "Please thank your wife for me."

"I will," Mr Ilmi said. "Now come with me."

Nuur followed Mr Ilmi into the hallway, in the middle of which were two doors facing each other. Mr Ilmi opened the one to their left to reveal his study. It was the one room that had not been decorated by his wife. On one wall hung reproductions of two abstract paintings by Mark Rothko. Mr Ilmi told Nuur that they were souvenirs from his visit to the Museum of Modern Art in New York some years ago. The window, facing the door, had a white, sheer curtain across it and next to it were a sleek white desk and a black swivel chair. Under the reproductions were a brown leather armchair and a standing lamp. But the most amazing feature of the room for Nuur was the wall across, which was entirely covered with bookshelves.

"We're going to be turning this room into a nursery for our baby. So feel free to take any book you like," Mr Ilmi said to Nuur.

"For real?" Nuur asked, shocked but elated.

"For real. Take whatever you like."

"I don't know what to say, Mr Ilmi."

"I think I know what you might like," Mr Ilmi said, trying not to make a big deal out of his gift. He walked the length of the shelf, carefully pulling books out and placing them on the desk as though he were making the literary equivalent of a mixed tape for Nuur, who scanned the titles hungrily. He saw works of fiction, philosophy, science, biographies of African American luminaries. Nuur picked up *A Portrait of the Artist as a Young Man*. He flipped through it, came across a few passages highlighted in a fading yellow marker.

"I almost took this title out from the library last week. It seemed interesting."

"It's more than interesting. It's life-changing," Mr Ilmi said with a chuckle, then looked embarrassed.

"I'll make sure to read it then," Nuur said.

Mr Ilmi pulled out one more book from a shelf.

"This is enough, Mr Ilmi. What you've given me is more than . . . "

"You sure?"

Nuur nodded. "This is more books than I've ever owned. Thank you."

Mr Ilmi gave him the book he had just pulled out. "Just one more. Are you familiar with Kahlil Gibran?"

Nuur answered with a blank expression.

"Some of it might seem a bit esoteric—"

Nuur took the book from Mr Ilmi. It was called *The Prophet*. "Cool. Thanks, Mr Ilmi."

"I'll get you a bag to carry them," Mr Ilmi said and left the room. A few moments later, he returned with two tote bags and saw Nuur sitting on the swivel chair, reading from *The Prophet,* holding it open with both hands. For a fleeting moment, Mr Ilmi saw himself sitting in that chair, holding a book in that very fashion, and in his eyes, the same searching look, the look of a young man yearning to unlock the secret of the meaning of life, or at least his own life. And for that fleeting moment, he was Nuur and Nuur was him.

Nuur was beginning to get the distinct feeling that he was lost. He was on the third floor of the Toronto Reference Library. A nice Indian librarian with a little red dot on her forehead had told him to go to the third floor when he asked her for help with finding guide books for applying to universities. "How to write a great admission essay, stuff like that," he had said to her.

He had come to the library determined to learn how to write the best admission essay he could. Getting into the university of his first choice was an ambition that had fueled and guided him for years. He had passed at least five shelves when it became clear to him that he had made a mistake. *Maybe she said the fourth floor*, Nuur thought. As he was walking toward the elevator, Nuur's eye caught the spine of a book. The name sounded familiar. A few months ago, the name would've meant nothing to him, but ever since he read *Descartes' Error*, the book that Mr Ilmi had given him, Nuur had been coming across the name Descartes a lot in textbooks and online articles.

The name jumped out at him and he stopped. He turned around and read the spine: *Descartes' Bones* by Russell Shorto. Nuur took it out and stared at the cover, which had a picture of a skull. He found the unnaturally large eye sockets disturbing. *Is this what my skull will look like?* he thought.

Nuur leaned against the shelf behind him, flipped the cover and read the first lines on the flap of the jacket. He mouthed the words as he read them. "One brutal winter's day in 1650 in Stockholm . . . " He remembered that his aunt Jamila lived in Stockholm with his little cousins Nowaal and Waise. *I would love to visit them*, he thought. He continued reading: "The Frenchman René Descartes, the most

influential and controversial thinker of his time, was buried after a
cold and lonely death far from home . . . ”

Nuur continued to read, eager to know more about the story of
Descartes’ bones. “To understand the natural world, one needed to
question everything. Thus the scientific method was created, and religion overthrown. The great controversy Descartes ignited continues to
our era . . . ” Nuur tossed his knapsack on the floor beside him and sat
down in the narrow space between the shelves, cross-legged the way
he sat in Imam Yusuf’s Sunday class. He flipped to the back jacket to
continue. “*Descartes’ Bones* is a historical detective story about the creation of the modern mind.” Nuur stopped reading for a moment and
went over the words again: “the creation of the modern mind.” What is
a modern mind? How does one create a modern mind? he wondered.
Did he have a modern mind? Nuur asked himself. He longed to know
the answers to these questions more than he wanted to know what factors to consider when applying to university. He leaned back, made
himself comfortable, and went to the first page of the book.

———

A loud male voice on the intercom announced that the library would
close in fifteen minutes, lurching Nuur back into real life. He got up,
gathered his school bag and jacket and headed for the first floor. It
occurred to him that he had spent the last four hours sitting on the
floor of the library, reading the book he was holding in his hand. A
part of him was irritated that he hadn’t accomplished the task that had
brought him to the library. But he was also elated that he had found
a book so engrossing that nothing else had mattered. Nuur wanted
to check out the book, but it was marked “Reference.” He desperately wanted to finish the book; stealing was wrong, it was a sin. Nuur
watched his hand shove the book deep inside his backpack and conceal it among his school texts.

Once outside, Nuur stood still and tried to reorient himself to the
world. He had emerged from seventeenth-century Europe, and now

needed a moment to acclimatize himself to the throngs of people and the endless lines of traffic. The last rays of the sun cast a soft, golden glow over everything, and the world was at once beautiful and disorienting. Nuur crossed the street and walked down Yonge Street toward Bloor Street. It was a long time since he was last in this part of town, and he felt as though he had been beamed into the centre of some lovely, gleaming universe.

When he was little, in the summer, when the weather was nice, his father would take him and Ayuub around in his taxi. Their route usually included downtown. Nuur would beg his father to roll down the window so he could take in the soaring heights of the glass towers. When his father was in a good mood, he would indulge him and allow Nuur to peek his head out and crane his neck up to see if he could make out the tops of the skyscrapers.

As Nuur stood at the intersection and glanced westward, he tried to remember when and why those drives with his father stopped. The evening city lights were already on, imbuing him with a sense that the world was indeed a beautiful place—a feeling he found hard to come by in his own neighbourhood. These days, Nuur's life consisted of his school, the mosque, his job at the restaurant, and his weekly visits to Albion Library. The older he got, the more acutely Nuur felt that the physical space he occupied in the world was dwindling down to an insignificant dot. As he walked westward on Bloor towards Avenue Road, it occurred to him that without him knowing or consenting to it, he had allowed his life to become as restricted as that of a prisoner.

Nuur enjoyed his walk through this beautiful part of his hometown. In some inexplicable way, he was reminded of the far away European cities he had spent the last four hours reading about. Places he had never visited but yearned to see. He wanted to walk the narrow cobblestoned lanes of London, Paris, and Vienna. He recalled a word he had once come across in an article—*flâneur*. He didn't know what it meant, so he checked it in the small dictionary he always kept in his backpack. The idea of being an observer of street life appealed to a nascent romanticism that he once possessed. As he walked down University Avenue towards Queen's Park, he was a flâneur, simultaneously in the thick of things and detached enough to observe and understand the world around him. More than anything else, however, he wanted to relish the sensory details of moving through time and space. This evening, for a fleeting moment, he experienced this. He felt the essential reality of himself as a man, however young, alone, independent of his mother, teacher, imam, and even his nemesis, James Calhoun.

He came to Queen's Park and sat on a park bench under a streetlamp. Despite the cold November weather, the bench made for an ideal place to continue reading the book he had stolen from the library. He buttoned up his coat and went back to *Descartes' Bones*. In no time, he encountered words he had never heard before. He took out the yellow highlighter he always carried with him and marked everything that was new to him. *Cartesian Dualism. Qualia. Aristotelian System. Agnosticism. Rationalism. Empiricism. Socratic Method.* He even underlined *consciousness*, which Nuur knew the meaning of thanks to Mr Ilmi's biology class but always had trouble fully grasping. He knew it was more than just the aggregate of thoughts, senses, and perceptions that his mind produced every minute of his waking hours, and even in his sleep, given that he dreamed often and vividly. But Nuur couldn't explain to himself the exact nature of consciousness. It seemed too slippery a concept. As soon as he tried to grasp it, he found himself reaching for spiritual terms, like *soul*. He wondered what the Quran said about the nature of human consciousness. He caught himself smiling, for he was trying to make sense of things without hearing either Mr Ilmi's or Imam Yusuf's voice in his head, attempting to direct him in one way or another. It was a fleeting moment of independence and he relished it.

Suddenly it was too dark to read comfortably, so Nuur closed the book and took a deep breath, as if surfacing from the murky bottom of a river. He put the book back in his school bag and got up to go home.

As he walked toward the subway station, his mind was still racing—he could feel the energy of the seventeenth-century world of Europe that the author had managed to recreate—a world buzzing with scientific ideas, debates, and controversy. Nuur couldn't help but feel the depth of his ignorance. He felt a sharp pain of realization that even if he read one book a day, it wouldn't be enough to make up for all the knowledge of history, physics, philosophy and other subjects that he lacked. As he descended down the stairs to the subway, he made a vow to himself: He would devote himself to the life of the mind.

11

I T ALL STARTED WITH A SIMPLE request. "Tell me a story," she said. Khadija and Mr Ilmi were having dinner at the long, mahogany table that was far too big for their small apartment.

"Tell me a story," Khadija said with a sigh that betrayed a quiet desperation.

She's already bored with me, Mr Ilmi thought to himself, but he was ready to oblige her request. Ever since she told him she was pregnant, Mr Ilmi had been doting on her. So this time he told her the story of how at ten he had gone missing for almost two days. Walking home from school one day, he saw a truck parked on the quiet dirt road leading to his home. He had always wanted to ride on one, so he tightened his knapsack around his shoulders and with some effort climbed up to the open back. It was full of flour sacks, and little Mr Ilmi lay down on one and watched the blue sky above. The engine came to life and the truck was soon racing down the road, the elated Mr Ilmi watching the tree branches whizzing by.

He fell asleep, and when he awoke, it was dark and the truck was locked inside a large garage along with many other trucks. At sunset the following day, exhausted, covered in flour, Mr Ilmi was brought home by the two truck drivers. His mother held him for what seemed like hours, sobbing. At last she released him, held up his face and slapped him hard, then kissed him repeatedly on the forehead.

When Mr Ilmi finished his story, he asked her to tell him one about her childhood. She told him about the day her best friend Fatima dared her to steal a bag of candy from a neighbourhood store, which she did; she was caught and taken to the police station.

Night after night, these storytelling sessions took place after dinner, at the table or in the living room as they sipped chai or shared a bowl of ice-cream like a couple on a date, until they started to yawn and sleep beckoned.

———

Mr Ilmi poured some sesame oil into the palms of his hands, rubbed them together and began to massage his wife's feet. Khadija's feet had begun to swell as her pregnancy progressed. She was lying on the couch, her back propped up with two pillows, her feet on her husband's lap on the other end of the couch. The television was tuned to Al-Jazeera English, showing a report about the worsening humanitarian situation in Syria's ongoing civil war.

"Ruffa?" Khadija said, unable to wrap her tongue around the name.

"No," Mr Ilmi said, laughing. "Rufus." He had gotten into the habit of suggesting strange names for their baby whenever she brought up the subject. The previous night he had suggested Chaka, after his favourite soul singer Chaka Khan, if the baby were a girl. She had laughed hysterically and told him, over her dead body. Tonight his suggestion was Rufus for a boy.

"Ruf-fus!" Khadija attempted to say the name. "People give their children such names?"

"Yes!" Mr Ilmi said emphatically. "There is a famous Canadian singer named Rufus."

"No. Really? No," Khadija said, shaking her head as though he had told her the most ludicrous thing. "It sounds like a dog's name."

Mr Ilmi laughed and nodded. Suddenly they both turned their heads towards the television. The newscaster had just mentioned Somalia.

Khadija reached for the remote control and turned up the volume. She listened intently, trying to understand the report. Her eyes widened when she heard the name Kismayo and turned to Mr Ilmi with a worried look. It was his cue to start translating.

"Twenty-five people were killed yesterday, many of them civilians,"

Mr Ilmi said, translating for her. "The African Union troops, supported by the Somali National Army, have entered the coastal city, which has been controlled by Al-Shabaab. Thousands of civilians have fled to neighbouring towns," Mr Ilmi continued, slowly and methodically. When he briefly turned away from the TV, he saw his wife holding her hand to her mouth.

"Do we have a calling card?" she asked. "We must call my father."

"It's three in the morning there, dear," Mr Ilmi said, reaching out to hold her hand. "We'll call them first thing in the morning."

It had taken Khadija and her family months to figure out the time difference between Toronto and Kismayo. She would call them at all hours of the day, sometimes waking her father up at two in the morning, and they had often roused up Mr Ilmi from the depths of sleep at four in the morning. Mr Ilmi pictured his wife's telephone conversations proceeding along a transatlantic umbilical cord that nourished her, and any attempt to sever it would likely result in his wife's unraveling. So he had learned to accept them as the price of admission into her heart.

For months after their wedding, Mr Ilmi had felt shut out of his wife's interior world, as though she were punishing him for taking her so far away from the only place and people she had ever known and loved. From one of his uncles he had learned some facts about her family. When Khadija was ten, a long drought had led to the complete destruction of her family's banana farm, a misfortune from which it never recovered. The entire country had suffered the most severe famine in its recent history. While still a girl, Khadija had planned to marry Nuruddin, a boy in her neighbourhood. A tall, broad-shouldered fellow her own age, his dark, wavy hair and performance in the town's soccer field had all the girls swooning. But it was Khadija who captured the young man's heart. Mr Ilmi had never found out what happened to that relationship and why Khadija had ended up marrying him.

He had heard the story of Nuruddin only two weeks before, in bed, after sex. As he lay next to her, looking up at the ceiling, one arm around her, he said: "Can I ask you something?" Khadija's head was resting on his chest, her fingers gently scratching the vertical patch of wiry hair on his chest. "Sure," she said, trying to suppress a yawn.

"Tell me about Nuruddin."

He felt her body get tense. He saw her raise her head and stare at him with a look of surprise. She gave a tiny smile that seemed to appreciate him for acknowledging that she had a life before him, that she had dreams for her life that didn't include marrying him or migrating to Canada. Mr Ilmi smiled back at her, to acknowledge her gratitude.

Khadija reached for the lamp on the nightstand beside her and turned off the light. In the dark, obscured from the intensity of his gaze, she told him the story of her love affair with Nuruddin. Freed by her husband's bold question, she told him the details of how she and Nuruddin met one day as she struggled to carry home a container of water—she had walked thirty minutes to collect it from a local pump, which sold water whenever the taps in the homes ran dry. Nuruddin had carried the water for her all the way home. He had possessed a deep and comforting voice and a cheeky humour. Conducted over months in a secret rendezvous in the one cinema house in town that played Bollywood movies, where they would sit together holding hands under her cotton garbosaar, the progress of their love was as slow as it was natural. But it came to an end after the death of her mother Nadifa. Khadija had left school to work to support her family and send her younger sisters to school. One night her father called her to sit down next to him on his sali, on which he regularly prayed. He asked her if she knew where Canada was. Her geography wasn't great but she knew enough, that it was far away and cold. Her father told her that a Somali man from Canada had asked for her hand in marriage. Khadija told her father that she would rather marry Nuruddin. Her father said that marrying Nuruddin would be nothing more than another mouth to feed. He told her to think about the proposal and what it would mean to her family. He gave her three days to consider.

Khadija stopped and put her palm on her husband's cheek. It was a gesture whose meaning confounded Mr Ilmi. Was it a gesture of sympathy for him? "Then what happened?" he asked.

"I knew what my answer would be even before he finished his request. But I took the three days he gave me. On the third night when he came home, after bringing him his dinner, I sat on the edge of his sali and told him I would accept the proposal. He nodded, smiled, and ate his dinner."

"Why did you say yes?"

Khadija became silent, perhaps searching for the right words, the proper way to tell him without hurting his feelings. "For my sisters," she said at last. "I did it for my sisters . . . I knew that what little money my father made wouldn't be enough to send all three of them to school."

Mr Ilmi gave Khadija's arm a gentle squeeze, as if to thank her. He was happy she had said yes to his proposal, not only because she was here with him, in bed, in the dark, her warm body pressed against his, but also because at the end of every month they drove to Dahabshiil, the remittance bank on Weston Road, to send her father four hundred dollars, so that three young girls in Kismayo could go to school.

Khadija rested her head on Mr Ilmi's chest. She remained quiet for a while, then cleared her throat and said, "Now you."

"Now me, what?"

Khadija tweaked his nipple. "Ouch!" he yelled and they both laughed.

"I told you mine. Now you tell me your story," she said.

In the darkness of their bedroom, Mr Ilmi felt his wife smile at him. He grinned incredulously as he considered her request. He debated just how much of his past would be wise to share with her. Should he tell her, he wondered, the real reason why he finally called his uncle Ahmed in Nairobi and accepted his oft-repeated offer of facilitating a marriage to a Somali girl? It was not a search for love but rather the deep loneliness that wrapped itself around him like a shawl that finally made him make the call one night and say the words his uncle had been waiting for. He remembered the shock he felt as he said yes to his uncle. He was stunned that he could cast away his deeply held convictions about romance, courtship, and love. He found it at once thrilling and unsettling that three months shy of forty, he still possessed the capacity to be shocked by his choices.

Mr Ilmi ignored his desire to confess everything and told his wife of the only one love that had really mattered. In details equaling hers, Mr Ilmi told his wife about Mikeila and about their deep and tumultuous three-year affair. When Mr Ilmi finished his story about the one that got away, as the saying went, Khadija didn't respond. Mr Ilmi's heart began to beat fast and instantly he regretted his frankness. He should not have gone along with his wife's dangerous storytelling game.

He had always suspected that total honesty was not a good idea in a marriage, and that night as he lay next to his wife, who had suddenly gone mute on him, his suspicion was confirmed.

"You should've told her," Khadija said at last.

Mr Ilmi tilted his head a little to see her better, but it was too dark to make out the expression on her face. "Told her what?"

"How much you loved her."

Now it was Mr Ilmi who turned mute. He didn't know what to say, so he remained silent and pulled her closer to him.

———

Their evening storytelling ritual became a part of Mr Ilmi's day that he looked forward to the most, because these sessions partly replaced his wife's Bollywood romances. But those storytelling sessions went deeper than romance. They were moments of shared intimacy.

One night Khadija told him about the day her mother Nadifa walked into the Indian Ocean. They were lying on the couch, their limbs entangled. Khadija had never told anyone about her mother's suicide. It was a secret which her family had kept from even their closest relatives. In their world, suicide was a sin for which the survivors of the deceased were shunned, as though self-killing ran in the family. That night, Khadija finally shared with her husband the secret she had carried with her from Kismayo to Canada.

When the famine of 1993 hit the country, it completely destroyed the family's banana farm. Penniless and hungry, Nadifa insisted that their only chance for survival lay in joining the caravan of people headed for a place called Dadaab in northeast Kenya. Her husband tried to dissuade her, saying the journey was dangerous, but she insisted, she would take the kids and walk with them by herself if need be. And so the entire family—Khadija, who was eight, her younger sisters Filsan, Samiira, and Nuurto, and her ten-month-old brother Zakhariye set off on foot across the parched lands of southern Somalia. Zakhariye could not cope and died three days into the journey. His dehydrated corpse was buried near a leafless acacia tree, his grave unmarked.

After a year in Kenya, when the family returned to Kismayo, Nadifa fell into deep, unyielding depression. She barely spoke and ate little. At the crack of dawn, one day, on a beautiful sunny morning, she put on her favourite white guntiino and announced that she was going for a walk. She never returned. Three days later, her body was found on the beach in a nearby village, tangled in her white guntiino and long strands of seaweed.

"When I think of my mom," Khadija said, her voice breaking a little, "I don't remember all the amazing things about her, like her fierce independence or beautiful singing voice or her high cheekbones. All I have is an image of her walking towards the water's edge, her back turned to me. Her white guntiino is blowing in the wind as she walks slowly into the dark blue sea. I call out to her but she doesn't look back. She walks further and further away until she is submerged." Khadija paused, then concluded, "That's the only thing that comes to my mind when I think of my mother . . . Isn't that awful?"

"There was more to her life than the way it ended," Mr Ilmi said as he took his wife's hand and held it to his lips.

"I imagine sometimes . . . I see my whole family in paradise. My dad, my sisters, my little bother, and we're all chatting and laughing together in heaven, remembering some of the funny things that happened to us in Kismayo. Except for my mom. She is not with us. She's not with us, because people who kill themselves don't go to heaven. They go to hell."

"We don't know that."

"That's what the Quran says. Allah punishes them with eternity in hell."

"Allah also forgives. He's most merciful. Most forgiving. The Quran tells us that repeatedly."

Khadija stayed quiet, as though counting the number of times the Quran calls Allah the Most Merciful, the Most Compassionate. The Most Forgiving.

12

Nuur was already in the back seat of the car, which was parked in front of the building. He watched his mother and Ayuub at the entrance, she holding him by the arms, talking to him, her face pressed to his head, whispering something into his ear as though his life depended on it. Nuur wished he could hear what she was saying. Tears were streaming down her cheeks.

Ayuub reached for the tip of her red garbosaar, wrapped around her shoulders over her winter coat, and wiped the tears from her cheeks. He kissed her one last time on the forehead and turned to walk to the car, his hand still clutched in her grip. She finally let go and walked back towards the entrance of the building, covering her face with her shawl. Nuur watched his brother approach, eyes downcast, dragging his giant duffel bag on the ground like a dead body. His eyes followed Ayuub, and finally through the back window, he saw Ayuub hoist the entirety of his worldly possessions and throw it into the trunk of the car.

Ayuub slumped into the front seat, next to his best friend Fathudin, who would drive. He turned around to look at Nuur, who quickly glanced away lest he burst into tears.

——

Two nights before, as Nuur was sitting up in his bed leaning against a pillow propped up against the wall, he heard a gentle knock on the door. He looked up from his homework to find his brother standing there.

"Sup?" Ayuub said and they exchanged one of their quick fist bumps. Ayuub threw himself on his own bed, which was no more than four feet away from Nuur's.

"How is Lisa?" Nuur asked, implying why his brother was not at his girlfriend's place where he had been staying the past few months.

"Good," Ayuub said and left it at that. He put his hands behind his head and stared at the ceiling. "They've gone to bed?"

"Mom is. Dad is out."

"Of course he is," Ayuub said, his voice dripping with contempt.

Another long awkward silence passed and Nuur wondered if he should go back to his homework or try to coax out of his brother whatever it was that was weighing on his mind. "Did you get into a fight or something?"

His brother turned to him, perplexed. "No. Why?"

"I don't know, you look like you're hiding from the police or something."

Ayuub laughed. "Sometimes you crack me up, bro. You've been watching too much local news."

Nuur turned back to his homework.

"I've decided. It's official," Ayuub said.

"What's official?"

"I'm moving to Fort McMurray in two days. We leave early Saturday morning."

"We?"

"Fathudin is coming with me."

Nuur closed his textbook, grateful for the intrusion of his brother's real world into the abstraction of his calculus homework. Nuur sat up in his bed, crossed his legs and turned to Ayuub, a gesture that said, "I'm all ears."

"Is that why you came home tonight, to tell mom and dad?"

Ayuub shook his head.

"You need to tell mom. You can't just leave. It would break her heart."

"I know. I will. Suleyman is coming with us too. We're picking him up in Kitchener."

"Three amigos hitting the road," Nuur said.

"Yeah, the three amigos," Ayuub said with a laugh. "It'll be fun."

Nuur smiled, happy that his brother would have companionship in his new life in what sounded like the other side of the world. He and his brother had shared their tiny bedroom from as far back as he could remember. Even when they had fought over toys or video games, when he had hated Ayuub with passion, the sound of his brother's breathing at night had been a comfort. That soft, steady hum had been the only constant in his life and made him feel less alone in the world.

"What about Lisa, what does she think?" Nuur asked.

"We agreed it was for the best. I can't get a job here and she can't raise a baby by herself. She barely makes enough as it is. When I suggested the idea, she said it was great, as long as I keep my dick in my pants and I visit her a couple of times a year."

"She sounds mature about the whole thing."

"Lisa is great, bro. I really want you to get to know her better."

"I would like that," Nuur said, already envisioning visits to his future niece or nephew. "So it's all set then?"

Ayuub nodded. After two years of meandering through life, he seemed happy to have finally figured out what he wanted and what he needed to do to get it.

———

It was Saturday morning, and Ayuub had offered to give Nuur a ride to the mosque where he was to meet Imam Yusuf, who had invited him to join him on a trip to Ottawa to attend a fundraiser to build a mosque in Baydhabo, Southern Somalia.

Ayuub glanced back again at his brother, who wore the same glum expression on his face.

"Oh, come on, bro! Stop looking so fucking sad. This is a good thing. Say it with me. This is a good thing!"

"This is a good thing," Nuur repeated after Ayuub.

"Bullshit! Say it like you mean it, man. This is a good thing!"

"This is a good thing!" Nuur said more loudly but still without conviction. His brother was embarking on a road trip across several provinces and time zones in search of a better life, but what would he find there? Would the two of them be the same when they met again? Were they parting forever? But as sad as he felt, Nuur wanted to celebrate with Ayuub, so he repeated the mantra, "This is a good thing!" after him, each time with a bit more heart.

"That's more like it!" Ayuub said. "Let's get some music up in here," he yelled as he reached for the CD player. K'naan's "Dreamer" blasted out of the speakers, giving Nuur a much needed jolt. He watched his brother dance in his seat, swaying his hands and singing along. Fathudin, who was silent up until then, joined in. They sang the chorus in unison at the top of their lungs.

The car pulled into the parking lot of the mosque, Fathudin and Ayuub singing along with K'naan the last bars of the song, which ended in an exuberant chant that had the power to make them feel as "good" as K'naan felt singing those lyrics. Every Somali boy of a certain age loved K'naan, if not for his music then for what he represented to them: a fellow Somali boy who grew up in the same neighbourhood and against all odds managed to ascend the heights of international stardom. Ayuub and his friend were young. They were best friends. And they were joining the westward exodus of young Somali men. A whole new world awaited them. It really was okay to feel good, as the song told them to. They chanted the words defiantly, telling the world to go fuck itself. They had nomad blood surging through their veins. It was in their DNA always to seek a better place, to find it, and make it their own.

The song came to a slow, rather anticlimactic end, Fathudin turned off the engine, and all three of them got out at once. The trunk was popped open and Nuur removed from it his frayed, navy overnight bag. He walked over to Fathudin, whom he had known for so long that he was almost like a brother. They gave each other a quick, manly hug. Lean in, chest pump, pat on the back, lean out. It took a few seconds, a choreographed expression of farewell, simple and devoid of drama.

Fathudin got back into the driver's seat.

Nuur walked around the car to where his brother waited, leaning against the passenger door. He put down his bag on the ground and watched Ayuub light the cigarette that dangled from his lips. Nuur caught a slight tremble in his brother's hand as he struggled with the lighter.

"Fucking wind," Ayuub snapped and flung the cigarette away. There was no wind. It was a sunny, unseasonably warm December morning with not a cloud in the sky. The kind of day where anything seemed possible and life offered itself up for the taking.

"Gonna come visit me?" Ayuub said.

Nuur nodded.

"Gonna take good care of yourself?"

Nuur nodded again.

"Say something, asshole," his brother said with his usual grin. Nuur felt tears rush to his eyes. He looked away and stared at the parking lot, which was empty, except for Imam Yusuf's black minivan.

"I'll pray for you," Nuur said and regretted it as soon as the words came out. He knew his brother didn't believe in prayer. The attainment of something good or the prevention of something bad with a simple prayer to Allah didn't make much sense to him. Nuur once heard his brother say, "I think God has better things to do than worrying about my exams," when their mother told them to pray as they left for school to write their final exam for the year.

"You do that, bro," Ayuub said. "I'm gonna need all the prayers I can get." He took out from his coat pocket a knitted toque, a red one with white letters that said ROOTS. He slipped it on Nuur's head, almost covering his eyes. Nuur took it off and gave it back.

"It's your favourite," Nuur said.

"Fuck you, put it back on."

"You're gonna need it up there in the North."

Ayuub ignored his brother's protest and slipped the toque back on Nuur's head.

"All right, bro. I gotta skip. We've four days of driving ahead of us."

Nuur nodded like a little boy.

"Take care of mom, okay?"

"I will."

They both made a fist followed by one last bump. Ayuub got into the car and Nuur hurried towards the mosque, as if trying to escape something. In his head he repeated, "Don't look back, don't look back," like a mantra. He failed his own command. Just before he reached the door of the mosque, he looked back and got a glimpse of the speeding car carrying his brother to another life.

———

The sun rallied valiantly against the gathering clouds as Nuur and Imam Yusuf left the city later that morning. Gradually, the suburban townhouses and shopping plazas gave way to empty fields and the occasional farm house. The multilane highway had yielded to two single lanes. Nuur took off the red toque his brother had slipped on his head. He brought it up to his nose and took in its scent of hair oil, cigarette smoke, and weed. He glanced at Imam Yusuf, who was shaking his head in disapproval.

"And this Lisa girl, what's her religion?" the imam asked.

"Not sure. Catholic, I guess. She's Italian."

The imam started another round of head-shaking. "So what are they going to raise this child as, a Muslim, a Catholic?" It was a shocked statement more than a question.

It's a baby. What difference does it make? Nuur thought. He began to regret telling Imam Yusuf about Ayuub's baby. "How long is the drive?" Nuur asked, desperate to change the topic.

"This is why I sent my children away," Imam Yusuf continued, relentlessly. Nuur had heard that the imam had sent his wife and six children to Hargeisa, the capital of the Republic of Somaliland, which had broken off from the rest of Somalia. That was the big trend in the community these days; men relocating their families to Hargeisa, the only stable, peaceful part of Somalia, while others shipped them away to Muslim countries like Egypt or Saudi Arabia. Even as far away as Malaysia.

"What about the other two?" Nuur asked, feeling an inexplicable rush of anger at the imam. He had taken a second wife in the city as soon as he had sent away his first wife, and he had had twin girls with her a few months ago.

"They're too young," the imam said. "I'll move them as soon as they reach school age. Before the brainwashing starts."

"Brainwashing?"

"The school system, they have them learning about 'alternative families' before they even leave kindergarten," Imam Yusuf said, taking his hands off the wheel long enough to make his quotation marks in the air. "Men marrying men, women marrying women. Raising children. And they have the gall to call it a family." The imam made a sound with his mouth to show his repulsion.

"You know what the Quran calls these people?"

Nuur shook his head. He knew the answer, for he had read the Quran from start to finish many times, but he knew how much the imam liked to pontificate. So he let him go on.

"Qaum-e-Lut. The city of Lut was their base. Like San Francisco or New York. Or Toronto, even. And Allah sent them a messenger." The imam quoted a verse from the Quran in Arabic as he often did when he wanted to buttress his arguments. "'Do ye commit lewdness such as no people in creation (ever) committed before you? For ye practice your lusts on men in preference to women: ye are indeed a people transgressing beyond bounds.'"

Whenever the imam quoted a verse from the Quran in Arabic, the tenor of his voice changed to one of great solemnity and melody. Nuur thought that Imam Yusuf could have been an impressive actor in another life.

"Allah's messenger warned the people of Lut," the imam continued, his voice coming back to its usual banal English tone. "He warned them of the coming punishment if they didn't give up their sinful ways and repent. They said to him: 'Bring us the wrath of Allah if thou tellest the truth' and so he did. Allah rained down on them stones of baked clay and turned the whole town upside down. That's how grave their sin was . . . is. And to this day, the area where the city of Lut was located bears the mark of Allah's wrath."

Nuur glanced at the imam. This part of the story was new to him. "Where is that?" he asked.

"The Dead Sea. Archeologists have confirmed that the cataclysm took place there all those thousands of years ago." He paused for a moment, then went on, "Now they call it, 'alternative families,'" his anger rising again.

It always struck Nuur as odd, the fixation that imams and preachers and most religious figures had on the sex lives of others. He found it comical, their obsession with who was sleeping with whom and in what fashion. He wanted to ask the imam why this was the case, but instead found himself saying, "You could've put your children in Islamic school here, if you didn't want them learning that stuff."

Imam Yusuf gave a familiar chuckle, reserved for when he wanted to belittle a pupil's naïveté. "Not enough. Not enough," he said. "The schools are just one part of the problem. It's the whole system that is corrupt, rotten from within. The kids come home from school to find more filth on television. Naked women in every commercial. They can't even sell a packet of gum without a naked woman." The imam continued his rant, his gestures gaining new levels of animation. "Tell me, Nuur. You're a smart young man, what on earth has a woman in a bathing suit got to do with selling gum?"

Nuur thought about the question for a moment. It had been a while since he watched television, and he thought he must have missed the commercial showing a naked woman selling gum. He wanted to tell the imam that he was not familiar with this particular ad, but thought the better of it, lest Imam Yusuf got the impression that he was mocking him. Nuur opted for the safer answer: "Sex sells, I guess."

"So what does that say about a culture so base, so indecent they have to dishonour the sanctity of a woman's body to sell things?"

The imam's cell phone rang before Nuur had a chance to answer the question. Not that he had a good answer. Imam Yusuf picked up the call with the little gadget that clung to his ear. Nuur turned his gaze to the farmland whizzing by, his attention half turned to the imam's conversation. It seemed to be about the amount of money they expected to raise in Ottawa and the means by which the money would be transferred to Somalia. "We have to send it in smaller amounts. Safer that way," the imam said. Nuur was enjoying the countryside. A few cows grazing. Horses standing still, heads close together, as though sharing the latest farm gossip. He was glad he had left Toronto even if only for the weekend.

Nuur tried to remember the last time he had left the city. He must have been ten or eleven, when his father rented a van smelling of leather and pine scent and drove the whole family to Syracuse to visit Uncle Jamal, his father's best friend from his university days in Casablanca, where they had studied architecture together in the 1980s. Nuur was jolted back to the present when he heard the imam saying, "So where were we?" He seemed to have become rejuvenated by the phone call and was eager to continue their discussion.

"I think you were saying something about the culture here."

"Oh yes!" the imam said and took a long pause as if figuring out where to go from there. "Will you promise me something?"

"Sure. What?"

"Promise me that if Allah blesses you with children, you will not raise them here."

Nuur was taken aback by the abrupt turn of the conversation from the general to the personal.

"I would love to have kids someday, but I'm not thinking about that now. I still have school to worry about."

"Listen to me, son. Marriage is the cloth that protects us from the evils of shaytan. You must marry as soon as you can. Next year, if possible. In this country, it's the only way to survive the temptations that a healthy young man like yourself faces every day."

Nuur smiled and nodded. He agreed with the imam about the abundance of temptation that surrounded him. Everywhere he went, there it was. At school he lowered his gaze every time he was confronted by the sight of pretty girls wearing next to nothing. There was Samira in particular, the honey-skinned Somali girl who had spent most of her childhood in Turin, Italy before coming to Canada; she sat next to him in English class and her locker in the hallway was next to his. Nuur tried his best to avert his gaze from the low-cut blouses she always wore, which did little to conceal the lacy top of her bra that accentuated her beautiful breasts. Despite his efforts, Nuur often found himself stealing glances at Samira's cleavage whenever she spoke to him about a particular book she was reading. There was always some book that "shook her to the core." *The Revolution from Within* was one. *The Second Sex* was another book that changed her life, and she gave it to Nuur as a gift, to read it when he felt "ready to experience it."

During their brief encounters by the lockers, when shaytan got the better of him, Nuur often imagined Samira without her constricting bra, his hands cupping her breasts, while she went on about Gloria Steinem or Simone de Beauvoir or other recent discoveries of women whom she called her "sheroes." After each encounter, Nuur made sure to perform an extra prayer in the evening and begged Allah for forgiveness from the hellfire he deserved.

And when Samira was not tempting him with her sweetly beguiling smile and lacy bras, temptation came through the general atmosphere of the school. It seemed to Nuur that wherever he went, sex was in the air. In the locker room, he overheard boys bragging about their latest blowjobs. These constant reminders of sex were a torture. But he had recently tried Imam Yusuf's suggestion for relieving the thoughts and urges that plagued his nights. Fasting, the ultimate libido killer.

"Women are a gift to men," Imam Yusuf continued next to him. "But they are also a curse. You must guard against their temptation."

Nuur nodded, unable to think of what to say.

"In a Hadith narrated by al-Bukhari, it's said that the Prophet, peace be upon him, said that womankind will form the majority of people in hell."

Nuur turned from the window and stared at Imam Yusuf. "Why?" he asked.

"Because women are susceptible to shaytan," Imam Yusuf said as if that were all the proof he needed.

"So are men?"

"Yes. But women much more so than men."

"Why?"

"Because they're emotional creatures. They're led by fleeting emotions rather than intellect or reason. And we are at our weakest to the lure of shaytan when we allow our emotions to rule us. Think about it, son," Imam Yusuf said, putting a gentle hand on Nuur's shoulder. "Envy. Anger. Lust. Deceit. What do they all have in common?"

Nuur's mind was blank.

"They are all emotions," the imam said with a chuckle. "And women are by nature more emotional. You do the math."

Nuur wanted to point out to the imam that technically deceit was not an emotion the way, say, anger was. But he couldn't bring himself to contradict his teacher. Instead, he thought of his mother. Would she be one of the women to make up the majority of people in hell? She was always at the mercy of her emotions, which ran through her like a hurricane, but as soon as the storm passed, she was back to her kind, giving, and intelligent self. All the qualities the imam praised highly. The thought of his mother suffering the torment of hellfire filled him with sorrow. He turned away from the imam and looked out the window. It was getting dark outside, the trees and rocky hills forming menacing shapes. He thought about his brother and father, each in his own way at risk of hellfire. He read a short, silent prayer in his head for Allah to forgive them both. He would do anything to save his family from eternal punishment.

Nuur glanced away from the darkening countryside and looked at Imam Yusuf. "Thank you, thank you for bringing me today . . . I wish the others came with us," he continued, wondering why the other boys from Imam Yusuf's Sunday class didn't come.

"I didn't tell the others about this," Imam Yusuf said with a sly smile. "Just you."

Nuur tried not to show his disappointment. "But I think Nuruddin and Idris would've loved a road trip."

"A road trip?" the imam said with a touch of derision in his tone as though the very concept was obscene. "This is not a road trip, son. I invited you for a very important reason. To show you the wonderful work we're doing at the Ottawa mosque. I think you'll be very impressed with the work of your brothers and sisters in Ottawa."

"The others would've enjoyed seeing the wonderful work too."

The imam let out a snort. Nuur couldn't tell if he was amused or frustrated. "Do not misunderstand me, Nuur. The others boys, they are very good boys, mashallah. But they lack something . . . a quality I see in you."

Nuur had it at the tip of his tongue to ask what it was that the imam saw in him, but he stopped himself for fear of seeming too eager to hear of his special qualities. He waited for the imam to tell him what this quality was that set him apart from the other boys in his Sunday Quran class.

"You have the potential to be a leader," the imam said at last.

Nuur chuckled. *Cut the bullshit*, he thought. He knew himself well enough to know that he was never the leader of anything. Even as a child, when he and the neighbourhood boys played outside, he was the last to be picked for games, the last to be asked for ideas. He had always been perfectly happy to follow.

"You have the potential to really contribute to your community, and more importantly, to your diin, your faith."

"Thank you," Nuur said. He was surprised that a part of him, however small, loved hearing this. There was at least the possibility that he might someday fulfill the potential Imam Yusuf saw in him.

"You do want to contribute, don't you? To your diin, and reap the rewards in paradise?"

Nuur smiled. "Yes. Of course."

"I thought so. So many of Muslim men your age have no such desire. They are more concerned with going to university and getting jobs and buying nice things. But as you and I know, for a true Muslim man, his house is not in this dunya. A true Muslim seeks a home in paradise."

"But I do want to go to university," Nuur said, a touch of worry creeping into him, fearing he might have tarnished the image the imam held of him. But he felt it would be a worse sin to lie to Imam Yusuf and present himself as something he wasn't. "I've already applied to U of T."

"U of T?"

"University of Toronto. My teacher Mr Ilmi said he wrote me the best recommendation letter he had ever given a student. He thinks I have a pretty good shot at med school. If I maintain my A average. I'm kinda worried about calculus though. It might drag down my GPA, but I think—"

"This Mr Ilmi, your science teacher—"

"Biology teacher—"

"Is he Muslim?"

"Of course," Nuur said, perplexed by the question. Somalis are known to be 99.9 percent Muslim.

"Just because you have a Muslim name and you say you're a Muslim doesn't mean you are a Muslim," the imam said, speaking harshly, enraged by the effrontery of those Muslim people who claim to be Muslims. "You agree with me on that point, don't you?"

"Yes," Nuur said, not wanting to seem like he didn't know this apparently obvious fact.

"Does he pray?"

"Does who pray?"

"Your biology teacher, does he pray?"

"I don't know. I don't think so."

"You have Khudba prayer on Fridays at your school, no?"

"Yes."

"Does he come to your Friday Khudba prayer?"

"No."

"Then he doesn't pray."

"Well, maybe he prays at home. Maybe—"

"No. Praying without Khudba is pointless."

Nuur was quiet for a moment. He felt like he was letting down his teacher, the best teacher he ever had, by not being able to defend him properly against what sounded like an excommunication—if such a thing existed in Islam. Nuur thought about his brother Ayuub, who had prayed as a boy until he discovered girls, and his father, whose attitude towards religion alternated between indifference and outright hostility. And there was his mother. Surely, Allah took note of her valiant and sincere struggle to pray and fast and cover her hair, not to mention her efforts to send whatever extra money she saved back home to the countless relatives who called her at all hours of the day, begging for help. Surely, Allah witnessed her struggle. Surely, she was a good Muslim even if she fell way short in the eyes of Imam Yusuf.

"This teacher, Mr—"

"Mr Ilmi."

"Yes, Mr Ilmi. How much does he know about Islam?"

"I don't know."

"Don't you wonder, though?"

"He teaches biology. It never occurred to me to wonder."

"My dear son, teaching is a sacred act. When you teach a pupil, you're molding his character. It's a serious enterprise. Do you agree?"

Nuur nodded uncertainly.

"And though it might seem to you like he's just your biology teacher, he is far more than that."

"What do you mean?"

Imam Yusuf was silent for a moment. "Do you admire this Mr Ilmi?"

"Yes. Very much."

"Why?"

"Because he's one of the . . . no, he is the best teacher I've ever had," Nuur said and quickly added "at school," just in case Imam Yusuf took offense.

"That's great. That means he's good at his job. But what do you know of him?"

Nuur looked at the imam, confused, unable to understand the question.

"I mean to say, what do you know of his character? Do you know if he gambles or commits zinna?"

"He's married. I met his wife. She's very nice."

"One can be married and still fornicate, son."

"He's not like that. He is a very nice man."

"I'm sure he is. There are plenty of nice people in the world. But we must be more than that. As Muslims, Allah, the almighty and all-knowing, expects us to be more than just nice." Imam Yusuf said *nice* as if it were a dirty word.

Nuur shifted in his seat and felt a sudden chill. He lifted the collar of his coat and crossed his arms, hugging himself.

"On the day of resurrection, after the great and final horn is sounded and the earth is rolled up like a carpet and the dead are resurrected from their graves, do you know what will happen?"

Nuur shook his head.

"We will be raised from the grave with our own kind. We will come forth in separate groups. The idolators in one group. The abortionists in another group. Those who profit from usury in another group. And so on and so forth. On that final Day of Judgment, you will want to be with the righteous and not just with those who were nice. To be among the chosen, you'll have to be more than just nice. Being a Muslim, my son, is a serious business. Nice will not cut it. You can't choose which of Allah's commandments to obey and which to ignore. You can't be just a little bit Muslim. You either are or you are not! It's become so fashionable these days to be one of those so-called progressive Muslims and go on television and say . . . " Imam Yusuf put on an effeminate voice, "Oh but we are just like you. We are Muslim but secular. We are Muslim but queer." He broke into riotous laughter. "Can you believe that, Muslim but queer! What is that? But my favourite one is, Oh we are Muslim but we believe in democracy."

Nuur turned around and stared at the imam's profile. "What's wrong with democracy? Isn't it a good thing for people to choose their own leaders?" he asked. Nuur did not like contradicting the imam, but he had always believed that democracy was what separated prosperous countries from failed states like Somalia.

"It would be, if democracy were just about choosing a leader. But trust me, son, when I tell you this. Democracy is a ruse. A mirage! It's the great mendacity of the West, an illusion, that mankind's problems can be solved in the parliamentary offices of their capitals. And let me tell you, my son, the infidels, they are the masters of mendacity. Every day they insult the glorious legacy of our beloved Prophet Mohamed in their filthy media, and when we complain peacefully, they say, Sorry: freedom of speech. What does that even mean? Freedom of speech? But if you so much as ask one question about their precious Holocaust, the Zionist media will destroy you. They will call you every ugly name in the book. So you see, their so-called freedom of speech is a hoax. A pack of lies! We must defend the honour of our Prophet Mohamed, peace be upon him, by any means necessary."

The imam paused for a moment, as if to recall where he was going with his diatribe. "You know, that day when I heard about that filthy magazine in France that was attacked and twelve of their infidels were killed, it was one of the happiest days of my life. It showed the unbelievers that you cannot insult our beloved Prophet Mohamed and get away with it. Wallahi, they will not get away with it. Protecting the honour of our diin is the solemn duty of every Muslim man. When it comes to defending our faith, jihad is not an option. It is an obligation! It is a compulsion!"

As Imam Yusuf continued his lecture, his voice betrayed a cool, steely anger unlike the theatrical gesticulations of his Friday sermons. Nuur had noticed that Imam Yusuf never gave political sermons at the mosque. Even during the so-called Arab Spring, when it seemed that after prayers everyone in the mosque was talking about what they were watching on Al-Jazeera, or during the war between Israel and Hamas in Gaza, when pictures of dead Palestinian children were scattered all over the news, Imam Yusuf never strayed from his usual sermons of the need for repentance and the fortification of faith. Nuur once overheard a group of Somali men at the restaurant where he worked, saying that the mosque had a mole, a regular mosque-goer whose job was to report back to the RCMP and inform them of any radical activities. No details were given, but from what Nuur could observe, they all seemed to agree that there was indeed a mole among them.

"Their democracy, this thing they want to infect us with, is not a simple case of choosing a president or prime minister," the imam continued. "Oh no, son. I wish that's all it was. What they want from us, no, what they demand from us is nothing short of the removal of the word of Allah from all public life. They're fine with our faith as long as we keep it hidden in our homes, locked away like a dirty secret. Nothing threatens the infidel more than the mention of Sharia. But taking away the Sharia from a Muslim is like taking a fish out of water. It is death. That's why you see our ummah from Indonesia to Morocco flailing around aimlessly, trying all manner of man-made systems of government. Secularism, oh that sounds nice. Communism, oh let's try a bit of that. Capitalism, what a lovely idea, let's give that a go. All to no avail! But what these so-called Muslims fail to understand is that we can never rule the world again the way we did in the Golden Age of Islam without the Sharia. It's our armour against their lies. It's our only hope for reward in this dunya and the hereafter. Never forget that, son."

Imam Yusuf took a deep breath and became silent. He turned his gaze away from the road and stared at his pupil. After a while he spoke again. "Do you know why I continue to live here even though it makes me sick to my stomach?" he asked.

Nuur tried his best to hide the fear that was gathering inside him. He wanted to tell the imam to focus on the road. He sensed a vague, almost imperceptible wish in the imam's eyes, a death wish. "Why?" Nuur asked, his voice shaking a little. "Why do you continue to live here if you hate it so much?"

Imam Yusuf finally turned his gaze back to the road and said in a soft, conciliatory tone. "I'm performing my jihad, propagating the word of Allah in the land of the unbelievers. I'm fifty-six years old. I'm too old for the battlefield. But I'm not too old to spread the message of God. Allah has given us all a struggle, a jihad. Find your jihad, Nuur," Imam Yusuf said in the soft voice of a father to a son or a therapist to patient. "Once you find your jihad, embark on it with all your heart. That will be your path to paradise."

13

"WHY YOU GOTTA BE SUCH a bitch about this?" Kamar Antoine was saying to his friend and sometime foe, Khasim, when Mr Ilmi walked by. Kamar was the shooting guard of Thistletown Collegiate's basketball team, while Khasim played centre. It was Mr Ilmi's day to monitor the hallways during lunch break, a duty he resented. As Mr Ilmi saw it, his job was to teach these kids science, not wander around the hallways of the school, breaking up fights.

"Fuck you, man!" Khasim said, responding to Kamar.

"Hey, Khasim. Language please!" Mr Ilmi said with a little extra effort to sound authoritative.

"Sorry, Mr Ilmi," Khasim said and busied himself with opening his locker. It always amazed Mr Ilmi how these boys, for all their threatening postures, bulging muscles under their hoodies, testosterone surging through their veins, could so easily be mollified by a few carefully chosen words. As Mr Ilmi continued meandering in the hallways, he couldn't help but feel sorry for these boys. Everywhere he went, he heard people complain about them: their contempt for rules, their proclivity for violence, and that they're destined for failure. But to Mr Ilmi, they seemed like little children, desperate to be noticed, to be seen, as if being seen were akin to being loved.

As he was heading outside, behind the school, where the more hardcore boys and their girlfriends hung out smoking cigarettes, the more daring smoking joints, Mr Ilmi changed direction and went down the long hallway that led to the cafeteria. It was eerily quiet. Normally this part of the school was the noisiest during lunch break. As Mr Ilmi continued at his casual pace towards the cafeteria, he heard voices chanting in unison, "Fight! Fight! Fight!" Mr Ilmi quickened his pace and was soon sprinting on the slippery hallway, his loafers practically gliding on the recently waxed tiles. The chant got louder the closer he got to the source of the commotion.

By the time Mr Ilmi reached the cafeteria, a sudden hush had fallen on the room. A large circle of students had gathered, and at its centre, some ghastly thing was going on that had silenced the forty or so students. Some of them held their hands to their mouths in shock. In the seconds it took Mr Ilmi to breach the wall of the circle, his imagination managed to construct a number of frightening scenarios: a stabbed student holding his belly, the stabber clutching a knife in his bloodied hand; a student shot in the head, his or her eyes wide open. As Mr Ilmi pushed through, there it was—a sight he could never comprehend.

James Calhoun was lying on the floor, his body contorted, a pool of blood surrounding his head. A few feet away from him, two male teachers were holding Nuur on the floor, hands behind his back, face pressed against the cold floor. He was not struggling. He seemed to Mr Ilmi to have given up.

Mr Ilmi could hear the pounding of his own heart and he had the dizzying sense of walking underwater. Suddenly, as if a gunshot had gone off, his ears popped and in came the deafening howl of an ambulance approaching the backdoor of the cafeteria. The sound seemed to have freed his limbs. He ran towards James's still body. He stood over him and looked into his eyes. They were wide open, staring blankly at the ceiling, but Mr Ilmi could see that he was still breathing, though faintly, and that gave him a surge of hope. "Don't worry, James. The paramedics are here," Mr Ilmi said. James didn't respond. His eyes were closing. "You'll be alright," Mr Ilmi added, sounding unconvinced.

Suddenly, two paramedics, a young blond woman and her equally blond male partner came rushing towards James and Mr Ilmi was pushed aside by the woman. Mr Ilmi moved back to give them room; a feeling of uselessness and irrelevance took hold of him. Mr Ilmi turned his attention to Nuur. But there was no sign of his pupil or the two male teachers who had held him down. Mr Ilmi frantically maneuvered through the still shocked crowd of students. There was no sign of Nuur. Mr Ilmi felt as though someone was playing a joke on him. "Nuur! Nuur!" he called out, his voice getting louder, more desperate with each call.

One of the students, a Guatemalan girl whose name had escaped Mr Ilmi, mutely pointed to the glass window outside. He turned and saw through the rain-covered glass window Nuur being lowered into the back seat of a police cruiser. Mr Ilmi dashed towards the fire exit of the cafeteria, the closest route to the parking lot. As he swung the door open, the fire alarm went off. When he finally got to the parking lot, the police vehicle was already backing out of the lot and into the street. A desperate need to tell Nuur that he would come for him after school seized Mr Ilmi. He ran after the police car but soon realized the futility of his effort and gave up. He stood motionless in the parking lot, a cool mist of drizzling rain falling softly on his face.

———

Mr Ilmi had been lying on the sofa of his living room, staring at the ceiling for over an hour. He lay there covered with a blanket that did little to warm his cold, tired limbs. He felt as exhausted as he was sleepless. Every time he closed his eyes, a montage of the scene at the school cafeteria came at him in rapid succession. A pool of James's blood on the floor. Nuur's frightened eyes. Two teachers holding him to the ground. All these images accompanied by the monotonous soundtrack from the wall clock over the dining table, a garishly decorated timepiece that his wife had fallen in love with when they were decorating the apartment. The harder Mr Ilmi tried to ignore the robotic tick, tock, tick, tock, the louder it seemed to get until it drowned out his thoughts.

Adding to Mr Ilmi's consternation was the fact that he and his wife had had their first big fight in a long time. Fearing that he might say something he would later regret, he decided to leave the bedroom for the quiet of the living room. But as he lay there, cold and sleepless, he wished he was back in bed beside Khadija. Mr Ilmi could count with one hand the number of times they had quarreled since they got married. These had been fights over mundane misunderstandings or unacknowledged acts of kindness or, most comic of all, one partner's need for silence when the other needed to talk.

Earlier that evening, when Mr Ilmi got into bed, his wife was sitting on her side, brushing her hair. This was one habit of hers that drove him crazy. He had never brought it up with her for fear of hurting her feelings, but he could never understand why she brushed her hair in bed when there was a huge mirror in their ensuite bathroom. The last thing Mr Ilmi wanted was an argument, so he didn't say anything about her annoying habit. All he wanted was her silent, comforting presence beside him. But Khadija had an urgent matter to discuss.

"I was thinking," Khadija said, and stopped, expecting him to ask what she was thinking. Mr Ilmi, however, had a "good for you," look on his face. After some moments, as he lay quietly with his back to her, Khadija asked him:

"Don't you want to hear what I was thinking?"

"Can we talk about it another time? I've had a really bad day."

"Why? What happened?"

"It's a long story," Mr Ilmi said wearily. "I will tell you about it tomorrow." Normally a big dramatic incident at school would be just the sort of news Mr Ilmi would have brought home with excitement. But this night he was too disturbed to tell her what had happened at school. He didn't wish to recount Nuur's misfortune for her entertainment.

"No, tell me now," Khadija insisted, as she braided her long hair into a ponytail.

"It's too complicated to get into now. I'll tell you all about it tomorrow."

Khadija got out of bed and headed for the washroom. "Is it about that boy?"

"What boy?"

"That religious boy you like so much?"

Mr Ilmi got annoyed. The way she said "religious" didn't sit well with him, as though being religious were a suspicious trait. He also didn't like the implication that he liked this boy any more than his other students. Mr Ilmi believed that he was fair and treated all his students equally. He was also perceptive enough to know that deeply held beliefs such as his were often the most suspect. His wife's casual description of Nuur as the boy he liked wounded Mr Ilmi in a way he found incommensurate with what had been a throwaway line. Why, he wondered, did Khadija's words bother him so much?

"You know, that boy who barged in that afternoon," Khadija continued.

"He didn't barge in. I invited him in."

"Something about him gives me the creeps," Khadija said.

Mr Ilmi stared at his wife's profile as she brushed her teeth at the sink. He tried to suppress a sudden, irrational rage. "Like what?" he asked.

"Don't know, something about him," she said, spitting into the sink. "Maybe it was his beard," she said between gargling and spitting. "He reminds me of those little fanatic boys who used to run around in Kismayo, telling women, 'Cover your hair! Don't do that! Don't act like that!' Tyrannical little zealots."

"Nuur's not a fanatic or a zealot. Just religious. There's a difference."

"His name is Nuur?" Khadija asked with an ironic chuckle as she turned off the washroom light and got back into bed.

"Why is that funny?" Mr Ilmi asked, anger seeping into his tone.

"Have you seen his complexion? He's dark, really dark like one of those Sudanese boys."

"What Sudanese boys?"

"You know, those lost Sudanese boys. They wrote a book about them."

She was too busy rubbing lotion on her face to see the flash of anger that spread across her husband's face.

"That's not funny. And it's immature," Mr Ilmi snapped.

Khadija gave a puzzled look. "What's your problem?"

"How would you like it if someone made fun of the way you look?"

"What's wrong with the way I look?" Khadija asked, offended now.

"Nothing. There's nothing wrong with the way you look. Just like there's nothing wrong with the way Nuur looks," Mr Ilmi said and leaned forward to kiss her on the cheek. She turned away.

"I'm sorry, okay? I'm tired. You're tired. Let's just go to sleep."

"Speak for yourself. I'm not tired. How could I be tired when I don't do anything? You go off to work and I sit here in this tiny apartment all day. How do you think that makes me feel?" Khadija burst out.

"Well, tell me then. How do you feel?"

"I feel trapped. That's how I feel. I worked. I had friends. I had a life in my country."

"This is your country now," Mr Ilmi said and winced at the sound of his own voice. He sounded like one of those sweet, reassuring Canadians he used to encounter as a newcomer back in the late 1980s. "This is your home now," they would say, dripping with patronizing kindness, as though being an immigrant boy from Africa was a form of handicap. "Everyone is welcome here," they said, often with a reassuring pat on the back. Later he came to recognize this solicitousness as a well-meaning people's clunky attempts at multiculturalism.

"No, it's not my country!" Khadija yelled. "I didn't—" She paused. "This isn't the life—" She stopped herself again. It seemed to Mr Ilmi that his wife was trying to express a thought she didn't quite have the language for. She was speaking Somali, but the ideas behind her words sounded foreign. "I don't know who I am anymore," she said at last. It came out as a simple statement of fact, said with a sense of resignation.

"And this is my fault?" Mr Ilmi said, raising his voice at Khadija for the first time since they got married. He felt pierced by her words, as though she were accusing him of having robbed her of her life. "You make me sound like I've abducted you." He didn't know what more to say and got out of bed, snatched his pillow, and left the room.

14

Nuur opened his eyes slowly. The room was dark, except for the light pouring in from the skylight in the middle of the ceiling. The light had a soft, ethereal quality as though it were entirely of another world. Nuur watched the stream of tiny dust particles suspended in the light. *How beautiful*, he thought. Then it hit him. His bedroom never had dust mites dancing in a spotlight. *Where am I?* he thought. He sat up too quickly and felt a sharp pain shooting up from his belly. He was at the mosque. He looked down where his head had been and saw his spring jacket folded to form a pillow. Nuur asked himself why he had slept at the mosque, and struggled for an answer. He tried to stretch but was confronted with an unbearable pain in his shoulder. He felt as though he had been run over by a truck in his sleep. His neck hurt. His ribcage ached when he took a deep breath, and there was a dry cut on his lower lip.

For the first time since he was a boy, Nuur felt a desperate yearning for his mother's arms. He recalled the sensation of her embrace from when he was a child. It was a full, open embrace that enveloped the whole of him, at once firm and tender, always there waiting for him every day when he came home from school. But when he was around twelve, he had found himself pulling away from her, not wanting her to embarrass him, and she stopped hugging him altogether.

Nuur got up and told himself to be strong and disregard the sharp pains he felt everywhere. The mosque was empty at this morning hour. Thuhur, the afternoon prayer, wasn't for another five hours, and Imam Yusuf usually came in around ten to do some administrative work like writing cheques. Nuur walked into the washroom and turned the lights on. He headed instinctively for the mirrors over the two sinks and let out a gasp. There was a bump on the left side of his forehead that was turning brown. One of his eyes was red around the iris and his lower lip was swollen. But what shocked him the most was the large bald spot on his chin, which had been covered by his full beard. He wondered what had happened to it.

Nuur lifted up his sweater and the white t-shirt under it and saw the dark bruise on his chest that was making it hard for him to breathe. He continued taking an inventory of all the aches and pains he felt, trying to remember how he got them. His memory became clearer as he recalled a distant chant that got louder and louder. Fight! Fight! Fight!

He closed his eyes and saw about forty or so students in a circle, their faces contorted with bloodlust. And there he was, in the middle of that circle yelling something incomprehensible. James Calhoun's face was an arm's length away, the pink knuckles of his closed fist coming at him. It landed on Nuur's forehead. Another closed fist followed and landed on his chin, just under the bottom lip. An agonizing burst of pain. He felt dizzy and defeated. He fell to the ground, his knees hitting hard the tiled floor. He heard James's voice taunting him. "Come on, pussy! Show me what'ya got! Is that all you got, Al-Qaeda Boy!"

The chants and the laughter got louder and the room was spinning around him. Amidst all that commotion, Nuur heard the voice of Imam Yusuf telling him to get up and defend himself. "Self-defense is the duty of every Muslim man," the disembodied voice soothing and yet eerily distant. "Jihad is the path to Allah, honour yourself and your ummah!"

Nuur willed himself to get up on his feet and as he did so, his hands reached for the two back legs of the metal chair he had been sitting on a few minutes ago, reading Kahlil Gibran poems about love. He lifted the chair up above his head and swung it with all his might upon James's head. He heard a collective gasp. James was on the floor. The circle fell silent. Nuur felt giddy. His hands were shaking, his heart swelling with pride. James got up and staggered towards him. Nuur swung the chair again. Suddenly, he felt the powerful grip of invisible hands holding his arms behind him, pulling him down to the floor. He felt a second set of arms holding his legs together. He struggled to free himself of the infidels holding him down. Realizing the futility of his resistance, he gave up. He looked up at the crowd around him; it seemed to have grown. Some people held their hands to their mouths, their eyes wide with shock. He saw familiar faces. There was Tanisha, next to her friend Lola. Nuur followed their eyes and craned his neck to find James splayed upon the floor, his body twisted. A stream of blood was flowing from his head.

——

Nuur was sitting in Imam Yusuf's crammed office, having soup from a Tim Hortons cup. He bit into a stale piece of bread.

"What do you mean you don't know what happened?" Imam Yusuf asked, as Nuur struggled to chew the bread without hurting his lip.

"It all happened so fast," Nuur said. "It felt slow, like in a movie, when it was happening, but looking back, it all happened so fast. One minute I was on my knees, the next minute James was down. I don't know how else to explain it."

"But why did it happen in the first place?" Imam Yusuf asked, slowly, like a prosecutor in a court, trying to reconstruct the events leading up to a crime.

Nuur tried to remember the sequence of events. He had gone to the cafeteria at lunch time, which he rarely did because something bad always happened to him there. One time, he took his lunch tray and tried to sit at one of the few tables available. Chris Jensen threw a piece of muffin at him. "Take a hike, weirdo," he said, then he and his friends laughed like it was the funniest thing they had ever seen. Another time, he tried to sit down with three Somali boys. They were talking about the basketball game at their school the night before. One of them was bragging about making a three-point shot with seconds left on the clock. Nuur attempted to join in by saying he had heard about what happened and asked how it had felt, saving the game. But they simply got up without a word to him and walked out. That was the day Nuur understood that rejection had a physical, palpable sensation. On the few times he had ventured out to the cafeteria, he had come out feeling bad about himself as though he had a deformity only others could see. And so whenever the weather was good, he would take his sandwich and juice box outside and eat his lunch under the big maple tree by the track field behind the school and watch the activities there. In the winter he took his lunch to the special room on the second floor which was used by Muslim students for their Friday prayer.

But this time, Nuur had overslept on account of staying up late studying for a test. By the time he showered and got dressed, there was barely enough time for breakfast let alone time to make lunch. So when lunch time came, Nuur forced himself to go to the cafeteria. Not certain of how halal the cooked meals were, Nuur settled for chocolate milk and a bowl of fruit. He took his tray and sat by himself at the far corner of the cafeteria.

—

"I was eating my lunch, reading *The Prophet*, a book that Mr Ilmi gave me."

"The Prophet?" the imam asked.

"A book of poems," Nuur replied. "I don't understand all of it, but it's beautiful. Have you read it?"

"How can you say something is beautiful if you don't understand it?"

"I don't understand all of the Quran, but it's still beautiful."

"It's not the same," Imam Yusuf snapped. "One is the word of Allah. The other . . . poems." He said the word as though he had bitten into a bitter fruit. "This Mr Ilmi you keep mentioning, does he do that often, give you books, I mean?"

"Yeah. He gave me like twenty books."

"What kind of books?" the imam asked, like a jealous husband who has found out that his wife was accepting gifts from another man.

"Some famous novels. A few books of poetry, but mostly popular books about the brain, because he knows I'm very interested in the human brain and consciousness."

Imam Yusuf chuckled. "Consciousness?"

Nuur had trouble interpreting the imam's snigger. Was he amused or was he belittling Nuur? He ignored it. "Anyway, there I was reading my book—"

"Why do you suppose he gives you these books?" Imam Yusuf asked, leaning back in his chair, his hands behind his head.

Nuur was silent for a moment. "I . . . I guess because . . . I don't know."

"Don't you think it's strange, a science teacher giving one of his students poetry books?"

Nuur was puzzled. Why are we talking about Mr Ilmi, he wanted to ask? But he replied, "I don't know. I never thought about it. He has a lot of books. All kinds of books that he has already read, so I guess he just wants to share . . ."

"Does he give other students poetry books?"

"Not sure. I don't think so . . . Why?"

"Just a question. Go on. Tell me what happened at the cafeteria."

Nuur struggled against a strange feeling of being all over the place. Even he started wondering why Mr Ilmi was so nice to him, giving him books when, from what he could tell, he never gave his other students so much as a pencil.

"So you were sitting there, then what?" Imam Yusuf asked, sounding impatient.

"Oh, sorry. Yeah, so I was eating my lunch and reading my book. Suddenly, I saw James sitting in the chair next to me. He reached for my plate and took a grape from my bowl. 'What'ya reading, Osama?' he said."

"Osama?"

"That's what he calls me. Osama or Al-Qaeda Boy or—"

"Why does he call you that?"

Nuur shrugged.

"Did he do that often, make fun of you?"

Nuur nodded. "He and his friends tried to beat me up last year in the washroom."

"Have you reported him to your teachers, the principal?"

Nuur shook his head.

"Not even to this Mr Ilmi fellow?"

Nuur shook his head again, like a little boy.

"Why not? This is very serious. They have a name for this. *Bullying*, they call it these days."

Nuur remained quiet for a moment, trying to figure out why he didn't tell anyone about the incident in the washroom at the start of the school year, when James and his friends had abused him. "I don't know why," he said finally. "I thought if I just ignored him, he would eventually get bored and leave me alone." He felt a lump in his throat. He knew that tears would not be too far behind, so he cleared his throat to banish them.

"Go on, what happened then?"

"I ignored him and continued to read my book. He grabbed it from me and looked at it. 'Poetry,' he said in disgust and laughed hysterically. 'I knew it, I knew it,' he said. 'Knew what?' I asked, grabbing my book from him. 'I knew you were a little faggot,' he said."

Imam Yusuf looked incredulous. "Then what?"

"He started saying other stuff."

"Like what?"

Nuur hesitated.

"What did he say?"

"'Yes, you are,' he said really loud so that others could hear it. 'You are one weird, poetry-loving, dress-wearing faggoty Al-Qaeda Boy,' he said."

"Dress-wearing?" Imam Yusuf asked.

"He calls my qamiis a dress," Nuur said, touching the white qamiis he was wearing. "Then he said," Nuur stopped then started. "'I bet you love to suck cock. A big, juicy cock."'

"Subhanallah," Imam Yusuf said, evidently scandalized.

"'I bet you love to take it up the ass too,' he said."

"Okay. Okay. I get the picture," Imam Yusuf said, as he got up from his chair and looked out the window. He stared out for a while, his back turned to Nuur.

"By then there was a crowd forming around us and he wouldn't stop. I told him to shut up and that's when it happened."

"That's when what happened?" the imam asked, without turning around.

"That's when I pushed him. I didn't mean to do it, but I was so upset, and they were all laughing at me. I know I shouldn't have but—"

Imam Yusuf turned around and stared at Nuur. "You did the right thing, son. You were defending your honour. He's lucky it wasn't me. I would've slit his throat."

Nuur chuckled, but soon realized the imam was dead serious.

"Then what?"

"Then it gets all hazy after that. I don't really know what happened. I remember he hit me in the chest after I pushed him and . . . " Nuur took another long pause. "Next thing I know, I'm on the floor, two teachers are holding me to the ground, and James is lying there, bleeding."

"And how did you feel then?"

Nuur looked at Imam Yusuf, unable to make sense of the question.

"When you saw James lying there on the floor, bleeding. How did you feel?"

"Bad, I guess?"

"Why? You did nothing wrong."

"I hit him with a metal chair. That's wrong. There was a lot of blood."

"That's what happens when people fight, son. People bleed," Imam Yusuf said as he came back from the window and rested a hand on Nuur's shoulder for a second before reclaiming his seat.

Nuur stared at the imam, confused but also awed. All day yesterday, everyone had looked at him with a mixture of shock, fear, and disappointment; everyone, from the students in the circle, to the two male teachers who broke up the fight, to the principal and, most of all, to Mr Ilmi. But now, a day later, sitting in Imam Yusuf's office, he was getting a look that validated him, a look that saw what happened from his perspective. He felt vindicated. "I don't know what's gonna happen to me now," Nuur said in a weak voice. He was on the verge of tears again. "I'm expelled from school. I don't know if I'll be able to take my final exams. Without exams, I won't be able to start university in September."

He tried not to break down. His efforts, however, were no match for the fear and sadness that engulfed him. Going to university had been the one constant goal that had given his life direction and solidified the ground beneath him when everything else felt shaky, liable to fall apart. Without warning, tears rolled down his cheeks, and whatever efforts he made to compose himself resulted only in more sobbing.

Imam Yusuf got up, walked over to Nuur, and put one hand on the crying boy's shoulder and the other on his crown. "This is God's will," Imam Yusuf said. "What God wills, no man shall alter."

Nuur looked up at Imam Yusuf, who was towering over him, looking down with a compassionate smile. "My son, say Alhamdulillah," the imam commanded. Nuur looked up at him, bewildered.

"We are Muslims, my son. When good things happen, we say Alhamdulillah. But more importantly, when bad things happen, we say what?"

"Alhamdulillah," Nuur mumbled.

"No son, do not thank Allah in that weak voice. Say it like you believe it!"

Nuur cleared his throat and repeated the phrase, "Alhamdulillah," with as much conviction as he could muster.

Imam Yusuf put his hand under Nuur's chin feeling with his finger the bald spot in Nuur's beard. The imam tilted Nuur's head up a little as though he were about to kiss him. "What happened to your beautiful beard?" the imam asked. "Did this James boy do this to you?"

Nuur shook his head. "My dad. My dad did it."

The previous night when his father and mother drove him home from the police station after posting bail, neither of them said a word in the car. They walked into the apartment in a procession of glum faces. Nuur put his school bag down on the floor next to the closet and went to the kitchen for a glass of water. He was standing by the sink when his father barged in, followed by his mother, who was telling his father to calm down.

"So this is what it's come down to now? I have to get a phone call from the school principal telling me to get my son from the police station. *The police station?*"

"Ismail Adan, let's find out what happened first," his mother said, calling her husband by his full name which she only did when she was angry with him.

"What is there to know, he's turning into his brother."

Haawo came over to Nuur and turned his head up to get a better look at his swollen lip. "He did this to you, this kid you had a fight with?"

Nuur nodded.

"And what did you do to him?" she asked as she licked her thumb and wiped a speck blood from Nuur's chin.

"I hit him with a chair."

"What were you thinking, doing a thing like that?" his father yelled. "Why didn't you at least hit him with your hand or better yet, walk away? Thanks to you some kid is lying in a hospital tonight with a severe concussion."

"Concussion," Nuur repeated. He felt the power of the word, the danger it connoted.

"That's right, a concussion! I'm sure his parents are going to press charges. Do you have any idea what that could mean?"

"What are we going to do now?" his mother said, putting her hands on her head the way she did when she got bad news from back home like the death of her mother a few years ago.

"I will tell you what we're going to do. Nothing!" his father yelled. "Let him go to jail. Let him join those other useless Somali gang boys rotting in jails across this country."

"Stop it, Ismail Adan. You're scaring him."

"Good!" his father shot back. "He should've thought about it before he started going around, acting like a big man, hitting people with chairs."

"I wasn't acting like a big man," Nuur snapped. "I was in the cafeteria, minding my business. He's the one—"

"Shut up! Just shut up. I don't wanna hear any more of your lies."

"I'm not lying, wallahi!" Nuur yelled. Nothing his father had ever said to him before had hurt as badly. The one thing Nuur knew about himself, the one thing he held on to like a life raft was the knowledge that he was an honest person. A good person.

"Don't you raise your voice at me, boy!"

"Then don't call me a liar!" Nuur shot back.

He saw his father coming at him and he stepped back until his back was fully against the kitchen wall. His mother tried to stop her husband, but he swatted her away like an insect. Nuur and his father stood face to face.

"I will call you whatever I please as long as you live in my house."

"It's not your house. You left! You left us. Remember?" Nuur screamed. He was shocked at the ease with which the words flew out of his mouth. He felt something give way deep inside. There was a time when he would never have dared to speak to his father like that. But something had happened to him at the cafeteria, just before he picked up that chair and swung it at James's head. Some part of him broke loose and he lost that confining desire that had been with him all his life, that need to be thought of as "baari." His desire to be an obedient son had been a driving motivation all his life. It was how he distinguished himself from his older brother. But picking up that chair had freed him in some way that was as unfathomable as it was unforeseeable.

"Why don't you go back to her!" Nuur yelled at his father. "Why did you even come back? Did she kick you out? Is that why you came back—'cause she kicked your sorry ass out?"

Nuur felt his father's slap as soon as he said the words. The sting of it filled him with an exhilarating rush such as he had never experienced before. Or perhaps it was the elation that came from being able to say the words he had been longing to say to his father for so long but never possessed the courage to utter them.

"This is what they teach you at that mosque, to talk to your father like that? This is what that fraudulent imam teaches you?" Ismail yelled and slapped Nuur again.

"Stop it! Ismail Adan, stop hitting him!" Haawo yelled.

"You're the fraud," Nuur yelled back.

Without warning, his father grabbed Nuur's beard and dragged him towards the kitchen drawer, ignoring Nuur's screams of pain and his wife's pleas for him to stop. "You grow a beard and you think you're better than me?" Ismail screamed as he opened the kitchen drawer with his free hand and took out a scissor. Despite his wife's attempts to pry the scissor from her husband's hand and Nuur's struggle to free himself, Ismail somehow managed to shear a fistful of his son's beard from his chin. Freed at last from his father's grip, Nuur staggered back and fell against the kitchen wall, creating a dent in the thin plaster.

Nuur held his hand to his chin, feeling with his fingers a round, bald spot. For a brief second, father and son held gaze. Suddenly, Nuur lunged at his father's throat and pushed him against the fridge with a strength that surprised and scared him. "You ever lay your filthy hands on me again and, wallahi, I will cut your throat," Nuur shouted. A part of him was calm enough to register the tone of his voice. It sounded at once recognizable and alien, as though it belonged to someone else. Nuur also noticed a look on his father's face which struck him as layered. Beneath the shock was horror and deeper beneath the horror was one of disappointment that looked ancient, biblical.

"Get out of my house," his father said, seething with rage, his voice sending a tremor through Nuur's fingers that still clutched at his father's throat. "I don't ever want to see your face again." Nuur slowly let go of his father. He looked to his mother, certain of her response. But she stared at him with a look of resignation. Nuur walked out of the kitchen. He went into his room and filled his duffel bag with whatever items of clothing his hands fell on. Moments later, he was out of his room; he snatched his coat from the floor by the closet where he had flung it. As he left, he threw a look at his mother. She was still standing against the kitchen counter where her husband had pushed her; he stared into her eyes, hoping to see something familiar, something that he yearned to see. But there was nothing there, just the cold, distant gaze. *Was this the mother he loved?* Nuur thought as he opened the door, paused for a moment, then stepped over the threshold.

With his coat in one hand and his duffel bag in the other, Nuur walked the narrow, dimly lit hallway to the elevator. With each step he took away from his apartment that had been his home all his life, he felt a part of him receding into his past and another propelling him forward to his future.

15

Mr Ilmi sat on one of the chairs outside the principal's office. He looked up at the clock on the mushroom-coloured wall. He hated everything about this office, the dirty grey carpet beneath his feet, Mrs Anderson, the obese secretary whose smile was as fake as the blond wig on her head, and most of all, he hated Principal Terry, whose hardline approach to problem-solving he found parochial bordering on the dictatorial. It was almost five in the afternoon. He had been waiting for over twenty minutes. Mrs Anderson told him that Principal Terry was on the phone dealing with "the situation." She said "the situation" as though referring to a terrorist attack or a mass shooting.

Perhaps it was the amount of blood on the floor or the sight of James Calhoun splayed out on the cafeteria floor that shocked both the student body and the administrators. Rumours started spreading throughout the school that James Calhoun was dead, when in fact he had been unconscious for about forty seconds before the paramedics arrived. Mr Ilmi blamed himself for the whole mess. He truly believed that if he had been in the cafeteria, he could have prevented "the situation" or at least mitigated it somehow. He had been on his way to the cafeteria, and he would have been in time to prevent the fight had he not stopped to talk to Kamar and Khasim.

"Come on in, Mr Ilmi," he heard a voice say. He looked up and saw Principal Terry standing by the door of his office. An officer of the Royal Canadian Navy, the principal was a tall, broad-backed man with a bald head and close-cut goatee that was either red or blond depending on the light. He had a habit of wearing dress shirts that were a tad too small for him and clung to his biceps and forearms. His large blue eyes had an unblinking glare that intimidated students unfortunate enough to encounter him in the hallways.

"Have a seat. Have a seat," Principal Terry said quickly as though anxious to get started. His baritone voice gave him the kind of gravitas any politician would kill for.

"My apologies for keeping you waiting. I've had my hands full with this fiasco," he said, joining his hands behind his shaved head. Mr Ilmi averted his gaze from the sweat stains on the principal's blue shirt and looked straight into his unblinking eyes.

"I've come to speak to you about Nuur, the boy who—"

Principal Terry cut him off saying, "It's all taken care of. No need to worry about it."

"I know. I'm sure it is, but the thing is—"

"He's lucky the boy's mother will not press charges," the principal said, interrupting Mr Ilmi again. "Expulsion will sound like a bargain considering what he might have faced in court."

"Expulsion?" Mr Ilmi shot back in a voice that was way too loud for the small office.

The principal let his hands drop, placed his elbows on the edge of his desk, and leaned forward. "Mr Ilmi, you will watch your tone in my office."

"I'm sorry, Principal Terry. But with all due respect, don't you think expulsion is overkill?"

"Overkill? Are you kidding me?"

"Principal Terry—"

"That's right. I'm the principal of this school. I'm the one in charge of enforcing the rules," he said, his voice getting louder with every word. "And I'm the one who has to answer to the School Board. So don't come into my office and tell me how to do my job."

Mr Ilmi took a deep breath in a desperate attempt to calm himself. The cordial discussion he had prepared for with all the goodwill he could muster had barely started before disintegrating into an acrimonious exchange. "Again, Principal Terry, my apologies. I would never presume to tell you how to run *your* school," Mr Ilmi said, hoping his emphasis would be enough to stroke the principal's fragile ego. "All I came here for was to implore you, beg you to reconsider your punishment. Nuur is one of the brightest students I've ever had the pleasure of teaching. He has a hunger for learning that most teachers would do anything to have in their students. By expelling him from—"

"Mr Ilmi, I sympathize—"

"Just hear me out, please. Nuur is one of the most well-behaved students at this school. And I'm positive every teacher here will agree with me—"

"Again, Mr Ilmi—"

He had on the tip of his tongue to say to Principal Terry, "Just shut the fuck up and listen for a minute!" But luckily, he managed to swallow his rage and said instead, "Please just let me say one more thing."

Principal Terry sat back on his chair and folded his arms in a grand gesture of listening that struck Mr Ilmi as rehearsed for occasions just like this.

"Nuur asked me for a reference letter. He has already applied to three top universities and with his grades, I'm sure he'll probably get a full scholarship, which is frankly the only way he'll ever afford to go to university. His father has left the family and his mother is a cashier at Walmart. His older brother has already dropped out of school. He wants to study medicine and become an oncologist. Do you know how rare it is to see such a crystallized dream in these kids? Please, all I'm asking you is to consider these factors and not just his one transgression, as large as it may be. If you expel him now, with just a few months away from the final exams, he won't be able to go to university this year, maybe ever. Expulsion will kill his dream. You will kill his only dream. You might as well kill him."

Mr Ilmi regretted those last words as soon he said them, for fear that the principal would interpret them as accusing a white principal of killing the dream of another black kid. Which would not be far from the truth.

But instead, the principal said: "Mr Ilmi, I admire your passion and commitment. I wish all my teachers went to bat for their students the way you just did."

Mr Ilmi's heart flickered with the hope that he might just have saved Nuur from expulsion.

"But you can't ask me to ignore the fact that this student beat another student unconscious with a metal chair," Principal Terry continued, his voice measured and compassionate. "I cannot in good conscience allow such a serious offense to go unpunished. That would be an abdication of my responsibilities as head of this school. There will be a full investigation into the incident and Nuur can tell his side of the story then, but for now, he must be punished—"

"I agree. I completely agree, what Nuur did was wrong. Very wrong. But expulsion is—"

"Expulsion is my only option, Mr Ilmi. You know the school's policy on violence as well as I do. Zero tolerance means zero tolerance."

"Oh, come on. You're the principal. You have discretion. You can—"

"Mr Ilmi, my hands are tied. We're not dealing with a fist fight here. An innocent boy lies in a hospital tonight with a serious head injury."

Mr Ilmi broke into loud laughter that sent alarm across the principal's face. "An innocent boy? Are you fucking kidding me?" Mr Ilmi said, no longer caring how loud his voice got.

"Mr Ilmi, you'll watch your language in my office."

"James Calhoun is a psychopath in training. The boy enjoys torturing students weaker than him. Everyone in the school knows it and every teacher in this goddamn school looks the other way. And frankly, I'm surprised it took this long for someone to beat the shit out of him with a metal chair."

The principal jumped to his feet. His large, unblinking eyes practically bulged out of their sockets. "We're done here, Mr Ilmi. Have a good evening. Clearly you have lost all objectivity in this matter."

Mr Ilmi stood up too and for a brief moment the two men looked like they might just pounce at each other across the desk separating them. Mr Ilmi grabbed his satchel, stormed out of the room, and slammed the principal's door so hard, he heard a loud yelp from the secretary who was still at her desk. The door swung open and Principal Terry stood at its threshold and yelled, "You'll apologize, Mr Ilmi."

"And you will blow me," Mr Ilmi said as he left the office.

16

Nuur woke up at six in the morning, just before the call to morning prayer. He stretched, sat up, and watched the soft, ethereal light streaming down from the skylight onto the centre of the prayer hall. He had been sleeping at the back of the mosque ever since his father threw him out.

Nuur knew he couldn't go back home as long as his dad was there, and the thought of going to a shelter for homeless teens made him want to sleep and never wake up. So when Imam Yusuf told Nuur he could sleep at the mosque, Nuur felt immense gratitude. When the imam added further that Nuur would have to earn his keep and do some chores around the mosque like mopping the floors and keeping the ablution area clean, Nuur felt as close as he had ever come to the grace of God. He felt that every chore he did to make the mosque a cleaner, more welcoming place for his Muslim brothers and sisters would bring him one step closer to Allah's love.

Sleeping on the floor was not easy on Nuur's body. His back ached and his neck was tight. He yawned and stretched some more, doing his best to ignore the aches and pains. His eyes fell on the stream of light again, and he wondered what it would feel like to sit at the centre where it fell. Nuur got up, stepped forward, and sat down cross-legged under the skylight. Bathed in that soft light, he tried to empty his mind of the past and future and just sit and be. Soon he experienced that dull, low-grade feeling of being utterly alone and unmoored. Silently he recited a few verses from the Quran. When he finished his recitation, he cupped his hands before him, head raised slightly to the heavens, and begged for Allah's mercy and compassion. He closed his eyes. Never before had he felt so close to his creator.

"Asalamu alaykum," Nuur heard a voice say. He turned around to find Imam Yusuf coming towards him with a radiant smile. The imam sat next to Nuur, the circle of light large enough to accommodate them both. "I bring good news," Imam Yusuf said, placing a soft, warm touch on Nuur's knee.

"You do?" Nuur said. Allah seemed to have answered his prayer.

"A bed has become vacant in the house. If you wish, you're welcome to stay."

"Your house?"

The imam chuckled. "No son, not my house. *The house.* A few good Muslims, may Allah bless them, contribute money to keep the house functioning. You're welcome to stay there, if you wish."

"I do," Nuur said, faster than he had ever accepted any offer before.

"There is one thing," Imam Yusuf said and paused.

"I will do anything," Nuur said. "I can clean. I'm a good cook. I'll make myself useful."

Imam Yusuf smiled one of his sweet, benevolent smiles. "I have no doubt you will make yourself very useful. But what I was going to say is, you must be sure that you want to live there. Are you really sure?"

"Yes," Nuur said, nodding for emphasis. "I . . . I have nothing to go back for."

"Very well then," Imam Yusuf said and got up on his feet. "Tonight, after the Isha prayer, I will drive you there. Be ready."

———

Imam Yusuf was silent as he drove his minivan on Highway 401, headed west. Nuur, in the passenger seat, looked out in fascination at the passing scenery, the malls, the isolated tall buildings, the cars leaving and entering various neighbourhoods of the city that he had never seen. By the little digital clock on the dashboard of the car, it was 10:23 PM in the evening. Playing on the CD was a lecture by an imam in Arabic. He sounded outraged about something, and Imam Yusuf let out a sardonic laugh and turned towards Nuur.

"Sheikh Abdulkareem of Nairobi. A great man! One of the foremost Islamic scholars in the world," he said. "How is your Arabic?"

"Not good," Nuur replied sheepishly. He had started taking Arabic lessons at the mosque on Sunday mornings, but that wasn't enough and his progress had been meagre. He felt that by reading the Quran in English, he was missing the beauty and poetry of the holy text in its original language, and he longed for the day when his Arabic would be good enough.

"Is he an Arab?" Nuur asked, pointing to the CD player as though the sheikh were actually in there.

"No. He's Somali. Reer Hamar. But he was raised in Saudi Arabia, then he apprenticed in Karachi with the great Pakistani scholar Sheikh Mustafa Chaudry. But now he lives in Eastleigh. You know Eastleigh?"

Nuur nodded. It was hard to be Somali these days and not know of the sprawling district in Nairobi that was home to hundreds of thousands of Somalis in Kenya. Nuur had heard stories about the vast amounts of money that changed hands in Eastleigh on a daily basis, even though from pictures he had seen of it on the internet, it looked like any old African city slum. He had also read online about the mass arrests, extortions, and beatings of Somalis in Nairobi by the Kenyan police and paramilitary. Eastleigh sounded to Nuur like a little hell on earth.

"You must go there one day," Imam Yusuf said. "You would love it there."

Nuur thought that unlikely but said, "Yeah, sounds like an amazing place." He wasn't sure where they were headed or what he would find once he got to wherever Imam Yusuf was taking him. All he knew was that they were going to a place the imam simply referred to as The House.

Nuur had wanted to let his mother know that he was all right. Early that evening, an hour before they began their journey, he went to the mosque foyer, where a payphone hung on the wall next to the entrance; it looked like it hadn't been used in years. Holding the receiver to his ear, Nuur fed two quarters into the machine and dialed his home number. He didn't know exactly what he wanted to say to his mother, but *Keep it short. Keep it short*, he told himself.

"Hello?" he heard his father say. "Hello?"

"Hi Dad, it's me," Nuur wanted to say, but instead his index finger, as if by its own volition, pressed down to disconnect the call. He stood in front of the payphone, unable to move. He felt as though he had just experienced the end of something. As he turned around and forced his legs to climb the stairs up to the prayer hall, Nuur also felt that this was the beginning of something new.

———

Imam Yusuf took an exit and after a few turns pulled into a narrow, winding lane of attached townhouses. They came to the last house on the lane, where the imam parked in the driveway. "Here we are," he said, turning off the ignition.

Nuur walked a couple of steps behind Imam Yusuf, who insisted on carrying Nuur's duffel bag. He slowed down and looked around. The neighbourhood was dark and cocooned in silence, but for the distant barking of a dog. "Come on," Nuur heard the imam say. "The boys are probably sleeping."

"The boys?"

"Yes, the other boys."

"Oh," Nuur said, having failed to realize that there would be other boys at The House.

"I live in the next block. This house belongs to a friend of mine, another imam, who is in Somalia now," Imam Yusuf said as he opened the front door and stepped aside to let Nuur in first.

"So who are the others?"

"Oh, you will meet them," Imam Yusuf said and switched on the light in the hallway.

Nuur didn't ask anymore questions. He took off his shoes and hung his coat in the closet next to the front door.

"Come, I'll introduce you," the imam said in a cheerful voice like a man giving a tour of his new house to his guests. He went down a flight of stairs to the basement, Nuur following gingerly behind, for fear he might tumble down. He heard the imam knock on a door and open it without waiting for a reply. "Asalamu alaykum," he said in his booming voice, which sounded even louder in the small space. Nuur heard several voices from inside greeting the imam. "Come in. Don't be shy, son."

In the room were four Somali boys in t-shirts and sweatpants, their angular bodies casually stretched out on a long, green fadhi carbeed the mattress-like seating that ran the length of the wall. Pillows of various sizes and colours were strewn about. They were watching a grainy video on a large, flat-screen television screwed to the opposite wall.

"This is Nuur. Come greet him," Imam Yusuf instructed the boys, who stood up right away and greeted Nuur warmly one at a time. First, there was a lanky, dark-skinned boy with a crew cut and an impressive full beard who introduced himself as Salah. He was followed by a chubby-faced boy who looked about fifteen and was named Abdi. Unlike Salah's, Abdi's beard was patchy and uneven. His smile was so broad and welcoming that Nuur felt like hugging him, for a mere handshake felt too impersonal, despite the fact that he had never met the boy before. Abdi was followed by Hussein, a short, skinny fellow with round glasses who looked even geekier than Nuur. The last one to introduce himself was Mohamed, evidently the eldest of the group. He was about the same height as Nuur, but he was stout and muscular. He might have been a wrestler in his previous life. His handshake was as strong as his physique suggested. Mohamed put his hand on Nuur's shoulder as they shook hands the way politicians did on the campaign trails.

"Nuur will be staying with us," the imam said, jingling his car keys in the pocket of his white qamiis. "Make him feel welcome. Okay?" The boys said "okay" in unison, like obedient little school boys. "Mohamed, show him the spare bed in your room and give him a clean towel." Mohamed nodded. Imam Yusuf turned to Nuur and said, "Mohamed will be your roommate. Don't be shy. There's plenty of food in the kitchen. I will see you tomorrow, Inshallah."

"Thank you," Nuur said.

"And set your alarm clock for the morning prayer," the imam said without turning back.

Nuur listened to Imam Yusuf pounding up the stairs. He was rooted to the same spot where the boys had taken turns greeting him; they had already turned their attention back to the television screen. Nuur didn't know what to say.

"Have a seat, bro," Mohamed said, patting the spot next to him. Nuur felt an ache in his chest. No one had called him bro since his brother left for Alberta. He sat down next to Mohamed and watched the flickering images on the screen. Twenty or so men were running in a long line, jumping over what looked like sandbags. Their faces were covered with a black cloth on which ran white Arabic writing. Nuur recognized the pattern as the flag of the group Al-Shabaab. Dangling from their shoulders were automatic rifles. Playing over the images was a loud but beautiful recitation of a Surah from the Quran that Nuur recognized immediately as Surah An-Nisa. "And what is wrong with you that you fight not in the cause of Allah and [for] the oppressed among men, women, and children . . . " Nuur felt as though Allah was addressing him personally in that Surah.

"What are we watching?" he asked.

"We got it today. Someone brought it from Nairobi," Mohamed said. "It was filmed in a camp in Hudur."

Where is Hudur, Nuur wanted to ask, but Mohamed answered his question. "In Southern Somalia." Nuur wanted to know where these boys sitting with him in the room came from. Did their fathers also kick them out? His mind was full of questions, but he didn't say anything. He figured he had time. So he leaned back on the cushion behind him, stretched out his legs and watched the masked men in the video.

17

Mʀ Iʟᴍɪ ʀᴇsᴛᴇᴅ ʜɪs ᴇʟʙᴏᴡs on the metal railing of his twen-tieth-floor balcony, its cold surface sending a shiver through him. He zipped up his hoodie to protect himself from the evening chill of late April. He looked out into the darkness that concealed the shabby houses, office buildings and industrial storage facilities that in the daylight ruined the view. But in the evenings, all he saw were little amber lights shimmering as far as the eye could see. He could even make out the tiny blue runway lights of Pearson International. In the ten minutes he had been standing there, he had counted five planes flying low overhead on their way to their controlled descent onto the ground.

Mr Ilmi and his wife Khadija had gone to bed two hours before. She fell asleep as soon as she hit the pillow, but worrying about Nuur had kept Mr Ilmi awake. Where could he be? Why hadn't he called or emailed? He finally got out of bed and left the room. Khadija, as expected, was oblivious to his departure. She used to complain end-lessly about the noise from the planes when she first came, but over time, she had lost that sensitivity. Mr Ilmi pictured her sleeping, her once petite body now substantial, emitting the hormonal scent that kept him awake at night with a dull desire. He could still remember how nervous they both were on their first night together as they began their honeymoon at Sarova Whitesands, a beach resort in Mombasa. He was nervous because he couldn't believe he had married a woman he had never slept with, a woman whose body and its quirks and pro-clivities he was as ignorant of as she was of his. And she was nervous, Mr Ilmi presumed, because he would be her first.

Sweet memories of the night at Whitesands weren't enough to abate the sorrow he felt for Nuur and the rage he felt against Principal Terry. The word expulsion and the consequences it implied for Nuur's life kept nagging him. After his disastrous meeting with the principal, Mr Ilmi had gone home, parked his car in the underground lot and walked over to Nuur's apartment to see how he was doing. But when he knocked on the door, there was no answer. He tried for five minutes and finally gave up and left, resolved to return the next day.

Had Nuur been told about his expulsion? Mr Ilmi wondered. What was his future now? He had to find a way to help him. Nuur was bright, he was brilliant. He had to be convinced that all was not lost. There were ways, and Mr Ilmi would fight for him.

Mr Ilmi became conscious of the metal railing biting into his forearm. He straightened up, turned around and slowly, reluctantly went back to bed.

———

And here he was. Mr Ilmi looked around the living room as he waited for Haawo, who was in the kitchen making tea. Despite his protests, she had insisted that he sit down and have tea. He stared at the heavy drapes over the windows. It was a beautiful Saturday afternoon and he couldn't understand why Haawo kept the apartment dark, refusing to allow even a sliver of natural light to come in from the outside.

She returned carrying a plastic tray with two cups of black tea, milk, and a sugar bowl with a little spoon sticking out of it. "How do you take your tea?" Haawo asked in Somali.

Her blandly pleasant tone struck Mr Ilmi as the kind that came from years of training. "Just a little milk. No sugar. Thank you."

Haawo looked surprised. "No sugar?"

Mr Ilmi could imagine what Haawo might be thinking: *What kind of Somali man drinks tea without sugar?* As she poured the tea for him, Mr Ilmi couldn't help but notice how young she looked. When he stood at the door a few minutes ago, waiting for someone to open it, he expected a homely, overweight mother of two grown sons, but instead he saw a slender woman with a cascade of black curly hair, wearing a pink baati and garbosaar. Haawo's beauty had a kind of muted, less-is-more quality to it.

"Subah wanaagsan," Mr Ilmi greeted her.

"Subah wanaagsan," Haawo replied in a voice that was thin, almost on the verge of tears. "How I can help you?"

"My name is Bashiir Ilmi, I'm Nuur's biology teacher—"

"Oh, yes, yes. Mr Ilmi. Come in, please," Haawo said in Somali with a warm smile. "Nuur told me so much about you. Come in, please."

As Mr Ilmi walked in, Haawo was already off to the living room quickly tidying up the sofa. She turned on the two lamps on the side tables at the ends of the overstuffed sofa.

"Please don't trouble yourself. I won't stay long—"

"No, sit, sit," Haawo said.

Mr Ilmi found the way she spoke endearing. Having lived in Canada so many years, she still retained that direct, brusque tone peculiar to Somalis of a certain age.

He took a sip of his tea; the taste of ginger and cinnamon with a touch of cardamom immediately improved his mood. His wife was not a tea drinker and he was often too tired after work to go to the trouble of preparing a "real" cup of Somali tea for himself. He might have changed a great deal over the decades he had lived in Canada, but the one thing that would never change in him was his love of Somali tea. He could never appreciate what was called "tea" in Canada. To him, dipping a tea bag in hot water was not tea.

"Nuur talked about you all the time," Haawo said in a wistful tone as though remembering a wonderful bygone era. "One day he came home so happy. Look hooyo, he said and showed me all these books. My teacher, Mr Ilmi, gave me all these books." She let out a soft laugh, then, embarrassed, she covered her mouth with the hem of the garbosaar on her shoulders.

Watching Haawo cover her mouth reminded Mr Ilmi of his wife's habit of smothering her loud, joyous laughter with the palm of her hand. It was a little disconcerting that even so far away from Somalia, his wife and now Haawo were still performing the traditional gestures of proper female etiquette. Growing up, his mother would admonish his older sister whenever she heard her laugh. "Stop laughing like a sharmuuto," she would say, as if prostitutes were the only women allowed to have fun in life.

"I think you are the only person in that school whom Nuur liked," Haawo continued. "It's very strange," she said and stopped, as though lost in thought.

"What is strange?"

"My other son Ayuub is so, bulsho, you know? So many friends. He brought them home all the time. Boys. Girls. Gaalo. Muslims. Everybody. But Nuur, he was always so quiet, so serious. Even as a little boy. I used to say to him, go out, have fun with friends. But no. He never did. He never brought friends home."

"I think books are his friends," Mr Ilmi said.

Haawo let out a little snort as though books were a sad substitute for friendships. Mr Ilmi put his tea cup down and turned to Haawo. "I came by yesterday around six. I wanted to see how Nuur was doing but no one opened the door."

"My husband and I went to Windsor to visit his aunt in the hospital. We got a telephone call from the school telling us Nuur was at the police station. We were so confused. Shocked. I said: No, this must be a mistake. Not Nuur, not my little Nuur. He was such a good boy."

Mr Ilmi frowned and tried to hide it. He wondered why she said *was* as if Nuur was no longer a good boy.

"As soon as we heard, we drove like crazy. His father was so, so angry. I've never seen him angry like that. We got to the station and we paid the money, how do they call it in English?"

"Bail."

"Yes, we paid the bail and we brought him home."

"Is he sleeping now?"

"No. Nuur never sleeps this late in the morning. Ayuub, his older brother, sleeps until one or two in the afternoon. But Nuur, never."

"So where is he now? I want to talk to him."

Haawo stayed silent. Mr Ilmi could see the tears beginning to fill her eyes. "Is everything alright?" he asked, alarmed.

"Please help me—" Haawo said and broke down before she could finish the sentence. She covered her face with her garbosaar. "He doesn't have a cell phone to call me. I don't know who to call. I don't know any of his friends, if he has any . . . "

"It's all right. It's all right." Mr Ilmi said. He reached out his hand to pat her shoulder or hold her hand, but it felt too presumptuous a gesture so he stopped himself midway. "Tell me what happened."

Haawo snatched a tissue from the ornate, gold plastic container. She blew her nose and took a deep breath. "When we came home, his father was furious with Nuur. He screamed and shouted at him. 'What's wrong with you? You wanna become a bum like your brother?' So he hit Nuur. He hit my Nuur."

Mr Ilmi felt his stomach drop. He pictured Nuur coming home, his face already bruised from James Calhoun's blows only to be hit by his father again. "We have to find him," he heard himself say. "We have to find him, now."

"I don't know where to find him," Haawo replied.

Mr Ilmi was at a loss for words. His mind was blank, devoid of any ideas about where to start. He found himself standing. His mind always worked better when he was on his feet, pacing a little, as he did in his classes. He saw Haawo standing as well, watching him expectantly. Mr Ilmi wanted to go on pacing, release the tension from his limbs, but he feared he would only look deranged in front of this woman he had never met before. So he sat back down. Haawo sat down as well.

"He worked at a restaurant, right?"

"Yes, two days a week, he worked at Hamar Cade, you know that restaurant on Rexdale?"

Mr Ilmi nodded, but he wasn't sure. He could never keep up with Somali restaurants. They seemed to open and close all the time. "Okay.

Let's start there. Hopefully they will know something . . . "

Haawo was on her feet before Mr Ilmi finished his sentence. He watched her disappear into the hallway. A moment later, she returned wearing a long, black cardigan that went down to her knees. The same pink garbosaar covered her head haphazardly, a few curls of her hair peeked from the edges. An oversized yellow leather bag dangled from her shoulder as she locked the door of her apartment and carelessly threw the keys into her giant bag.

Outside, as they walked towards his car, they passed a woman often seen wandering in the neighbourhood. She was wearing a black niqab, covering her from head to toe and, as she usually did, she was speaking in Somali to some imaginary person in a one-sided conversation. Sometimes she spoke in an earnest, pleading tone, at other times she would be yelling, her face contorted with rage. Today, she was happy.

"Salamu alaykum, Habaryar Maryan," Haawo said to the woman, who didn't look old enough to be Haawo's aunt, but she didn't seem to mind being called habaryar.

"He called me last night. He's met a wonderful girl," Maryan said, speaking in a Northern Somali dialect, her face beaming with joy.

"That's nice," Haawo said and gave her a quick hug.

"She has the most beautiful hair in the world," Maryan said, wiping her shiny face with the hem of her niqab. "I have a wedding to plan. You have to come to the wedding,"

"Of course. I wouldn't miss it," Haawo said. "Now don't stay outside too long," but the woman was already walking away, talking to herself, laughing.

As he waited for the car to warm up, he watched through the windshield the woman still carrying on her conversation, making hand gestures in the air.

"Poor woman," Haawo said.

"What's wrong with her?"

"She's crazy."

"I gathered that much," Mr Ilmi almost said, but opted for, "What happened to her?"

"Remember the boy who was shot at Eaton Centre last year?"

Mr Ilmi had a vague memory of the incident. A nineteen-year-old Somali boy was shot dead in the food court of the mall in broad daylight. Something about a gang feud.

"That's his mother," Haawo said. "People say that when the police came to her door, she refused to open it because she had dreamt of the shooting the night before. She saw her son lying dead in the street, and that's why she wouldn't let the police in. Since that day, she's not been . . . herself."

As on most Saturday afternoons, Hamar Cade Restaurant was crowded. Somali mothers had taken a break from cooking, fathers were running after toddlers happy to be let out of their small apartments. The waiting line was long and the noise was deafening. Mr Ilmi and Haawo went up to the cashier and Mr Ilmi asked if they could speak to the manager. The cashier, a short scrawny man with two front gold teeth told them to wait for Abdirahman Mohamuud, the manager, who was in the back room dealing with some emergency. As he waited, Mr Ilmi tried to ignore the aroma of warm basmati rice and roasted goat meat permeating the restaurant. He hadn't eaten since morning. He swallowed, met Haawo's eye. Her worry about her son had evidently been aggravated by his appearance at her door. He wondered what Nuur's father was doing to find his son.

He spotted a middle-aged man with short greying hair and a long beard coming towards them.

"Salamu alaykum," the man said, extending his hand to Mr Ilmi. "You're looking for me? I am Abdirahman Mohamuud, the manager here." He gave a tiny bow of the head to Haawo.

Mr Ilmi shook the man's hand, which felt wet and cold. "Can we talk somewhere private?" he said, looking around as if to bring to the man's attention the hordes of customers and their children and the clanging of silverware.

"I'm afraid there is nowhere better. It's even crazier in the back of the house."

"This is Haawo, Nuur's mother," Mr Ilmi said, giving up his hope of a quiet place to talk.

"Oh yes, Nuur's mother, mashallah, mashallah. You have a wonderful boy. Hard working. Very good."

"Where is he? I want to see my son," Haawo said as though the man was holding her son tied up in the pantry.

"I might ask you the same," Mr Mohamuud said. "As you can see, Saturday is our busiest day. Nuur was supposed to be here at eleven sharp. I planned to call him and ask him why he didn't show up. It's very unlike him not to show up."

Suddenly, Haawo broke down. She opened her mouth but no words came out.

"I'm sorry. Did I say something? Is something wrong?"

"My son is missing," the words finally dislodged from Haawo's throat. "Please help me."

The manager motioned with his hand for Haawo and Mr Ilmi to follow him outside, as though the mention of a missing boy might put his customers off their lunch. Once outside, they found a quiet spot in the parking lot of the plaza. "How do you mean, missing?" he asked.

"He left home a few nights ago. He never came back."

"Did you call his cell phone, his friends?"

"He doesn't have one."

"What, friends or cell phone?"

"Both."

"Did you call the police?"

She nodded. "They said it was too early to file a report. Something has happened to my son. I know it. I can feel it."

Mr Ilmi put his hand on Haawo's shoulder to comfort her, ignoring customary etiquette.

"When was the last you saw him?" Mr Ilmi asked the manager, who was now looking worried.

"Not since last week. He works on Fridays after school for the dinner shift and Saturday morning till around five. I offered him more shifts but he turned them down, saying he wanted to study."

Mr Ilmi understood that too well.

"Was he friends with any of the other waiters? Can you ask them if they heard from him?" he asked. "Can you please go and ask them?"

Mr Mohamuud nodded and walked away.

Meanwhile Mr Ilmi checked his cell phone in case Nuur had found his number and called. He hadn't, and Mr Ilmi shook his head at Haawo. Soon the manager returned. "I'm sorry," he said with a lot of concern. "None of the boys have heard from him."

Haawo grabbed his hand and put a piece of paper in it. "This is my cell number. If you hear from him, call me."

The manager looked like a religious man, but he didn't freak out at a strange woman touching him, as many Somali men would have done. He took the paper and put it in his wallet. "I'll pray for his safe return," he said and slowly walked away. Almost at the restaurant entrance, he turned around and came back to them.

"Yes?" Haawo asked anxiously.

"A few months ago, I asked Nuur if he could fill in for one of the waiters on Sunday. He said no. He said he didn't want to miss his lesson at the mosque with Imam . . . I forget the name of the imam. But here is the address of the mosque." The man took out a pen from his shirt pocket and scribbled on the edge of the paper that Haawo had given him.

Haawo looked at it for a moment. "It's not far. Let's go," she said to Mr Ilmi. They got into his car, and as they drove away, Haawo rolled down her window and yelled, "Mahhat sannid," to the owner. He turned and waved to them.

When Mr Ilmi and Nuur's mother reached the mosque, the afternoon prayer had already ended and the parking lot was empty but for a couple of cars. Neither of them had ever been to this mosque.

At the entrance, Mr Ilmi held the door open for Haawo. As she was about to go in, a man stepped out. She stood aside to let him pass, but he stopped and said, "This is not the women's entrance," in an accent that Mr Ilmi couldn't place. His features said Somali but his accent said something else.

"I'm not here to pray," Haawo snapped at the man in English.

He looked at her as though she had uttered a vile blasphemy, then he turned and walked away. Mr Ilmi and Haawo proceeded into a foyer. There was a staircase here leading to the main prayer hall. They went up to find a large square room with bare walls and a red carpet that might have been beautiful once. The only remarkable feature of the prayer hall was the skylight. An old man was sleeping in a far corner.

They came out of the prayer hall back into the long, narrow hallway. At the end of it was the figure of a young man in a white qamiis who held a mop and looked remarkably like Nuur. His slender back was bent as he mopped the linoleum floor. For a brief second, Mr Ilmi's heart leapt with joy until the young man turned around.

"Salamu alaykum," the boy said. He put aside the mop and came towards them. He couldn't have been more than sixteen. "We're looking for the imam. Is he here?" Mr Ilmi asked.

"Imam Yusuf?" the boy asked.

"Is there more than one?"

"Sometimes we have others when Imam Yusuf is traveling."

"Then we want Imam Yusuf," Haawo told him.

Mr Ilmi couldn't help but imagine what the boy thought of them. Perhaps they looked like a middle-aged couple looking for an imam to conduct a quick wedding ceremony in his office, so they could rush to their apartment having been made hallah for each other.

"Imam Yusuf isn't here now. He's usually here around Asir time," the boy said in the casual, slightly lazy tone of Canadian teenagers.

Mr Ilmi and Haawo looked at each other. Since neither of them prayed, the prayer times didn't come to them automatically.

"In like an hour," the boy said, making it easier for them.

"Do you know Nuur?" Haawo asked.

The boy was quiet for a second as though trying to pick Nuur from a long list of names he might have heard. "What does he look like?"

"About your age," Haawo said.

"Maybe a year or two older," Mr Ilmi added. "About the same height. He wears a qamiis like you and he has a beard a little bigger than yours."

The boy paused again. "That's pretty much all the boys here," he said sombrely. "I might've seen him around—"

"When?" Haawo asked.

"Not sure—"

"Think!" Haawo demanded. "Please, he's my son. He is missing."

Mr Ilmi was looking at the boy's face and he noticed a sudden change in his eyes. It looked as if some kind of a warning signal had been switched on. "So many boys come and go. Hard to tell," the boy said and went back to mopping the floor. Mr Ilmi and Haawo looked at each other, then turned and walked back to the stairs.

They decided to wait for Imam Yusuf in Mr Ilmi's car. It was parked facing the entrance so they could see people going in and out. In the car, Haawo turned to Mr Ilmi and said, "Thank you."

Mr Ilmi looked at her blankly. "For what?"

"For everything. For being kind to Nuur. For helping me find him."

They became silent and sat, staring at the door of the mosque. Haawo's fidgeting became more pronounced, Mr Ilmi observed, and he thought about what she must be feeling, sensing her son slipping away from her through some invisible crack from which he might never emerge.

"How long have you guys lived here?" he asked, to distract her.

"Too long," Haawo replied.

Mr Ilmi laughed, but stopped as soon as he saw the blank look on her face. "Why do you say that?"

"It's the truth. This was supposed to be temporary."

"What was supposed to be temporary?"

"The whole immigrant thing. It wasn't supposed to last this long. For twenty years my suitcase has been half packed, just waiting."

"Waiting for what?" Mr Ilmi asked, but he knew too well what she was saying, for that was how most older Somali immigrants lived, one foot here, the other back home.

"When we left Somalia, my home was fully intact. That morning, I had asked the maid to put new jooradi on the beds," Haawo said and let out a mirthless chuckle. "Who puts clean sheets on the beds and then abandons her house hours later? Who does that?"

Mr Ilmi mused to himself about how differently he himself felt. In Toronto he had always thought of himself as being essentially at home. His wife was another story. How at home she felt depended on her mood on a given day.

"The shelling was getting closer and closer. By four o'clock, most of the neighbours were gone. I waited for Ismail, that's Nuur's father, to come home. As soon as he arrived, we ran for our lives. There wasn't even time to pack our clothes. The shelling was so close you could feel it right here," Haawo said, placing her palm on her heart. "Ayuub, Nuur's older brother, was just five months old. I wrapped him around my chest with my garbosaar and we drove like crazy people." Haawo let out another tired laugh. "We drove fast on Maka al-Mukarama to a friend's house near the airport, but already checkpoints were going up, young thugs with guns stopped us, ordering us to get out of the car and asking us our qabiil. If you passed their clan test, they let you go. So they let us go. People were looting stores and hotels, running down the streets with powdered milk, curtains, lamps—anything they could lay their hands on." Haawo shook her head.

"How did you manage to escape the city?"

"Connections. I used to be a stewardess with Somali Airlines. So I managed to get tickets. They canceled two other people's reservation so my family could fly out. All commercial flights were stopped the next day. Sometimes I think about those two people who lost their seats on the last flight out because I used my connections. Sometimes I ask myself, what happened to those people? Maybe they got out by boat or car. Maybe they got killed waiting at the airport. I don't know. I'll never know." Haawo took a long breath, then said, "Maybe it's . . . you know, how do you call it?"

"Call what?" Mr Ilmi said.

"When you do something bad and it comes back to hurt you."

"Karma?"

"Yes. Karma. Maybe that's what is happening to me now. Maybe I lost my Nuur because I hurt those two people." Without warning, she covered her face with her garbosaar and her shoulders started convulsing, but no sound came out.

For the first time that afternoon he felt genuinely at a loss for words. He did not know how to help this distraught woman in his car, whose only connection to him was her son, his favourite and now missing student. "It's okay," he said meekly, "everything will be all right." Even he didn't believe that, but he added, "You will see. You will see."

Haawo composed herself and wiped her tears. Quietly they focused their attention on the mosque entrance. Some men were going in but none of them looked remotely like an imam, so they remained in the car.

"So where is Nuur's dad?" Mr Ilmi asked.

"I kicked him out the next morning."

"Why?"

"Two years ago, my son Ayuub and he had a big fight. He hit him really hard and there was blood. A lot of blood. I was a bad mother. I let him hit my son in front of me and I did nothing. He promised he would never do it again. Then he did it again, but this time, it was my baby. My Nuur. The next morning, I took out a suitcase and I put in all his things and I said, Go. Go back to her."

"To her?"

"Another wife. In Minnesota."

"I'm sorry," Mr Ilmi said. He didn't know what he was more sorry for: that her husband took another wife or that he beat her youngest son.

"It's all right. I should've listened to my mother."

"Yeah, why is that?"

"She used to say: You listen to what I tell you, my daughter. Never stay with a man who takes another wife because—" She stopped and pointed. "That looks like him." They both jumped out of the car and followed the man in the grey qamiis and khaki vest. "Imam Yusuf!" Haawo called out. The imam turned around and glared at what could only have seemed like two crazy people running towards him.

"Salama alaykum," Mr Ilmi said. The imam returned his greetings with a puzzled look as they shook hands.

"Imam Yusuf, my name is Haawo, I'm Nuur's mother." In her hurry to catch the imam before he stepped into the mosque, Haawo's garbo-saar had fallen from her head, and her massive black curls had come cascading down her shoulders. The imam stared at Haawo in horror.

"What can I do for you?"

"I'm Nuur's mother. I need to see my son."

The imam looked at Mr Ilmi, as if to say: Control your woman. "This is your wife?" he asked instead.

"No. I'm a friend."

The imam made a face. "He's a thin boy with a beard, around six feet tall," Mr Ilmi said gesturing with his hand.

"We have a lot of those here," the imam said.

Haawo rummaged in her bag for a photo of Nuur, but couldn't find any.

Losing his patience, Mr Ilmi looked at the imam in the eyes and said, "Don't you give Quran lessons every Sunday afternoon?"

"I do. I also give lessons on the Hadiths of our beloved Prophet, peace be upon him. Mashallah, we get many young and not so young boys who come to study with me. You should come. It's very benefi-cial, for this dunya and the one after."

"Yeah, that's nice. So you're saying, you've never met this boy named Nuur?"

Imam Yusuf was silent for a moment. "I didn't say that," he replied.

"So you have seen him?" Mr Ilmi asked, sounding like a frustrated detective.

"No. I didn't say that." Imam Yusuf said.

"Stop toying with us and tell us what you know!" Haawo snapped.

Mr Ilmi glared at her, in an attempt to calm her down, fearing they might scare the imam away.

"Imam Yusuf, Nuur's mother, as you can see, is sick with worry. Can you tell us the last time you saw Nuur?"

The imam inhaled dramatically and looked at both Mr Ilmi and Haawo. He took a minute as if trying to remember. "I have not seen Nuur in over a week," he said at last. He looked at his watch and made a face. "It's time for Asir. Prayer comes before all else. Do you pray Mr . . . "

"Ilmi."

"Ah, excellent name. It means knowledge."

"I know what my name means," Mr Ilmi snapped.

"Now I really must go in. Brother Ilmi, Sister Haawo, I hope you come in and pray with us," the imam said in his most pleasant voice and walked into the mosque, leaving them standing at the entrance. They turned to each other with disappointment, then slowly walked back to the car. Inside, they sat motionless for a long while. Haawo turned to face Mr Ilmi.

"Are you thinking what I'm thinking?" she asked.

Mr Ilmi nodded. Although he had no way of proving it, something told him that the imam was lying.

18

A MONTH HAD PASSED SINCE Nuur came to The House. A month since he disappeared from his school and his home. Upstairs in the house were three bedrooms, each furnished minimally with two single beds and a shared bed table in the middle. Bed sheets nailed above the windows served as curtains.

On the first floor living room were two large green sofas that looked like they had been rescued from somewhere. There was a round glass coffee table in the middle on which sat a basket of plastic fruits. On the walls hung several large black tapestries of a velvet fabric, on which were written verses from the Quran, in calligraphy so ornate that it was impossible to decipher them.

It was in the basement, a large, uncluttered space, where the boys congregated when they weren't sleeping or cooking on the first floor. The basement was divided into sections. In one corner was the seating area with fadhi carbeed arranged like in a hookah bar, where the boys sat and watched Islamic DVDs, the only kind Imam Yusuf allowed in the house. In another section were a large desk with a computer and a flat-screen monitor. And in the third and farther corner was a gym of sorts, with a punching bag dangling from the ceiling, a few pairs of free weights, a dumbbell, and a bench press.

The boys spent their afternoons taking turns using the weights or holding the punching bag for each other. Mohamed, the eldest and the fittest, played the role of the trainer, encouraging and teasing the other boys as the occasion called for. He showed them the correct form to lift weights, or the right way to extend their feet when they practiced kick-boxing. Except on the rare occasion when a boy misbehaved and Imam Yusuf or Mohamed censured them, the atmosphere in the house was fun and from time to time even boisterous.

"Hold your hands like this," Mohamed said to Nuur, showing him how to protect his face against an oncoming punch. Nuur thought about the day in the school cafeteria when James's strong punch had sent him reeling to the floor. He wished Mohamed had come into his life a little earlier and prepared him for run-ins with the James Calhouns of the world.

"It's really important that you keep moving your feet around. Never give your opponent a chance to land a clean punch," Mohamed said. Nuur was awestruck as he watched Mohamed's feet gliding around the basement floor, defying the laws of physics. "Be on your toes. Be light and fast on your feet. Anticipate where the next punch is coming from," Mohamed said, throwing punches into the air.

Nuur followed Mohamed's instructions and in no time he had worked up a good sweat and laboured breathing. "You need to work on your endurance," Mohamed told him. "Do you do any cardio?"

"Does walking count?" Nuur asked with a sheepish smile.

"Yeah it does. If you're a grandma."

Nuur laughed out loud and caught himself. It was a long time since he had heard the sound of his own laughter. It was even longer since he had joked around with boys his age or with anyone else for that matter. At school he had heard other kids laughing in the hallways and wondered what it felt like not be on the outside looking in, to be in on a joke and not the butt of a joke.

"Come on, old man," Mohamed said, "move those feet. That's right, float like a butterfly, sting like a bee."

Again Nuur broke into laughter. And even though his muscles were aching, he felt a strange sense of expansion as if someone or something had breathed into his lungs, making him light and floaty, ready to take off. He gave into the feeling and wished it would continue forever, when suddenly he heard Salah and Abdi shout "Allahu Akbar" in unison. They were before the computer watching a clip on a website they visited daily. Nuur and Mohamed stopped their boxing and walked over to see.

"What is it?" Mohamed said.

"Watch this," Salah replied and pressed the replay button. They huddled around the monitor and watched. There was Al-Shabaab's black flag on the screen and underneath it graphics that read "Martyr's Spring." The sound of a melodious Arabic chant filled the room. Nuur knew it wasn't a recitation of the Quran. It was too rhythmic and lilting, a devotional song intended to inspire the listener.

"What're they saying?" Nuur asked Mohamed. Without realizing it, Nuur had come to assume that Mohamed knew everything.

Mohamed shrugged. "I don't speak Arabic, bro."

"Paradise is for those who lay their lives for Allah, the most merciful, the most forgiving," Hussein said. He listened for the second verse of the song. "Lucky are those who are called upon . . . And join the great struggle, jihad."

"You speak Arabic?" Nuur asked Hussein in surprise.

"Yeah. Not as good as it used to be though," Hussein replied modestly. "We used to live in Yemen before my parents came here."

They continued to watch the rest of the video in silence. A gangly Somali man in army uniform was looking directly into the camera. His face was covered with a red Arafat scarf showing only his large, black eyes. "The filthy infidels from Uganda and Kenya will beg for mercy," he said in Somali. "They will regret the day they set foot on our land, raped our girls, and infected them with AIDS." The clip cut to the same man standing on what looked like the rooftop of a white, dilapidated villa, on his shoulder, a rocket launcher. He aimed the weapon on his shoulder at a convoy of three army trucks slowly navigating an unpaved road. He pressed a button and there was a big flash. For about ten seconds dust obscured everything. When it cleared, one of the vehicles was engulfed in flames. The video pulled in for a grainy close-up showing two figures on fire staggering out of the burning truck. A few feet away on the dusty road lay several bodies. Suddenly, the camera got all jerky, as if the man with the camera was running for his life. The cameraman and the man with the rocket launcher began chanting, "Allahu Akbar! Allahu Akbar! Allahu Akbar!"

Nuur heard Salah and Abdi and Hussein start their own chant of "Allahu Akbar," echoing the men in the video. Nuur joined them. "God is great. God is great. God is great!"

Unlike the jovial atmosphere in the house during the day, the nights were difficult for Nuur, for it was at night when thoughts of his mother and brother and Mr Ilmi invaded his mind. Tonight was no different. Nuur went to bed before the other boys. He lay there for over an hour, trying to silence the voices in his head long enough to fall asleep. But the sweet delirium of slipping into unconsciousness continued to elude him. His mind alternated between thoughts of his old and his new life, which for the first time included friends and a sense of a larger, all-encompassing meaning.

Playing on a loop in his mind were the images of the men in the video they had watched earlier. The jubilation of the men after the direct hit on the army truck; the man whose finger hovered over the button of his shoulder launcher, waiting, holding it steady until the perfect time for a direct hit. In the man's eyes, Nuur saw a level of concentration he often tried to achieve in his own life but rarely managed. It was a single-minded devotion to a mission, and it was a thing of beauty to behold. That night, in that dark room, Nuur felt inside him a yearning for that thing, whatever it was, that the man in the video was experiencing.

Since he left home, no one had tried to contact or reclaim him. He didn't expect nor particularly wanted to see his father. But Nuur felt a deep wound that came with the realization that between keeping her son in the house and placating her husband so he wouldn't go back to the new wife in Minnesota, his mother had chosen the latter option. He wondered why his mother or Mr Ilmi had not come to see where he was staying. Did they not go to Imam Yusuf and ask where he was? *Surely he would bring them to the house if they asked,* Nuur thought as he tossed about in his bed.

Nuur tried his best not to dwell on his pain as he pictured his mother and father at home by themselves, watching television, holding hands. He pictured Mr Ilmi standing in front of his class, imparting knowledge to some other boy sitting in his old seat, centre chair, first row. It felt as though his presence in their lives, in their consciousness, had shrunk down to a dot that would soon disappear altogether. *Maybe that's how they want it*, Nuur thought. He was in the middle of making a vow to himself never to call or visit his mother, father, or Mr Ilmi when he heard the door open. It was Mohamed tiptoeing into the room, trying not to wake him up.

"I'm awake," he said.

"Can't sleep?" Mohamed asked.

"I've tried," Nuur replied, watching Mohamed getting into his bed. "Are the boys still downstairs?"

"Yeah. Still online, watching stuff from Iraq. Good night," Mohamed said.

"Night."

Nuur lay on his back, motionless, staring at the ceiling. If he concentrated hard enough, he could make out the shape of water stains on the ceiling. Peering at a stain, he saw that it had a shape. It resembled a large, many-branched tree, the kind of tree he had heard about as a child from his mother. After judgment day, the story went, when each person's deeds in this world are appraised, the wicked will be dragged to hell while the good will be escorted to heaven by a procession of angels. And in paradise, the good will find a tree unimaginable in size and beauty, its branches spreading millions of light years in all directions, and the righteous will sit under the cool shade of that tree with their loved ones and they will talk and laugh and spend as much time together as they pleased for all eternity. Reaching the end of this description about the tree in paradise, his mother would tell Nuur to close his eyes tight and pray to Allah that they would find each other in paradise and sit together under that tree. Nuur heard himself call Mohamed's name.

"Yeah," Mohamed said from his bed.

"Are you awake?"

"Kinda."

"Can I ask you a question?"

"Go for it, bro."

For a moment, Nuur remained silent. He didn't know exactly what he wanted to ask Mohamed, except that he wanted to talk to him. He liked talking to Mohamed. "Why are you here?" he asked.

"As in, why am I here on earth?" Mohamed said.

Nuur let out a soft laugh, realizing how vague his question had been.

"No, I mean here, in this house."

Mohamed took a moment to reply. "Imam Ali in Ottawa, a good friend of Imam Yusuf, saved me," he said almost in a whisper, like a naughty child talking way past bedtime.

"Saved you from what?" Nuur asked, lowering his voice to match Mohamed's.

"From myself."

"What was wrong with you?"

"Do you want the short or the long version?"

"The long," Nuur whispered. Listening to Mohamed's voice in the dark reminded him of those nights when as children he and his brother Ayuub would whisper stories to each other long after their mother had told them to close their eyes and turned their lights off.

"I was really fucked up," Mohamed said.

Nuur had still not gotten used to Mohamed's swearing. There was something incongruous about hearing words like *fuck* and *shit* come out the mouth of a young man who wore a white qamiis and kufi and grew a beard like himself.

"Fucked up how?" Nuur asked, getting a slight thrill from saying the word himself.

"Drugs," Mohamed said.

"Taking or dealing?"

"Both."

"What kind?" Nuur asked, curious to know as much as there was to know about this boy whose charisma he had gotten an intimation of the first night they met.

"Dope. Coke. E. Oxy."

"Oxy?" Nuur had heard of dope and coke and he assumed E meant Ecstasy but Oxy was new to him.

"OxyContin. It's a pill. A pain killer. An opioid."

"You took all that?"

"Not at once. I started with the occasional joint, you know, with friends. Then one night at a night club in Hull, a girl I was dancing with gave me E. She said I would see the world in a completely new way."

"Did you?"

"Yes. I've never felt anything like that before or since."

"Wow," was all Nuur could say.

"Then a joint or two just to bring me down a bit from the E."

"Bring you down?" Nuur felt like an idiot asking these questions. He pictured Mohamed in his bed, making faces at his dumb questions, perhaps wondering what kind of life he had led that he didn't know these basic things that any respectable tenth grader would know. But his curiosity got the better of his embarrassment.

"From the high of E," Mohamed said. "By the time I got into Oxy, I was so deep in that world, making some good money, at least enough to make me think I didn't need to finish school."

"You quit high school?"

"Yeah. Stupid, I know."

"My brother, Ayuub quit too."

"Are you close?"

"We weren't always. We used to fight a lot as kids. But once I got to high school, everything changed. Now we're more like friends than brothers. He moved to Fort McMurray."

"I hear they got good jobs there."

"Yeah . . . then what happened?" Nuur asked, so as not to miss out on the rest of the story.

"The usual thing, really. Same old scenario. Pretty soon, I had a whole new set of friends. Became a different person. Moody. Arrogant. Basically, an asshole. My mom gave me an ultimatum. Quit drugs, go back to school, or leave the house. So I left the house."

"What did it feel like, being kicked out?" Nuur asked. Did Mohamed feel the same way as he did when his father told him he never wanted to see him again?

"I don't blame her. Not really. She has two other kids, younger ones, with my stepdad. She didn't want me around them. Hell, *I* wouldn't want me around them. So I moved in with two buddies of mine, Isaaq and Jabriil. We partied a lot. Fucked as many chicks as we could."

Nuur laughed more out of nervousness than knowledge of what Mohamed was talking about. He had noticed that whenever the subject of sex came up, he laughed or chuckled and tried subtly to change the topic. It became a kind of shield from ever having to be frank about sex. Sometimes it hurt him to think that he had never kissed a girl, never known what it felt like, the sensation of a woman's lips on his, the taste of her tongue, the feel of her breasts in his hands. These thoughts always resulted in a couple of days of fasting, during which he was so hungry that all thoughts of sex miraculously disappeared.

"It was the best two years of my life," Mohamed continued. His tone was matter of fact, with no hint of shame, regret, or nostalgia. "But like all parties, it had to come to an end at some point . . . Two years ago, Isaaq was killed. I heard stories that a couple of guys he owed money to were looking for him, but I didn't take them seriously. I thought those guys were just gonna rough him up a bit, you know, make him piss his pants a little so he would pay them. It was a Sunday night. I had the flu, so I went to bed early. At six-thirty in the morning, there was a loud knock on our door. It was the police. Isaaq had been found in an empty parking lot. He had bled to death from a gunshot wound to the neck."

Nuur turned to Mohamed. There was enough light in the room for him to see the outline of his friend's body, lying on his back like himself, staring at the ceiling. He wanted to know if Mohamed could also see the tree of paradise on the ceiling. But he didn't ask, for fear that he might seem crazy.

"Anyway, they took me to the morgue to identify his body. I had to call his mother in Montreal to give her the news. It was so weird. She didn't cry or scream or anything. She just held the phone and kept repeating, 'Subhanallah, Subhanallah, Subhanallah,' softly, like she lost her voice or something. I was like, what the fuck is wrong with you, lady? I wanted to scream at her, Hello, your son is dead. Can you say something else please?"

"What was Isaaq like?"

"He was funny. One of the funniest dudes I ever met," Mohamed said, his voice soft, wistful. He took a long pause before continuing. "Every time we went to a club or something, he would end up chatting up some guy's chick, and the next thing we knew we were being chased out of the club by a couple of big Jamaicans. Or we would go into a convenience store, and even though he had the money, he would pocket a chocolate bar or something, anything. Even random shit he had no use for. Like this one time, we get back into the car after buying some cigarettes and he gives me a look and I just know he stole something. He digs into his coat pocket and puts it on the dashboard. And you know what it was?"

"What?"

"A box of crayons."

"Crayons?" Nuur laughed. "Why?"

"He used to have this saying, this motto. A day without adventure is a day wasted. It's like he knew he didn't have much time, so he tried to cram as much life into his nineteen years as he could."

"So how did Imam Ali in Ottawa save you then?"

"When we finally got Isaaq's body back from the police, we took him to this Somali mosque in the Southend, this neighbourhood in

Ottawa, so that he could be buried properly, even though he hadn't set foot in a mosque since he was, I don't know, like seven years old. So they prepared the body for burial and prayed Janazah on him and then me and Isaaq's cousins and a bunch of other guys went to the cemetery for the burial. And there I was standing by the side of this pit, this gaping hole in the ground. And I watched a couple of guys from the mosque take the body out of the box. It was wrapped in a white sheet. And slowly, they put him in the hole. I could see the outline of Isaaq's body. It was like he was sleeping, except he wasn't. And this strange feeling came over me. To this day I don't know how to explain it. It was mysterious, otherworldly almost, like some kind of cosmic warning saying, That's what awaits you, Mohamed. That hole in the ground. And it just hit me. I was living like the party would never end. But it always does, and I hadn't done a single thing to prepare myself for that hole. Anyway, Isaaq was buried and I went back to my life but I could never shake off that image of his body in that hole in the ground. And for months, that image followed me everywhere, stalking me. I would go to a club with a friend and I'd be dancing with some hot chick and boom. The image of the body in the hole. Kinda hard to dance to a Jay-Z track with that in your head. Or I would be in bed with Sadie, this girl I used to see, she would be trying to blow me and nothing, there would be nothing happening down under, if you know what I mean. So one day I decided to go back to the mosque and Imam Ali was there. And I told him what I'd been experiencing and you know what he told me? He said, 'That is your soul wanting something more.' I said, 'What?' He said, 'That's your soul longing for more than the pleasures of this world.' I told him, 'I wanted to start praying but I didn't know how.' So he started teaching me how to pray and I started going to Friday prayers and pretty soon I was going on Saturdays to learn how to read the Quran and on Sundays I went to Imam Ali's lectures on the Sharia and the Hadiths. Before I knew it, I was practically living at the mosque. In less than a year, I went from clubbing and doing drugs and fucking around almost every night to living at the mosque. I got fired from my job at this call centre for a cable company and it didn't even matter. Nothing mattered anymore except aqira. Suddenly my little, insignificant life had meaning. I could help, be of service to my ummah. I'm just waiting now."

"Waiting for what?"

"My chance to serve."

Nuur was quiet for some time. He didn't know exactly what Mohamed meant, but on some fundamental level beyond words, he understood Mohamed's yearning to serve, for he too had that longing. He too had been plagued by that feeling, an indescribable sense of wanting to give himself, all of himself, until there was nothing of him left to give, until he, as he knew himself, ceased to exist. "Me too," Nuur said at last. "I'm waiting, too."

"Inshallah," Mohamed said.

"God willing," Nuur repeated. And they never spoke of the matter again.

Nuur couldn't fall asleep at all that night. He lay in bed, staring at the ceiling for what felt like hours. The darkness of the room reminded him of the grave that awaited him. Like for any good Muslim, thoughts of the grave were never absent from his mind for too long. He thought about the day he would be buried in the ground, his body turned towards Mecca. He thought about all the stories he had heard about the grave. The one story that haunted him the most was the one about how as soon as the earth was placed on him and his loved ones started to walk away, he would be brought back to life and he would hear the receding footsteps of the last mourner.

Giving up on sleep, Nuur got out of bed and left the room as quietly as he could, making sure not to wake Mohamed, whose soft snoring he could hear as he closed the door behind him. Nuur went down to the basement and sat at the computer desk and turned it on. He sat motionless as he waited for the machine to come to life.

Nuur opened his Google email account for the first time in over a month and saw that he had thirty-seven unread emails. His eyes scanned the list. There were a few from his brother Ayuub. A few more from Mr Ilmi. But most of the emails were from his mother. He placed the cursor on one of his mother's many emails. Just as he was about to open it, he changed his mind. He went to the menu bar and selected "All." He moved the cursor to the button "Delete Forever." His finger hovered over the mouse. He waited for a few seconds, giving himself a moment to change his mind. Click. Gone.

Nuur expected to feel sad or relieved—with the click of a button, he had managed to obliterate his former life. He waited for a rush of euphoria or exhilaration, but all he felt was a cold detachment. He opened YouTube and stared at the thumbnail pictures of previously viewed videos. A few of them showed Arab imams. A few showed Al-Shabaab fighters. Nuur's eyes fell on the picture of a young, light-skinned Somali boy in a white qamiis and white kufi like his. The boy was looking directly into the camera, his eyes big with excitement or happiness. Nuur clicked on the video. The young man's deep, melodic voice filled the room and Nuur quickly turned down the volume, afraid he might wake up the others. He watched, mesmerized by the young man who seemed to be in his early twenties. His face was glowing as if lit from within.

"I was directionless, unhappy, and of no use to me or anyone else," the young man said. He spoke with an accent that Nuur recognized to be British in someway, but it sounded different from the British accents he was used to from the movies. "I ran round the streets of Manchester, going to clubs, drinking all night and sleeping all day. When I was awake, I was busy distracting me mind watching every Man U match on the telly. I was unemployed and treated like a second-class citizen in me own so-called country. The kafir talk the talk about multiculturalism and all that rubbish, but they don't walk the walk, do they? But I warn you, my young Muslim bothers, don't believe their lies. Their land will never be our land, yah. I believed in their lies till I was saved by the words of Allah, Subhana Watallah and the Sunnah of our beloved Prophet, may peace be upon him. I'm at peace now 'cause for the first time in me life, I have a direction, I know who I am. I know me place in the world."

Nuur watched, enthralled by the words and the strange accent. The boy beamed at him as if speaking directly to him. "Now I live here in Barawe, the birthplace of me father, doing me part to help me brothers in their great struggle to free our land from the infidels. And I tell you, me brothers, I never felt more alive. For the first time in me life, I'm part of something bigger, something more meaningful. I know me mission in life and I'm willing to give me blood for it. Do you have something you believe in so much you're willing to die for?"

Nuur wanted to say yes. But yes to what, he wondered. What would he die for? The question hung in the air, hovering over his head like a thought bubble, taunting him, making him feel like a fraud. "Thanks to me brothers here in Barawe, I've got a community, people who luv me and care for me. I'm among my fellow shabaab," the boy said and paused for a moment. "I am . . . We *are* the youth of God."

Nuur felt a sharp jolt in the heart when he heard the boy say, "We are the youth of God." He had never heard it put quite that way. It was at once beautiful and blasphemous. A part of Nuur wanted to be among "the youth of God" but a part of him scoffed at the presumptuousness of the phrase. But the more he thought about it, the more Nuur marveled at the notion of belonging to God. He wanted to be one of them, but the idea also frightened him. He turned off the computer and went upstairs. Before going back to the bedroom, he went into the washroom. He turned on the light and saw his image in the mirror over the sink. He stared at himself as if seeing himself for the first time. The boy staring back at him looked vaguely familiar, like someone he had once known but could not remember from where. The longer he gazed at his reflection in the mirror, the less familiar he seemed to himself. He loved the feeling.

19

IT HAD BEEN A DIFFICULT labour. For seven hours, Mr Ilmi watched Khadija writhing and screaming in pain. He held her hand, wiped away sweat from her forehead with a small towel, made loving gestures that she swatted away like she would an irritating fly. Seven hours into it and with the life of his unborn child in danger, the doctors were in the middle of preparing Khadija for a cesarean section when out of the blue, her womb surrendered the life it had been holding on to. In seconds, the baby, a boy seven pounds and two ounces with a full head of hair, was exiled out of the only home his short life had known into what must have felt like a cold, bright, inhospitable universe.

Mr Ilmi was standing behind the doctor and the nurse, who were coaxing the baby out, and was treated to an uncensored glimpse into the trauma of bringing a new life out into this world. Even with the adrenalin rushing through him and the drama unfolding before his eyes, Mr Ilmi was still lucid enough to marvel at the spectacle of it all. He watched in astonishment the tiny human form fighting to come fully into being, gasping for its first breath, the addiction to life already taking hold. Through a thick film of tears in his eyes, Mr Ilmi held the bundled up little being in his arms. He felt the pat of the friendly Ethiopian nurse on his back. "Congratulations, you have a son," she said, a battle-hardened smile on her face. Mr Ilmi didn't thank the nurse, for his eyes were focused on his first-born, who with his incessant cries had already started a lifetime of demands to be loved.

Memories of those frightening, exhilarating hours of labour played in Mr Ilmi's mind as he looked across the glass window separating him from his son. He wanted to hold him and tell him stories. Stories of what, he didn't know. It occurred to him that he and his wife still had not decided on a name for the baby. They had each written a list of five names for a boy and another five for a girl on a piece of paper, but that was as far as they got. After days of debating, they decided it was best to wait till the baby showed up and introduced himself or herself to them, thus making the task of naming easier. And even though Mr Ilmi had been standing there by the window for about thirty minutes staring at his sleeping son, no particular name came to his mind. Something about the boy resisted the act of being named, of being saddled with whatever impossible qualities, hopes and dreams a name conferred. Mr Ilmi briefly fantasized about the idea of keeping the boy unnamed, unburdened until he was old enough to decide for himself what he wished to be called.

Mr Ilmi was astonished at his mind's ability to tune out all the other babies lined up next to his son. As the other fathers, relatives, and grandparents came to the window, stared and pointed out their particular baby in pink or blue and left soon after, Mr Ilmi stood, leaning against the wall opposite the window, and observed the sleeping boy. Finally, he glanced at his watch, saw that it was almost midnight, and thought he'd go back up to his wife's room and sleep on the chair next to her bed.

Having first spent some minutes walking outside in the hospital grounds, the cool fresh early June air clearing his mind, he headed for his wife's room. On the ground floor, on his way to the elevator, he came across the prayer room. He peeked through the square glass window in the door and saw a dimly lit carpeted interior, the soft chairs and the silence more enticing than the hard-backed chair by his wife's bed.

Mr Ilmi opened the door and walked in quietly, for fear of disturbing whatever lonely soul had decided to take refuge there. It was empty. Four rows of chairs faced the front, where there was a cross in one corner, a menorah in the other, and on the floor a few prayer mats for Muslims. Mr Ilmi took a seat at the very back, facing the front, as though waiting for a performance to begin. He thought about walking over to a prayer mat to pray and express his gratitude to Allah, but he felt too drained to get up, so he sat and said his prayer in his head. It had been a long time, too long, he felt, since he had prayed. He thought about all the warnings he had heard growing up about those who claimed to be Muslims but didn't say their five daily prayers. Neither he nor his wife prayed, and it dawned on him that his newborn son would be raised in a household without prayer. Mr Ilmi was seized by an unfamiliar spasm of shame for neglecting his most basic of duties as a Muslim. He closed his eyes and vowed to change that as soon as he returned home with his wife and new baby.

Even as a boy growing up in Mogadishu, an aspect of Mr Ilmi's constitution had resisted the organized form of Islamic worship. At the mosque in his neighbourhood where he went with his father or older brother for Friday prayers, he always found it awkward to perform the intricate choreography of the prayer. He simply went through the motions, standing up, kneeling, prostrating, and repeating the whole process over and over. He couldn't help thinking that if the prayer had been simpler, he might have been more emotionally engaged in it, more spiritually present. He often felt he was missing that gene that made some people open to spiritual experiences. Once, and only once, did he ever have a truly spiritual experience. It was in New York City, of all places.

—

It was a few years into his teaching career. Feeling lonely and frustrated in Toronto, Mr Ilmi decided to spend his March break vacation visiting his friend Hamzah, a gregarious Iraqi he had met at Queen's. The two had often shared their dreams of medical school. But unlike Mr Ilmi, Hamzah did end up in medical school, and was a resident at Beth Israel in New York. Mr Ilmi stayed at Hamzah's apartment in Harlem, and since Hamzah was a resident, he was barely in there and Mr Ilmi had the place pretty much to himself for the duration of his stay.

Every morning, he took the A Train downtown and explored the city on foot, devoting an entire day to a particular neighbourhood. West Village one day, East Village the next, Soho the following day. He made a point of visiting all the museums on the Upper East Side. He visited Stonewall Inn and had lunch in Christopher Park and took pictures of the white statues in the park. On one of his excursions, he got lost. Directionless, he took the subway and got off at Canal Street. On his map he discovered that the trendy neighbourhood he had stumbled upon was Tribeca. He ambled down West Broadway, passing bustling shops and crowded bistros, snapping the occasional photographs of architecturally rich, rehabilitated industrial buildings turned into pricey lofts. In the periphery of his vision, Mr Ilmi saw two women in hijab crossing the street. Caught off-guard by the sight of two such women in that neighbourhood of movie stars and hip-hop moguls, Mr Ilmi quickened his pace to see where they were heading in a hurry. He saw them enter through the green door of a slender three-storey townhouse. Unable to curb his curiosity, he followed them. To his great surprise, the building, nestled between an elegant restaurant and a noisy bar, was a mosque.

Mr Ilmi walked in, took his shoes off and proceeded towards a prayer area no larger than his living room. A small group of about fifteen worshipers sat in a circle. The first thing that caught his eye was the makeup of the group. There were a few Arabs, several South Asians. There were also two African American men and a few white women, their hair uncovered. They all sat cross-legged on a blue Persian carpet, their eyes focused on a thin, frail woman who looked to be in her late sixties, her pale skin made paler by her black qamiis. A few clumps of wispy white hair peeked out of the shawl on her head. Mr Ilmi exchanged a look with the woman, who offered a hint of a smile and motioned for him to take a seat. He obeyed. She looked around the circle as if to make sure the gathering was complete.

"Asalamu alaykum," she greeted the small congregation.

"Walaykum salam," they said in unison. It was then that it dawned upon Mr Ilmi that the woman was the imam of the mosque. He tried his best to suppress his surprise and pleasure. Never before had he witnessed a woman imam.

"My name is Sheikha Fatima. It's my joy to welcome all you seekers to our gathering," she said in a frail but surprisingly authoritative voice. "This evening, I would like to speak to you a little about a subject dear to my heart," she said, placing a gentle hand on her chest. "What does it mean to be a Sufi? When you say, I'm a Sufi, what are you saying?" She paused. "What you're really saying is that you're in love with God even though you don't know God. It means you have a strong love of God in your heart that isn't satisfied by earthly love, as beautiful as that may be. It's a yearning, a quest, and that is Sufism."

Mr Ilmi asked himself if he had "the yearning," and decided that he did in fact have it, but his particular longing had the tendency to be diffuse and vague, a general yearning for something greater but which he would be hard pressed to define.

"A Sufi is one who is guided by his heart. In fact, this is the highest Sufi directive. It says, listen to your heart. Follow your heart, because Allah says: I do not fit into all worlds that I manifest, yet I dwell in the hearts of my believing servants. So the heart is the primary centre and focus and vehicle to meet Allah and to immerse and disappear into Allah. In the Sufi path, you go into the interior because that is the grand universe. A Sufi is one who is not bound by space and time. A Sufi is a person of inner experience."

Mr Ilmi felt as if Sheikha Fatima were speaking to him, for he had always imagined himself to be a deeply interior being. Even as a child, playing with other kids had bored him, while getting lost inside his own thoughts satisfied a mysterious yearning for solitude.

"Know yourself and you will know your Lord. The Sufi path is about knowing oneself and that is a journey that can take a lifetime. It's a lifetime's devotion to self-analysis and self-correction. You're absorbed in yourself and looking at your own faults instead of the faults of others. A Sufi believes that before you take a speck out of your brother's eye, take the beam out of your own eye." Sheikha Fatima paused long enough to take several sips of water from a reusable bottle. "So what is that beam?" she asked between sips. "It's the limited self, the ego, that little part of us that thinks it's a little God. There are seven levels of the self that have been defined by Sufi science. Seven basic levels, and the first level is the tyrannical self. And the second level is the self that is questioning and critical of itself, that recognizes human frailty."

Mr Ilmi wondered which of the seven spiritual levels he was at. Probably the bottom one, he thought.

"We are all actors," the Sheikha continued. "Every one of us is acting out the divine desires, but at which level? Are you acting out the demonic part of the divine game or are you acting at the heart level, at the love and compassion?"

Mr Ilmi continued listening, occasionally nodding his head at something he thought or felt or noticed in his own life. Everything Sheikha Fatima said felt true, because it confirmed his religious or spiritual worldview, however muddled that was. For the first time in his life, he felt at home in a mosque.

Mr Ilmi could feel something rising in him, a peculiar, all-encompassing sense that he was not alone. Even in the midst of the loneliness that had driven him to New York, he felt the presence of something greater than himself.

"The Sufi focuses on love," Sheikha Fatima said, her voice barely over a whisper now. "How do you turn off the darkness? You turn on the light. You can beat the darkness. You can scream at the darkness. But the easiest way to extinguish the darkness is to turn on the light."

Mr Ilmi closed his eyes and focused on the soothing voice of the Sheikha beckoning him inward, deep into a part of himself he didn't even know he possessed.

"The light is there but it's covered by layers of conditioned existence," she continued. "And the easiest way to turn on that light is with . . . love. Only love."

Suddenly, something happened, shattering Mr Ilmi's state of semibliss. He tried to cry out, as he felt his chest constrict and cave in.

He held his hand over his mouth to muffle his cries of pain. People stared at him. Tears filled his eyes. "Sorry. I'm sorry," he mumbled and jumped to his feet and rushed to the door, where his shoes lay among a pile on the floor. He slipped them on and stumbled out into the evening.

———

Mr Ilmi heard the door of the prayer room creak open, jolting him out of his memory of Sheikha Fatima and how her words had entranced him and broken open his heart and sent him reeling onto West Broadway in Tribeca. He turned towards the door and saw a short middle-aged man. "I'm sorry. I didn't know the room was occupied," the man said.

"Oh no, please. Come in. I was just resting here. It's so quiet," Mr Ilmi said to put the man at ease. He seemed to be in distress.

"I was just about to leave," Mr Ilmi said and got up to go. The man had not moved from the door when Mr Ilmi reached it. For a brief moment, as they stared at each other, it seemed that they were about to embrace, but that moment passed.

"I just came to say a few prayers for my grandson," the man said in a weak voice. "He was only a few days old. We hadn't even gotten to know him . . . "

"I am very sorry to hear about your grandson," Mr Ilmi said and watched the man walk on to the front of the hall towards the cross. He watched him kneel, and stepped out of the room. He quietly closed the door behind him and wandered over to the hospital's waiting room. It was deserted.

Mr Ilmi put some money into a coffee machine and listened as it struggled to pour and mix his coffee. The wall TV was on mute but tuned to BBC World News. It showed a recap of a soccer game. Mr Ilmi took his coffee from the machine and picked up the remote from a table to turn on the volume. Just then a Breaking News sign flashed on the screen followed by a clip of a fiery explosion. Terrified African men and women were spilling out of a burning building. Mr Ilmi turned up the volume to hear the newscaster's voice giving context to the gruesome scenes on the screen. "The twin explosion ripped apart a popular café in central Nairobi, where a large crowd had gathered to watch the final of the Africa Cup. The death toll stands at twenty-three but is expected to rise. The Somali Islamist group Al-Shabaab has claimed responsibility for the attack on its Twitter page."

Mr Ilmi felt the burning pain of scalding coffee on his hand. He went and dropped the cup in a trash bin and returned his attention back to the horror unfolding on the TV screen. Two men were dragging a bloodied woman out of the building. Mr Ilmi stepped back and sank down on a chair, and for reasons he was too afraid to contemplate, he thought about Nuur.

20

Nuur tried to slow down so that he and Mohamed wouldn't arrive at the KLM check-in counter together. He wasn't carrying much luggage, just a medium-sized four-wheel bag that he pulled along without effort. Over his shoulder hung a beautiful brown leather satchel that Imam Yusuf had given him as a going-away present. He slipped his hand into the satchel to check for his passport and e-ticket. It was the third time he had done so in the last ten minutes.

Nuur saw a long moving sidewalk. He knew of the existence of such things but had never seen one before. This would be a day of many firsts. His first time on a plane. His first time out of Canada. He made a mental note of them all, thanks to Imam Yusuf and his faith in him.

When he came to the start of the moving sidewalk, he froze. He knew that it was just like an escalator, the kind he had hopped on to without worry since he was a child. But it was the flatness of the thing that intimidated him. He wanted to get on, to see what it felt like to be carried by it, but he didn't like the idea of the earth moving beneath his feet. He heard someone behind say, "Pardon me," and was practically pushed aside by two tall men in smart pilots' uniforms as they got onto the contraption. He decided to go for it and placed one foot on the moving belt. He wobbled a bit before regaining his equilibrium and was pleasantly surprised by the sensation of being propelled forward into his future, as though the machine were encouraging him on his mission. As he stood waiting to reach the end of the belt that was conveying him to his destiny, Nuur caught a glimpse of himself in the glass wall that ran along one side of him. He saw a vaguely handsome, preppy boy who looked like he had walked right out of a department store catalogue. It was he, but not. He wore a red polo shirt, dark blue jeans and black sandals that gave him an air of casual boredom with the tedium of air travel.

A few weeks earlier, Imam Yusuf took Nuur and Mohamed to a shop in a dingy plaza in Mississauga to have their passport pictures taken. The night before, the imam had come to the house and brought with him an electric razor in a black case. He put it on the dining table where Nuur, Mohamed, and three younger boys were sitting, reciting the Quran aloud from the open books before them. They were completely engrossed, running their index fingers along the lines they read, their voices producing a chaotic chorus, their heads swaying back and forth. They stopped at once and stared at the case. The imam explained to Mohamed and Nuur that traveling with their long beards would inevitably attract attention. They needed be inconspicuous, look like other boys their age. Nuur and Mohamed took turns shaving in front of the washroom mirror and came out clean-shaven and with crew cuts. The imam also took them shopping and bought for them jeans, polo shirts, and two pairs of shoes each.

Sitting at a departure gate in Terminal 3, Nuur checked his watch. It was five-thirty in the evening; just another fifty minutes and he would be sitting in the window seat he had requested. He looked out the glass wall at the KLM airplane that would take him and Mohamed across an ocean and over two continents to their destiny, which for Nuur was as enthralling as it was mysterious. From his satchel, he took out the two boarding passes he had inserted into his passport, as he had seen people do in movies. They would land at Schiphol Airport in Amsterdam at 8:10 AM. Three hours later, another KLM flight would take them from Schiphol and deliver them to Jomo Kenyatta Airport in Nairobi the following evening. The rest of the details of the trip were written on a different piece of paper hidden deep in his suitcase. But Nuur didn't need to consult it, for he knew what it contained. Once they landed at Jomo Kenyatta Airport, they were to call a number which would be answered by a man named Osman Muse, who would drive them to a hotel in Eastleigh, the predominantly Somali area of

Nairobi. Once they were inside their hotel room, they were to take a pair of scissors and cut their passports into tiny pieces, put them in a metal bowl, open a window, and set fire to them until no trace of their identity was left. They were to wait for a few days until the next leg of their trip, which would be by car to the border town of Mandera, through which they would be smuggled into the land of their parents. A land neither Nuur nor Mohamed had ever seen.

Nuur glanced behind him to see if Mohamed was still there. He saw him reading a newspaper, and felt comforted. He scanned the area and marveled at the complex choreography of modern-day travel. Outside, he could see planes landing and taking off, throngs of flight attendants in little hats and high heels marching in groups, couples, friends, and lovers engaged in private conversations. He longed to walk over and sit next to Mohamed to continue one of their late night chats that had become the highlights of his days at The House. As he listened to the constant announcements of flights to cities he would never see, Nuur wondered if he and Mohamed would be separated once they got to Kismayo. He had asked Imam Yusuf this question, but the imam only said that they would go wherever Allah willed them to go.

He had been surprised by the ease with which they passed through security. He almost laughed at the needless trouble they had taken to rehearse their answers. Even on the drive to the airport, Imam Yusuf kept asking them the same questions over and over again.

What is the purpose of your trip?
To visit my dying grandfather in Nairobi.
Where will you be staying in Nairobi?
At my cousin's house in South C.
When will you be returning to Canada?
At the end of August before school starts.
What are you carrying with you?
Just my clothes.

Mohamed's questions were the same but the answers different. It was essential, Imam Yusuf explained in a stern voice that made Nuur nervous, that their answers be not only correct but also answered with natural ease. Nuur marveled at the speed with which events had unfolded over the two months he stayed at The House. There had been a great deal of talk about the possibility of a mission, and speculation about who would be lucky enough to be chosen for it. There were also stories about the three boys who had left for Somalia last year; emails about their mission came occasionally, and were greeted with great excitement and envy.

———

It all started one evening in early May. Nuur, Mohamed, and the other boys were in the basement, their eyes glued to a newly arrived DVD from Somalia that Imam Yusuf had brought the night before. It was recorded in the town of Baydhabo in southwest Somalia, and the imam characterized it as incontrovertible evidence of the war crimes committed by the evil allied forces. It showed a middle-aged man with a long, hennaed beard yelling in a southern Somali dialect that Nuur had trouble understanding fully.

Talking directly into the camera, the man started with the customary words of praise to Allah, the most forgiving, the most merciful. He told whoever was watching and listening, in whichever part of Allah's world they lived, be it England, America, or Canada, that with the permission of the infidel government in Mogadishu, the enemies of Islam were going from village to village conducting a crusade against the Muslim people of Somalia. After quoting several passages from the Quran, he switched back to Somali. He told the watchers of the DVD that with their help and the help of the Almighty, the infidels would meet their gruesome end in the arid soils of Somalia. Make no mistake, he warned, the armored vehicles of Kenya, the heavy artillery of Uganda, and the invisible drones of the Great Satan, America, will wither in the face of the righteous youth of God. The recording cut to the black flag of Al-Shabaab blowing in the wind. One of their signature religious songs started to play over static images of bloated corpses, including those of a woman and child lying in the dirt. A picture of a house on fire faded into an image of about ten Somali men sitting on the ground, their hands tied behind their backs, faces covered with dirty, white hoods.

Imam Yusuf came down to the basement with his usual greeting, "Asalamu alaykum." The boys greeted him back. "Please turn it off for a minute," he told Mohamed, who was holding the remote control. Mohamed obeyed. "Let us sit together," the imam said, to which the boys responded by sitting in a circle on an old rug. As was his custom, the imam started with a recitation of the Fatiha. Then he said, in a tone of great solemnity, "I bear great news . . . The time has come. Allah, the most forgiving, the most merciful has granted your dear wish to help our brothers and sisters in Somalia in their struggle."

Mohamed let out a deep sigh and said, "Alhamdulillah!" Nuur and the other boys followed suit.

"May Allah reward you and your families with paradise," the imam said.

"When do we go?" Salah asked, his face glowing with excitement.

"My sons, Hussein, Abdi, and Salah, inshallah, your time will come soon."

Nuur watched as Abdi's shoulders slumped and he cast his eyes down in disappointment. Salah, whose emotional outbursts in The House had earned the rebuke of Imam Yusuf on several occasions, didn't take the news well either—this was the second time he was being passed over—and to add insult to injury, in favour of the newcomer, Nuur.

"No! This is NOT fair," Salah said; he jumped to his feet and ran out of the basement. Thundering up the stairs, Salah could be heard saying, "I'm ready! What do I have to do to prove it?"

The boys glanced at each other in confusion and then at the imam. Finally, Abdi stood up, saying, "I'll go talk to him." Hussein followed Abdi.

Left alone with his new recruits, Imam Yusuf shook Nuur and

Mohamed's hands and patted their backs, congratulating them.

"When do we go?" Mohamed asked with an eagerness that made Nuur wonder if he too should show more enthusiasm.

"What will we do?" Nuur asked and immediately regretted his question lest Imam Yusuf interpret it as coming out of fear, or worse, ambivalence. Nuur was told on countless occasions that ambivalence was the enemy of true faith.

"Our brothers and sisters in the struggle are in great need of many different kinds of help. Bright young men like you can help them in many different ways. For instance, there is a need for computer-literate youths to distribute online material. We also need people who are good at producing videos and editing them. Someone to help with social media like Twitter," the imam said, giving the impression that they were starting an exciting summer internship. "But you must remember, Allah rewards those who strive to do more and give more in his name." Imam Yusuf paused. He put a hand on the shoulder of each boy and in a soft, fatherly voice said, "When the time comes and you feel ready and willing to assume more responsibilities, then it is up to you how much you want to give of yourself."

Nuur had more questions but he sensed in the imam's tone a kind of finality and for a fleeting moment, he cherished the feeling of pre-ordainment that came to settle over him. From that night on, things moved with a speed that Nuur found exhilarating. Within ten days, he held in his hands his first passport. Flipping to the first page, he stared at his photo, showing him without the full beard he had had for the last two years. Also missing in the photo was the kufi that had been his crown for as many years. He couldn't help but see this photo as evidence of a new him, at the start of a new life.

———

Nuur was jolted back from his thoughts by his name being called on the intercom. He strained to hear the name better, his heart pounding. He was certain that the voice did indeed say his name and that at any moment, airport security or the police would descend upon him and Mohamed. In that instant, he got his first and clearest intimation that the enterprise that he and Mohamed had undertaken was something that required, for its success, secrecy and lies. A shiver ran through him as he tried to reconcile the lies he had to tell—a sin in the eyes of Allah—with the righteous mission he had undertaken in the name of Allah. Amid the clamour of people and flight announcements, Nuur heard what sounded to him like a distant but familiar voice asking him: "What are you doing?"

In Nuur's mind, however, another voice managed to overcome this one. It was the same female voice as before, announcing KLM Flight 692 to Amsterdam. Nuur saw people around him rising to their feet. He got up too, gathered his satchel and joined the queue for boarding. There were seven people ahead of him, including Mohamed, moving inexorably towards the last obstacle between them and the plane. Nuur watched with relief as the woman in the sky-blue KLM uniform scanned Mohamed's passport and boarding pass. Nuur kept his eyes on Mohamed until he disappeared into the bridge.

Nuur's turn came. Surely the woman could hear the sound of his beating heart. She took his passport and observed it carefully. She looked at his face and back at the passport. She walked away to her computer and typed something. Nuur watched her as she spoke in a language he assumed was Dutch. He looked around and saw an immigration officer in a navy uniform walking towards him. He was certain it was the woman's call that had tipped off the immigration officer. He wanted to drop his satchel and flee, but his limbs felt heavy as lead, incapable of obeying the signals from his brain ordering them to run. Sweat began to form on his forehead.

The woman came back to him, "I'm afraid we have a problem," she said. Nuur felt vomit coming on. "There has been a mix up. You requested a window seat. I've just checked with my colleague on the plane and all the window seats are taken. We apologize."

Nuur sighed and whispered "Alhamdulillah" under his breath. "It's no problem," he said doing his best to sound nonchalant.

"Have a wonderful flight," the woman said with a pleasant smile to go with her pleasant words and gave him back the passport and the boarding pass. Nuur made his slow precession towards the boarding bridge. Once he reached the threshold, he stopped and looked back, expecting, or more accurately, hoping to find his mother Haawo or brother Ayuub or even Mr Ilmi there. He saw no one he knew. He turned and marched through the bridge into the tunnel and the plane that ushered him towards his mission.

21

M R ILMI TURNED AROUND from the window, leaned against its ledge, and watched his students writing their final exam of the year. He stood up and walked slowly around the room, making effort not to disturb his students' concentration as they struggled with multiple-choice and true-or-false questions about the human liver and the names of the many enzymes it produced, the human brain and its innumerable properties, and other organs of the body.

As Mr Ilmi made his way up and down the room, he paused to glance down at the heads of his pupils. There was Ryan, who had recently dyed his hair purple and started wearing black nail polish. Ryan was one of the bravest boys he had ever known and a constant source of inspiration for Mr Ilmi. He had come out proudly, in this school of all places, and he dished it back at the boys who tormented him as good as they dolled out theirs.

Next to Ryan was Duran, his afro as expansive as when the school year started. Mr Ilmi looked down at Duran's frantic scribbling, no doubt getting many of the answers wrong. He walked across the room and passed by the brilliant Janet, and across from her was James Calhoun, slumped over his exam paper. His head was shaved now and it showed the large scar where Nuur's chair had landed.

Three months had passed and still there was not a single word about the whereabouts of the boy. Mr Ilmi had developed a habit of walking over to Haawo's apartment on Saturday afternoons, and there would follow the same routine. He would knock on the door a few times, Haawo would open it and welcome him with a pleasant but sad smile. She would make Somali tea for him and as they drank it, he would ask her if she had any news. The answer was always the same: "Still no word." Until the previous Saturday. Haawo at last had news to share. Mr Ilmi almost choked on his tea.

"A Mr Mastracci, an officer from CSIS, came yesterday morning," Haawo said, her voice weak and emotionless.

Mr Ilmi sat up. It was he who had called CSIS and told them about his suspicion that Imam Yusuf may have sent one of his students to Somalia to fight for Al-Shabaab. The officer he spoke with asked if he had any evidence. Mr Ilmi told him he had only a strong suspicion. The man heard him out and told him they were already working on the cases of several other missing Somali boys and they would look into this case too. Mr Ilmi gave him Nuur's full name and social insurance number, and sent him a scan of the most recent picture that Haawo had. While he was glad for any news coming from CSIS, he also dreaded to hear what they might have found.

"Mr Mastracci said they tracked Nuur's passport—"

"That's great. That's fantastic . . . and?"

"But that's all they could find."

"I don't understand."

"He said that when they tracked Nuur's passport, they found that he had landed in Nairobi. But there is no more record. They suspect he entered Somalia through the Kenyan border but they have no proof."

As Mr Ilmi put down his cup, his hand was shaking. He felt as though someone had punched his heart. All these twelve weeks he had been hoping for news of Nuur, but as he sat in Haawo's cramped, airless living room, he felt a kind of hopelessness he had never felt before. He had always prided himself on his ability to see something good in even the direst of circumstances. But hearing Haawo's words now confirmed his worst fears for Nuur and made him doubt the very concept of hope.

"I'm going to Somalia," Mr Ilmi heard Haawo say.

"What?"

"Actually, it was Ayuub's idea."

"What was Ayuub's idea?"

"I called Ayuub in Alberta and told him what the officer said, that they think Nuur was taken to Somalia. Ayuub said we should go to look for him."

"Look for him? In Somalia?"

"Yes."

"It's a big country to look for one person," Mr Ilmi said and immediately wished he could take back those words. The task of finding someone whose whereabouts were unknown in any country would be difficult enough, Mr Ilmi thought. But searching for a boy in towns and villages all over Somalia in places controlled by a murderous terrorist group, where battles still raged and suicide bombings were a regular occurrence, seemed to Mr Ilmi like a fool's errand. Or a mother's.

"When's Ayuub coming?" he asked, in an attempt to dismiss his mindless comment.

"He's waiting for his last paycheck and will fly home next week."

"What will you do?"

Mr Ilmi watched her intently. There was a calmness about her fortified by a deep resolve. Tears began to well in her eyes and a small, uncertain smile formed on her lips. She shrugged and let out a sigh. "I'll bring my Nuur back," she said.

A mother's vow, Mr Ilmi thought and smiled back at Haawo. He saw his hand reach out to her as if independent of his will. He grabbed her hand and held it for a moment. "I'm very happy to hear you and Ayuub will go," he said. But as he released her hand, thoughts of the improbability of their search mission invaded his mind again. But he knew she had to follow her heart.

Mr Ilmi rose to his feet. "I must get going," he said, "I have to buy some things for the baby."

Haawo got up and followed him to the door. "How's the baby?"

Mr Ilmi stopped and answered, "He cries a lot."

"It gets better. You will see. The first time your baby smiles at you . . . " Haawo stopped as if remembering the first time Nuur smiled at her. "You will be a very good father, I can tell."

"Thank you," he said and stepped out the door. Outside, he stopped and turned to her.

"May I see it?" Mr Ilmi asked, gesturing towards the rooms in the hallway.

Haawo gave him a puzzled look.

"His room," Mr Ilmi said. He felt a surge of embarrassment at his sentimentality, an emotion he had often suspected had been surgically removed from his people. He felt Haawo's hand in his as she led him down the hallway. She opened the door to one of the rooms and turned on the light. Mr Ilmi went in and stood at the foot of the two single beds that were separated by a night stand with a lamp on it. He noticed the bare, white walls. It looked nothing like what he thought teenage boys' rooms looked like. There were no posters of soccer players or pop stars. No photos of any kind.

"He made his bed every morning before school," Haawo said, standing by the door. "Everything is the way he left that night. When his father told him to leave, he ran into his room. Two minutes later, he came out with his bag and ran out." Haawo leaned on the frame of the door as though she feared she might faint. "Do you ever have this one moment from your past that you keep playing in your head?" she asked.

Mr Ilmi was silent for a long moment. He thought about the moments in his life he most regretted, like the time Mikeila told him that perhaps they needed to take a break and every cell in his body wanted to scream "NO!" But pride or stupidity made him nod and effectively they agreed to a breakup he knew he would regret for the rest of his life. Mr Ilmi wanted to tell Haawo about that moment with Mikeila so many years ago, a moment that came back to him when he least expected it. But he simply shook his head and said, "Not really."

"I do," Haawo said. "When Nuur's father told him to get out of the house, Nuur looked at me. It was brief. I saw it. He wanted me to say something. Anything. But I didn't. I just looked down. I'll never know what that did to him," Haawo's voice cracked. She cleared her throat.

"I'll never forgive myself for that."

"You have to. You have to forgive yourself."

Haawo slumped down on the edge of one of the beds. "Sometimes I get so angry with him. Why? Why? I scream. Why didn't you come back the next day so you'd know I had kicked him out? So that you'd know I didn't choose him over you?"

Her voice had gone down to a whisper.

Mr Ilmi glanced at her eyes to see if she was crying but there were no tears. She just tilted her head to the side a little. She seemed like a woman too exhausted to cry.

Mr Ilmi turned and saw a narrow, white bookshelf in the corner of the room by the window.

"I bought it for him at Walmart where I work," Haawo said, smiling now. "When he came home with all those books you gave him. I said to him, you are going to need a shelf for all those books. He was so happy when I brought it home. It took him an hour to put it together and when he lined up all the books, he called me from the kitchen: 'Mom, mom, come look!' He was so proud of his books. Every night when I peeked in to say good night, he'd be in bed reading one of your books."

Mr Ilmi smiled to himself as he looked at the books neatly stacked on the shelf. They were all there, all the books he had given Nuur except one—*The Prophet*. Had he taken it with him to Somalia? Mr Ilmi tried to picture Nuur sitting somewhere in Somalia, perhaps under a palm tree near the beach, reading it, but no such image came to his mind.

———

"Time's up," Mr Ilmi said to his students. A couple of them moaned. "One more minute, please," Janet said, her thin baby voice earnest, almost desperate.

"Sorry, I've already added an extra five minutes. Bring your papers and place them on my table, please," he said, standing by the classroom door.

They got up one by one and stacked up their exam papers on Mr Ilmi's desk. They grabbed their bags and shuffled out of the class, their faces exhausted and expressionless.

"Any plans for the summer?" Mr Ilmi asked Ryan as he was leaving the class.

"My dad is taking me to the Van Gogh museum in Amsterdam in July," Ryan said, pulling a few curls of his purple hair away from his face. "He said, 'You can't be a real painter without seeing Rembrandt.'" Ryan imitated his father's voice.

"Your dad is right," Mr Ilmi said with a big smile. "Pay close attention to his use of light in his self-portraits. There is one he did in, I think, 1889. You'll be amazed."

"Thanks, Mr Ilmi. Have a great summer," Ryan said and disappeared into the hallway.

Mr Ilmi always asked each of his students about their summer plans before bidding them farewell. Janet had got a summer job at her mother's law firm where she hoped to brush up on constitutional law before starting at McGill University in the fall. Tisha would be working at the YMCA to save money for Seneca College to study early childhood education. James was the last to leave the class. He stopped and he and Mr Ilmi stared at each other for some time until James chuckled.

"What's so funny?"

James looked down, cupping his hand over his mouth. "You," he said.

"I'm funny, am I?"

"Yeah," he said. "But you're also cool."

Mr Ilmi laughed. "Thanks, James. I'm glad you approve."

"Have a great summer, Mr Ilmi," James said as he headed for the door.

"How're you doing . . . I'm mean, the head."

"It's cool. I get headaches sometimes. Nothing I can't handle, though."

"Good. I'm glad to hear that. Any plans for the summer?"

James was quiet for a moment. "Not sure yet. Thinking of taking a year off. Do some backpacking in Central America. We'll see."

"Take good care of yourself, James."

James gave Mr Ilmi a little salute and left.

Alone at last, Mr Ilmi let out a laborious sigh and walked over to the blackboard and erased it clean of any reminders of the long, eventful school year. He wished he could erase the entire year and all the bad things that had happened. He gathered the exam papers and stuffed them into his satchel. He closed the windows and made for the exit. He reached for the light switch by the door, and just before turning the lights off, he stopped and glanced back at his empty classroom.

Epilogue

M<small>R</small> I<small>LMI TRIES TO REMEMBER</small> the woman's name. She's walking towards him and he wants to call out to her. Haawo told him her name the day they went looking for Nuur. He remembers the story of how she lost her mind when her only son was killed in some kind of gang war. As she approaches him, her name comes to him in a flash. "Iskawaran, Habaryar Maryan," Mr Ilmi greets her in Somali.

The woman looks startled, evidently surprised that he knows her name, and stops to stare at him as he continues to push his son on the swing.

"How old is he?" she asks.

Mr Ilmi is taken aback by her lucidity. "A year and two months."

"My son has a boy just like him," she says.

"That's good," he replies, trying to keep his face expressionless, not to reveal that he knows the story of her son's death. "What's your son's name?" Mr Ilmi asks and feels ashamed for continuing the charade.

"Suleyman. Abdi. Daahir," she says, pronouncing the dead boy's names one by one.

"Well, say hello to him for me," Mr Ilmi says.

"He's hungry. I have to go home and feed him," the woman says and let's out a deep, guttural laugh. "He's getting married tomorrow. You're invited."

Before Mr Ilmi can respond to her invitation, she takes off. He can hear her faint voice as she mutters about the details of the wedding, about the hundreds of people who will come for the celebration of her dead son's wedding.

Mr Ilmi stands motionless behind his little boy. He has forgotten to push the swing and the child lets out a high-pitched "Daddy!"

followed by something that Mr Ilmi can't understand but interprets as a command for him to start pushing. He resumes.

As the sounds of his son's babble play in his ears, Mr Ilmi's attention wanders over to three Somali boys approaching in his direction. They seem to him to be around seventeen. One of them wears a white qamiis, the kind Nuur used to wear. For a fleeting moment, Mr Ilmi is convinced that the boy is Nuur. But as they get closer and pass him, Mr Ilmi realizes that it's just his eyes playing tricks on him again.

This has been happening on occasion. Nuur in his white qamiis and kufi, his school bag dangling from his shoulder, materializes out of nowhere. Just three days ago, Mr Ilmi and his wife Khadija were out with their son for his afternoon walk. Mr Ilmi was pushing the stroller. As they came to a black Toyota waiting at the traffic lights, Mr Ilmi suddenly froze. He was certain that he was seeing Nuur in the passenger seat of the car. Mr Ilmi stared hard at the profile. But as the light changed and the car started to move, the boy turned his face briefly, and Mr Ilmi realized that he was just another one of Nuur's many doppelgangers.

Fifteen months have passed since he last saw Nuur, and still there hasn't been a word about his whereabouts. Last July, on a muggy, humid day, Mr Ilmi had driven Nuur's mother and his brother Ayuub to the airport. As they said their farewells Haawo promised to keep him posted about the progress of their search. And for months, she kept her promise. Once every two weeks or so, he would open his email inbox to see a message from her and his heart would skip a beat. He would open it only to find just another update of her and Ayuub's whereabouts. They had stayed in Nairobi's Eastleigh for a few days, then taken a short flight to Mogadishu, where they hired a private detective, who drove them to the coastal towns of Marka, Kismayo, and Barawe. But as the months dragged on, the emails became less frequent, then stopped altogether.

The last email Mr Ilmi received came five months ago, on the morning of Easter Monday. Haawo in her usual terse update informed him that they had received a tip, and she and Ayuub were traveling to Baydhabo, the small city southwest of Somalia where a war of attrition was waging between Al-Shabaab and the African Union troops.

After that communication, Mr Ilmi sent Haawo several emails imploring her to keep him posted, but so far he has heard nothing. Sometimes he pictures them, and what he sees in his mind depends on his state. On good days, Haawo, Ayuub, and Nuur have reunited. They live in a little house by the beach in Mogadishu. But on days when optimism fails him, he sees Haawo and Ayuub lying on the side of some dusty country road, their bullet-ridden bodies rotting in the sweltering heat.

Peals of laughter from kids chasing each other bring Mr Ilmi back to the present. In two short weeks, school will start and these kids and their games will migrate back to their small apartments. As grateful as he is for his long summer break, which gives him the luxury of spending time with his son, Mr Ilmi looks forward to the start of the new year with a new batch of students. Each year that passes helps Mr Ilmi see the value of his work, the act of imparting whatever knowledge he has to a new parade of pupils, even though only a few of them will ever amount to anything noteworthy.

Mr Ilmi's eyes are drawn to the sky above his building. The long streaks of mauve, red, and orange cutting across it remind him of the sunsets over the Indian Ocean in Mogadishu. He looks away.

"Okay, Nuur, time to go home," Mr Ilmi says. In one gentle move, he lifts his son out of the swing and hugs him close to his chest. The boy protests with a few ineffectual kicks of his little feet and arms. Mr Ilmi looks into his large, watery eyes, his long lashes wet with tears. "I promise I'll put you on the swing tomorrow," he says. The boy calms down and points his finger to the ground. Mr Ilmi puts him down.

"Let's go home now!" Mr Ilmi tells his son. After a moment's hesitation, little Nuur reaches for his dad's hand and together they walk in the direction of home.

Acknowledgements

Writing a novel takes immense support from so many people and places. My thanks to the Ontario Arts Council and the Toronto Arts Council for their generous grants which have helped me write this book. I'm blessed to have the affection and assistance of dear friends too many to count. But special thanks to Timothy Gray, Bhakti Shringarpure, Abdi Latif Dahir, Debbie Wolgelerenter, Vickram Jain, Hoda Dahir, Gunnar Nime, Mary O'Connell, and Sieraaj Ahmed.

My deepest gratitude to everyone at Mawenzi House for their expert shepherding of this novel from a manuscript to a book I'm so proud to have my name on. I'm especially grateful to my editor M G Vassanji who is as brilliant an editor as he is a novelist. And lastly, to my family, you're the greatest blessing of my life.

Hassan Ghedi Santur emigrated from Somalia to Canada at age thirteen. He has a BA in English Literature and an MFA from York University, and an MA from Columbia Graduate School of Journalism. He has worked as a radio journalist for CBC radio and his print journalism work has appeared in the *New York Times*, *Yahoo News*, and *The Walrus*, among others. In 2010, he published his debut novel *Something Remains*, followed by *Maps of Exile*, an exploration of the plight of African migrants in Europe. He is currently working on his third novel, *Other Worlds, Other Lives*.